DEATH OF A CLAM DIGGER

The dogs didn't move.

They were both on all fours, heads lowered over the edge of the path, distracted by something, still barking.

"What's got them so riled up?"

When Hayley and Mona reached their two dogs, they stopped suddenly in their tracks, stunned.

The dogs were barking at a man lying face down in the clam flats.

Mona leaped over the side of the shore path down to the protruding rocks along the edge, slipping and sliding on seaweed until she managed to get her footing in the muddy flats. Hayley followed close behind, gingerly, trying to maintain her balance. Mona reached the man first. She bent down and grabbed a fistful of his plaid flannel shirt and tugged on it with all her might. The man's body slowly turned over, and the shock caused Mona to stumble back and fall flat on her butt. By now, Hayley had caught up to her and could plainly see the man's face. Although it was covered in mud, she instantly recognized him.

It was Lonnie Leighton.

And he wasn't breathing.

He was, Hayley feared, very much dead . . .

Books by Lee Hollis

Hayley Powell Mysteries
DEATH OF A KITCHEN DIVA
DEATH OF A COUNTRY FRIED REDNECK
DEATH OF A COUPON CLIPPER
DEATH OF A CHOCOHOLIC
DEATH OF A CHRISTMAS CATERER
DEATH OF A CUPCAKE QUEEN
DEATH OF A BACON HEIRESS
DEATH OF A PUMPKIN CARVER
DEATH OF A LOBSTER LOVER
DEATH OF A COOKBOOK AUTHOR
DEATH OF A WEDDING CAKE BAKER
DEATH OF A BLUEBERRY TART
DEATH OF A WICKED WITCH
DEATH OF AN ITALIAN CHEF
DEATH OF AN ICE CREAM SCOOPER
DEATH OF A CLAM DIGGER

Collections
EGGNOG MURDER
(with Leslie Meier and Barbara Ross)
YULE LOG MURDER
(with Leslie Meier and Barbara Ross)
HAUNTED HOUSE MURDER
(with Leslie Meier and Barbara Ross)
CHRISTMAS CARD MURDER
(with Leslie Meier and Peggy Ehrhart)
HALLOWEEN PARTY MURDER
(with Leslie Meier and Barbara Ross)
IRISH COFFEE MURDER
(with Leslie Meier and Barbara Ross)

Poppy Harmon Mysteries
POPPY HARMON INVESTIGATES
POPPY HARMON AND THE HUNG JURY
POPPY HARMON AND THE PILLOW TALK KILLER
POPPY HARMON AND THE BACKSTABBING BACHELOR
POPPY HARMON AND THE SHOOTING STAR

Maya & Sandra Mysteries
MURDER AT THE PTA
MURDER AT THE BAKE SALE
MURDER ON THE CLASS TRIP

Published by Kensington Publishing Corp.

DEATH of a CLAM DIGGER

LEE HOLLIS

Kensington Publishing Corp.
www.kensingtonbooks.com

KENSINGTON BOOKS are published by

Kensington Publishing Corp.
119 West 40th Street
New York, NY 10018

All Kensington titles, imprints, and distributed lines are available at special quantity discounts for bulk purchases for sales promotion, premiums, fund-raising, educational, or institutional use.

Special book excerpts or customized printings can also be created to fit specific needs. For details, write or phone the office of the Kensington Sales Manager: Attn.: Sales Department. Kensington Publishing Corp., 119 West 40th Street, New York, NY 10018. Phone: 1-800-221-2647.

The K and Teapot logo is a trademark of Kensington Publishing Corp.

First Printing: August 2023
ISBN: 978-1-4967-3651-2

ISBN: 978-1-4967-3652-9 (ebook)

10 9 8 7 6 5 4 3 2 1

Printed in the United States of America

For Debbie Parsons

Chapter 1

Hayley Powell's aging but still spry shih tzu Leroy suddenly sprang to attention as they took a leisurely stroll along the Shore Path, a famous pebbled path that stretched from the Town Pier next to Agamont Park and continued along the eastern shore of Mount Desert Island. It was early, the morning sun just now bursting over the horizon. It was going to be a gorgeous peak foliage October day in Bar Harbor, Maine.

Hayley glanced around, expecting to see a squirrel darting toward a tree nearby, which never failed to excite Leroy, but she didn't spot one. Still, something had alerted his keen senses, and then without warning, he took off running, the weathered red leather leash handle flying out of Hayley's hand.

"Leroy!" Hayley shouted.

But the dog paid no attention to her. He hardly ever did unless she was opening a box of his favorite doggie treats.

Leroy raced along the path, skidding to a stop and

peering over the edge at something down below, erupting in a spurt of short barks. Hayley sighed and ran to catch up to him so she could grab ahold of the loose leash and they could continue on their way. She wanted to be at her restaurant, Hayley's Kitchen, because she was expecting a beverage delivery, and she still owed Sal Moretti, the editor of the *Island Times*, her food and cocktails column for tomorrow's paper.

"Leroy!"

His tiny tail wagging, Leroy remained focused on some kind of commotion past the rocky edge of the shore, out in the low tide clam flats. The closer she got, Hayley could begin to hear labored grunts and growling. Had Leroy stumbled upon two stray dogs fighting?

When she reached the edge of the path and glanced down, her mouth dropped open in shock.

It wasn't two animals.

It was two people.

Both women, maybe.

Locked in an embrace.

Pounding on each other with their fists while rolling around in the muddy clam flats.

They were unrecognizable because they were both covered in mud. Hayley just stood there, mouth agape, watching as one of them, the bigger, heftier one, suddenly got the upper hand by managing to wrap her thick arm around the other woman's neck in a headlock. The smaller woman struggled mightily, reaching up with her fingernails, trying to claw at her assailant's face. That's when Hayley got a better look at the bigger woman's wild, furious eyes and determined grimace. She had seen that expression many times in an endless number of uncomfortable moments.

It was Mona Barnes.

Her BFF.

"Mona!" Hayley cried.

Surprised, Mona looked up, momentarily distracted. This allowed her opponent to wrench free from her grip and scramble to her feet. Mona tried hauling herself up as well, but the mud was too slippery and she had trouble balancing herself. It didn't matter in the end because the other woman had time to deliver a swift kick to Mona's behind with her hip-wader, black-rubber, clam-digging boot, sending Mona flying back down, her face firmly planted in the mud. The woman slogged over and picked up a sharp clamming rake, raised it over her head, and started marching back over toward Mona with the intention of beating her senseless with it.

"No! Stop!" Hayley cried.

Hayley knew she had to do something.

As Leroy continued to bark, Hayley crawled down the side of the shore path ledge and scrambled over the rocks until her sneakers sunk into the quicksand-like mud and she trudged toward the wrestling match as fast as she could. By now, Mona had managed to raise herself up enough so she was on her knees, wiping mud off her face with the sleeve of her sweatshirt. Spotting the crazy-eyed woman wielding a clam-digging rake, Mona grabbed hold of an overturned bucket and began wildly swinging it at the woman to keep her at bay. The woman, incensed, began taking stabs at her, like she was in a sword duel in medieval England.

When Hayley finally reached them, she hurled herself

in between them, knowing that she was risking getting impaled by the rake or whacked in the head with the clam bucket.

"I said *stop*!" Hayley screamed at the top of her lungs, so loud even Leroy ceased barking and watched the scene in dumbstruck silence. Hayley threw her arms out wide to keep the brawlers at a safe distance from one another, like a World Wrestling Federation referee calling out illegal maneuvers.

Finally, both women seemed to give up. They dropped their weapons, but still stood facing off, glaring menacingly at one another.

"It's a good thing Hayley got here when she did, or you wouldn't be able to stand right now!" Mona snapped.

The other woman rolled her eyes. "Don't flatter yourself, Barnes. It was over for you before it even got started." She wiped mud away from her face with her hands and Hayley finally got a good look at her.

It was Vera Leighton.

The oldest daughter of Lonnie Leighton.

Owner of Leighton Fish & Seafood, a local business.

And Mona's chief rival.

The situation was finally starting to slowly come into focus. The two seafood companies had been competing for decades. First with Mona's parents and Lonnie. Now the war was mostly waged between the second generation to run the businesses, Mona and Vera. Although Mona's parents had long retired, Lonnie was still very much involved with his company, although Vera, along with his two younger daughters, Ruth and Olive, ran the day-to-day business. The two companies constantly clashed, vying for the best restaurant contracts and tourist business, like a modern-day Hatfields and McCoys family feud.

"Would one of you mind telling me what's going on here?" Hayley demanded, her body still in the middle to keep them physically apart.

Vera pointed a gnarled finger at Mona. "She knows what she did!"

"Well, I don't, so why don't you tell me, Vera?" Hayley sighed.

"She's always trying to encroach on my territory, and I won't stand for it anymore!" Vera snarled.

Mona guffawed. "You're crazier than your demented daddy if you think this spot is your territory! If you didn't drop out of high school to elope with that loser Kenny Farley, you'd know this is public property!"

"You know I never married Kenny!"

That's because Vera's enraged father had stopped them before they even had the chance to reach the Trenton Bridge. But even though her marriage plans were curtailed, Vera never bothered returning to school to finish up and get her diploma.

"Not marrying you was the only lucky day that poor kid ever had!" Mona snorted. "I hear he's in the state pen for a botched convenience store robbery. You could always pick 'em, Vera!"

Vera eyed the rake lying by her feet.

"Vera, don't even think about it!" Hayley warned.

Vera flicked her eyes to Hayley. "My family has been clamming this spot since the nineteen seventies. It was an unspoken rule that Mona and her boys stay far away from here and do their clamming elsewhere. So, imagine my surprise when I showed up here this morning to find Mona in her hip waders digging for *my* clams!"

"These are not your clams, Vera! Mother Nature isn't part of the Leighton Seafood empire!" Mona snapped with a sarcastic sneer. "I have every right to be here!"

"You just came here to get my ire up, come on, admit it!" Vera yelled accusingly, her gnarly finger pointing again.

Hayley folded her arms. "Did you, Mona? Did you come to this spot this morning just to tick off Vera?"

There was a long pause.

Then, looking down at the discarded bucket and the closed-up clam shells scattered all around, Mona muttered, "I refuse to answer on the grounds that it will probably incriminate me."

"See? She just likes stirring up trouble!" Vera cried.

"Mona, why did you feel the need to come here and upset Vera? That seems awfully petty," Hayley said.

"Because she knew I was negotiating a contract with that new restaurant, the Greek one on Cottage Street, and she came in at the last minute and stole it away from me!"

"It's not my fault you charge too much. All I did was offer a fair price. Any decent businessman with half a brain would have signed with us."

"I hate you, Vera Leighton!" Mona wailed.

"Good, because I hate you too, Mona Barnes!"

"See? At least you're both on the same page about *something*," Hayley noted, trying to keep the peace. "Come on, Mona, let me drop off Leroy at home and take you to breakfast. Let's go."

Mona bent down and picked up her bucket and rake, and Hayley gently led her away by the arm.

"You have a nice day, Vera," Hayley chirped.

Vera called after them. "I'll let you know. It's been a crappy day so far, but if I hear Mona's dropped dead later, my day will be roses and sunshine!"

Mona was about to turn around but Hayley gripped Mona's arm tighter. "Keep walking, Mona. Just keep walking."

Chapter 2

Sunday night dinner at the Barnes family home was always a loud, rollicking, sometimes messy affair. Hayley had once naively believed that as Mona's brood got older and more mature, the ear-splitting volume and boundless chaos of these legendary gatherings would somehow slowly subside. But that was not to be the case. Even with half her children all grown up and living in other parts of the country, the offspring that remained in Bar Harbor were just as outspoken, boisterous, and rowdy as their matriarch, which made for a wildly entertaining evening with off-color jokes, delicious local gossip, and loud arguments over a wide variety of topics, except politics which Mona never allowed to be discussed at the dinner table. Whenever Mona invited Hayley and Bruce to join the family for their Sunday night dinner, they always instantly accepted. This was a fun night you never wanted to miss out on.

Tonight was no exception. Mona's three oldest sons, Dennis Jr., Digger, and Dougie, who helped their mother run her seafood business, were in the living room shouting at each other at the top of their lungs over a bad referee call during a baseball game they had watched that afternoon. They had dragged Bruce into the discussion, who was more than happy to offer his own strong opinion on the losing team, his beloved Boston Red Sox who he firmly believed had been robbed of a win because of a questionable call at the plate. Hayley watched with amusement as things got so heated, Dennis Jr. finally gave up trying to make his point and stormed off into the kitchen to fetch another beer from the fridge.

Hayley then wandered into the den where Chet and Jody, the two youngest of Mona's brood were glued to the large screen TV on the wall watching a Marvel superhero show on Disney+. Trying to engage the kids in conversation, she began peppering them with questions about who Hawkeye was and how did he get so good at shooting a bow and arrow, but their half-hearted one-word answers strongly hinted that they had no desire to talk to her. So Hayley decided to help Mona, who was busy carving the ham in the dining room. She quickly noticed Mona angrily hacking at the ham with her knife, tearing into it with grim determination, as if she was taking out all her anger on the poor pig's carcass.

Hayley folded her arms. "You're still thinking about Vera Leighton, aren't you?"

Mona didn't even look up as she kept violently slicing and dicing. "You're damn right I am! That awful, despicable woman just makes me so mad! I can't stop thinking about what happened today!"

"Mona, let it go. It doesn't matter. There is room for two seafood businesses in Bar Harbor."

"That's not the point. She needs to be brought down a

peg. She's been like this ever since high school. Remember when we were on the track team together?"

Hayley sighed. "Yes, Mona, I know what you're going to say. I've heard the story a million times . . ."

"She deliberately kicked me in the shin as she passed me during that track meet in Presque Isle, causing me to fall. My knee was never the same after that. It's still out of whack all these years later."

"It was an accident."

"Oh, Hayley, please, it was no *accident*! She couldn't let me beat her even though we were on the same team! And then with me down, the best athlete on the team mind you, the runner from Presque Isle managed to glide right past her and win the meet. We lost because of Vera's petty jealousy! It cost us the state championship!"

"Well, it's a good thing you don't hold grudges."

Mona gave her a curious look before registering the pointed sarcasm and then simply choosing to ignore it. "My point is, once a cheat, always a cheat, and I am not going to put up with her underhanded tactics any longer. She doesn't own the entire Atlantic Ocean. She can't order me not to dig for clams on public property! If it's the last thing I do, I am going to put that spiteful woman and her whole corrupt family out of business, and I will enjoy every minute doing it!"

"Mona, if you do that, think about the bad karma."

"Bad karma? I don't care about bad karma! Hayley, I was stuck married to that deadbeat Dennis for decades! I've had more than my share of bad karma! What's a little more matter to me now?"

Hayley shrugged.

She did have a point.

Mona finished destroying the ham and then shouted,

"Soup's on! Get your butts in here before everything gets cold!" She turned to Hayley. "I forgot the mashed potatoes on the stove."

"Don't worry, I'll get them," Hayley said, crossing to the kitchen as Bruce, Digger, and Dougie wandered in, still arguing over the baseball game. Mona headed to the den because it was obvious she was going to have to physically tear Chet and Jody away from the TV.

As Hayley entered the kitchen, she happened upon her other BFF Liddy, who had also been invited to join this week's Barnes family Sunday dinner, in the middle of what looked like a very private, intense conversation with Dennis Jr.

"What are you two whispering about so secretively?" Hayley asked as she began scooping mashed potatoes from the pot on the stove into a large glass bowl.

Startled by her presence, Dennis Jr. jumped back and blurted out, "Nothing!"

"Hayley, you can't just sneak up on people like that!" Liddy snapped.

"I didn't. I just walked into the kitchen to get the mashed potatoes."

Dennis Jr. nervously excused himself and scooted out of the kitchen. Hayley watched him; then turned to Liddy, curious. "What was all that about? Why did he look so spooked to see me?"

"It's nothing, really."

Hayley raised an eyebrow. "It didn't look like nothing."

"Honestly, Hayley, why are you always *so* suspicious? If you must know, Dennis Jr. has been sharing an apartment with his father for a few months now, and it's gotten a little old. Dennis Jr. wants his own space and is eager to be out on his own, and so he asked me to find a place for him to rent while he saves up to buy a house. It's what I do. I help people. I'm not going to even charge him a rental commission. He just has to promise to use me as his realtor when he's ready to buy. Okay?"

Hayley studied Liddy's poker face and then nodded. "Okay."

"Good, I'm starving!" Liddy said, grabbing a basket of freshly baked rolls and darting out of the kitchen.

Hayley finished scooping out the potatoes and followed her, thoroughly convinced that Liddy was not telling her the whole truth.

Chapter 3

It was unusually busy for a Monday night at Hayley's local eatery Hayley's Kitchen, but Hayley would never complain. Ever since she opened the doors to her new restaurant over a year ago, it had been an astounding success right out of the gate with both the locals and the tourists. She had dreamed for years about owning her own business, and the fact that she was not only surviving but thriving was just icing on the cake. Cake also happened to be on top of the specials board as tonight's dessert, a New England Johnny Cake with Homemade Vanilla Ice Cream. However, the really big hit on the specials board was a mouth-watering Clam Risotto with Bacon and Chives. Her customers were ordering the dish in droves, and Hayley started to fear they might run out of clams before the night was out. She knew her chef, Kelton, was going to need some assistance with all the orders pouring in so after stopping by her old boss Sal and his wife Rosana's table to say hello and drop off a calamari appetizer on the house, she made a beeline for the kitchen to offer a helping hand.

She immediately spotted the sweat running down her burly, lovable chef's forehead as he plated a steamed lobster with all the fixings. He was red-faced and Hayley knew his blood pressure was probably off the charts at this point. She circled around the food prep table and placed a comforting hand on his shoulder.

"What can I do, Kelton?"

He sighed, relief in his eyes. "You can get another pot of rice going. I'm almost out. And I need to slice more bacon."

"You keep plating. I'll handle the rest."

She got to work at the stove simmering clam juice in a medium saucepan, boiling more water for the rice and slicing the bacon strips. Twenty minutes later, they were caught up and Kelton gratefully felt the pressure on him finally receding. They were a good team, in Hayley's mind, and Kelton was her Most Valuable Player.

Betty, her hostess, flew into the kitchen. "Hayley, one of the customers would like to speak to you."

"Uh-oh, that does not sound good. Do you know what it's about?"

Betty shook her head. "She wouldn't say, she just wants to have a word with the owner."

Hayley glanced over at Kelton, who seemed to have everything under control. Then she took a deep breath and followed Betty out of the kitchen into the dining room. Betty pointed to an attractive woman in her forties, trim, perfectly coiffured auburn hair, in a sharp business suit, dining alone at a table near the stone fireplace. Hayley steeled herself and marched over to the woman. The woman was taking a sip of her Chardonnay when Hayley noticed her plate was scraped clean.

That might be a good sign.

"Hello, how was your meal?"

The woman locked eyes with Hayley. "Are you the owner?"

"Yes, I am. I'm Hayley Powell."

"Tabitha Collins, pleased to meet you, Hayley. I just have one thing to say."

Hayley braced herself.

"This Clam Risotto?"

She took an agonizingly long pause.

"Best dish I have ever tasted."

Hayley felt the tension in her whole body slowly draining away. "Thank you so much. This is the first night we've had it on the menu so we weren't sure how it would go over. Our clientele can be pretty finicky."

Tabitha chuckled. "Well, food is my business. I am the CEO of a national seafood company, Boston Common Seafood, have you heard of us?"

Hayley's eyes widened. "Um, everyone's heard of Boston Common Seafood, it's world famous. You're the CEO? I'm impressed."

"I like to think, given my position, people take my opinions about food seriously. I can be tough and I am not the type to dole out compliments freely. Something has to be extra special in order to get any praise out of me, but let me tell you, this clam dish is a masterpiece."

Hayley felt her cheeks flushing. She had never been good at accepting a compliment. She would get embarrassed and self-conscious. "I certainly appreciate you telling me that."

Tabitha looked around at the buzzing restaurant. "This place is a gold mine."

"Well, certainly not yet. It took a lot of money to get this place up and running. It's going to be a little while longer before I actually turn a profit."

"I think you should branch out. Open more locations, maybe one in Portland, definitely Boston. Start in New England and branch out from there."

A nervous giggle unexpectedly erupted out of Hayley. Tabitha gave her a curious look. "What's so funny?"

"Nothing, I just . . . nothing."

"I am dead serious, Hayley. Give it some thought. I know my company would be interested in doing business with you. We have a history of building small businesses from the ground up, then acquiring them for our brand. We are not just about selling bags of frozen shrimp at your local grocery store. We have restaurants all over the world. Play your cards right and you could end up a *very* rich woman." She paused and smiled at Hayley, as if she was reading her mind. "Martha Stewart–rich."

Wow, this woman was amazing.

That was exactly what she had been thinking.

Just *how* rich was she talking about?

Hayley's head was spinning. It was all too much to process at the moment. "Thank you so much for your kind words. I will definitely think about it. But I'm crazed running just one restaurant. I can't imagine taking on more work at this point."

Tabitha was still smiling. She was very good at dangling the bait, knowing the fish would eventually bite. She appeared to be a patient woman, confident that in the end she would get what she wanted.

Betty was passing by, and Hayley stopped her. "Could you have Kelton come out here, please?"

Betty feared the worst but nodded. "Yes, I'll go get him right away." Then she hurried into the kitchen.

Hayley turned back to Tabitha.

"I'm flattered you liked our Clam Risotto so much, but I can't take the credit. I came up with the recipe, but the real artist is my chef, Kelton."

Right on cue, Kelton appeared by her side, sweat still sliding down his face, and like Hayley had been just moments earlier, bracing for the worst.

Hayley gave him a reassuring smile. "This is Tabitha Collins, a very influential seafood company executive, and she just wanted to give her compliments to the chef."

Kelton nodded, not knowing what to say.

He was just like Hayley.

Uncomfortable with a compliment.

"Th-thank you," he stuttered.

But unlike Hayley, he was also quite taken with this stunning, confident woman. It was obvious to both Hayley and Tabitha that Kelton was suddenly smitten.

And as a result, he was totally tongue-tied. He opened his mouth to say something else, but no words came out.

Tabitha watched him, charmed and amused.

Hayley decided it was time to rescue the poor man. "You can go back to the kitchen now, Kelton."

"Th-thank you," he managed to get out before scurrying away.

Tabitha pressed a business card into Hayley's hand. "In case you change your mind."

Hayley glanced at it and then slipped it in her pocket. "I'm going to have your waiter bring you a Johnny Cake, with my compliments."

"That's very nice of you. But I'm not really a dessert person. Just an espresso would be lovely."

Of course she didn't eat sweets.

There wasn't an ounce of body fat on her.

Which was why they would probably never work together.

Hayley didn't trust anyone who would refuse a decadent, high calorie, sugary dessert.

Chapter 4

It was almost eleven o'clock by the time Hayley had managed to lock up the restaurant for the night. Bruce had texted her earlier that he was going to be up late finishing his column for the *Island Times*. He had been working on his notes for a true crime book he wanted to write and had been neglecting his work at the paper so he needed to play catch-up.

Hayley didn't want to be a distraction so she decided to swing by her brother Randy's bar, Drinks Like A Fish, and unwind with a glass of Burgundy. The bar was basically empty except for a couple of locals in the back guzzling down mugs of beer while playing a game of darts. Randy had dismissed his bar manager, Michelle, for the evening since business was so slow. Randy rinsed some cocktail glasses in the sink as Hayley chattered on about the unexpected and unlikely offer she had just received from Tabitha Collins.

"Why wouldn't you jump at something like that, sis? It would be my dream to expand my business, open a Drinks Like A Fish national franchise!"

"You've always been more ambitious than me, Randy. Just the thought of taking something like that on gives me heart palpitations," Hayley said.

"It's probably the red wine giving you heart palpitations. I read something about that online."

Hayley smirked at him. "I will admit, it made me feel good to know someone that important is a fan of my restaurant. It's very flattering, but I have enough on my plate right now."

"I wouldn't dismiss it out of hand. You never know when an opportunity like this might come around again."

Hayley nodded. "You're right, I know, but Bruce and I have been trying to spend more time together. We want to travel more when the summer season is over, he wants us to go to Europe, maybe rent an Italian villa for a few months so he can work on his book, and if I were to squash that dream by taking on more work . . ."

"What about *your* dream? What do *you* want?"

"An Italian villa sounds pretty dreamy to me. Spaghetti Carbonara every night? Heavenly."

Randy studied his sister, finally satisfied she was speaking the truth. "Okay, then, forget I said anything." He paused. "But I really think you should talk to Bruce about it. You could be surprised by what he might think of all this."

"I'm almost afraid to," Hayley chuckled.

Because she knew Bruce would be supportive. He might even push her to pursue such a life-changing opportunity.

And that's what scared her the most.

Suddenly the door to the bar slammed open, and Mona stormed in, apoplectic, eyes blazing, startling Hayley.

"Mona, what on earth . . . ?"

"I don't want to talk about it! Randy, I need a Bud Lite, now!"

Randy rushed to the cooler.

"No, wait! I'm going to need something a hell of a lot stronger than beer! I need a shot. Whiskey. Johnny Walker. ASAP!"

"On it!" Randy shouted, saluting like he was a soldier in Mona's infantry.

He raced to grab the bottle off the shelf.

"Mona, what are you doing up this late? You're usually in bed by eight thirty!" Hayley said.

Mona was always up before dawn to haul her lobster traps.

"I can't sleep! Not after the news I just got!" Mona wailed.

Hayley's stomach tightened. "What news? What happened?"

"Ethel McFarland!" Mona spit out.

"Oh no, did she have another stroke? Is she dead?" Randy asked with a sense of dread in his voice.

"No, she's not dead! She's fit as a fiddle as far as I can tell, and still sticking her nose into everybody's business!"

Ethel McFarland, a seventy-six-year-old retired kindergarten teacher at Emerson-Conners, was also known as Bar Harbor's biggest gossip.

Randy delivered Mona's drink and she gulped it down and slammed the shot glass down on the bar.

"Feel better?" Randy asked tentatively.

"No, hit me with another," Mona roared.

Whatever news Ethel McFarland had relayed to Mona was obviously not good.

Randy hustled off to grab the Johnny Walker bottle as

Hayley tried to get Mona to focus. "What happened, Mona?"

"I was getting ready for bed when I realized I had promised to pick up some Lotto tickets for Dennis Jr. at the Big Apple and I had forgotten to do it earlier. Well, the drawing is tomorrow so I just got in my truck and headed over there before they closed. While I was there, Ethel McFarland was picking up a pack of cigarettes even though her doctor warned her she was just asking for another stroke. While we were both waiting to be rung up, she casually dropped the bomb that Dougie is seeing someone!"

Randy returned with the second shot.

Mona snatched it out of his hand and downed it.

"Your Dougie?"

"Yes, Hayley, how many Dougies do you know?" Mona sighed loudly.

"I just wanted to be sure," Hayley said quietly.

"Dougie's got a girlfriend? That's wonderful!" Randy cooed. "We should be celebrating!"

"This most certainly is *not* a cause for celebration," Mona snapped.

"But Dougie's nineteen. This is the perfect time for him to be dating. I don't understand why this would upset you?"

"It's not the fact that he's got a girlfriend that I have an issue with, it's *who* the girlfriend is!"

"Who?" Hayley and Randy said in unison.

"What are you two, owls now? It's Olive Leighton!"

Finally, some clarity.

Of course Mona was upset.

Olive Leighton was the youngest daughter of Lonnie Leighton, her bitter rival.

"Olive's a lovely girl, very pretty," Randy said. "I can totally see why Dougie would like her."

"She's a *Leighton*!" Mona roared.

Hayley smiled. "I think it's kind of sweet. Two young people falling in love despite the feud between their families. It's like *Romeo and Juliet*."

"This isn't some high-falutin' Shakespeare play I can barely understand, this is my life we're talking about! And I don't want my Dougie anywhere near that corrupt, cheating brood!"

"Dougie's an adult, Mona, he's going to make his own decisions," Hayley said.

"Not if I have anything to say about it!"

Randy gingerly picked up the empty shot glass and set it down behind the bar, deciding it would be best to cut Mona off at this point. "What are you going to do?"

"I'm going to go home right now and tell Dougie he needs to break it off with that girl first thing tomorrow morning."

"Mona, that's a terrible idea! You might alienate him. I know if my mother told me not to see someone, it would only make him more attractive to me!" Hayley warned.

"Well, Dougie's always been a mama's boy, he worships the ground I walk on, he'll listen to me and do what's right," Mona said, nodding, trying to convince herself.

Hayley, however, was not at all convinced.

Nobody can control who they fall in love with.

Nobody.

If Mona expected Dougie to just walk away from something good in his life, she was just deluding herself. And Hayley instinctively knew that things were about to get very messy in the Barnes household.

Chapter 5

The following morning, Hayley was sitting in the waiting room of her physician Dr. Cormack's office, a few minutes before eight o'clock. She was kicking herself for making the appointment so early. When she worked at the *Island Times*, she had to report to the office at eight so she got in the habit of scheduling her doctor's appointments for as early as possible so she could get straight to work after her exam. Those days were over. Running a restaurant was an entirely different lifestyle. After working until ten or eleven at night, sometimes she didn't show up at the restaurant to begin her day until eleven in the morning or even noon, depending on whether or not she had food deliveries. But this checkup had been on the book for months now so if she had tried to change it, she might not get another slot until maybe weeks or even months from now. So she had just dragged herself out of bed, downed two cups of coffee, and hustled over in order to get this whole thing over with. She had already taken a blood test. Cholesterol, glucose, liver, all decent numbers, so there were no worries on that front. She knew when the nurse took her blood pressure it would be sky-high. She had what the doctor described as "White Coat Syndrome." Whenever she was in Dr. Cormack's office, she got incredibly nervous and anxious and so her blood pressure would just shoot off the charts. But then, hours later when she took it at home, it pretty much ran normal. She sometimes had a fast heartbeat, but mostly that occurred when Bruce came out of the bathroom shirtless.

Hayley felt perfectly healthy today and hoped Dr. Cormack would not keep her here too long.

The door to the examination rooms swung open, and Lonnie Leighton shakily stomped out, heading for the exit. Hayley was taken aback and troubled by his appearance. His face was gaunt and pale, his hands were trembling, his thin body fragile and weak. Lonnie had always looked much older than he actually was due to decades of hard living, but today his appearance was particularly startling for Hayley, who barely recognized him.

As Lonnie tentatively made his way for the door that led out to the parking lot, Dr. Cormack's loyal, bubbly nurse, Tilly, shot to her feet from behind the reception desk. "Lonnie, wait! The doctor wants to see you again in two weeks!"

Lonnie waved her away dismissively with a bony, cracked, wrinkled hand. "I'll call you later and schedule something!"

Tilly was undeterred. "But you're here now, so why not save us both the trouble?"

Lonnie spun around so fast, he nearly lost his balance. Hayley could plainly see the sudden sharp move had

made him light-headed and dizzy. She jumped up and
hurried over, taking him gently by the arm to help steady
him.

He glowered at her, eyes narrowing. "What do you
think you're doing?"

Hayley instantly released her grip. "I thought you
were going to fall and so I—"

"I was *not* going to fall!" Lonnie bellowed. "I'm perfectly fine! I don't need your help! I'm not some in-
valid!"

"No, of course not. I never meant to imply you were,
it's just that—"

He turned his back on her, focusing his anger now at
poor Nurse Tilly. "I said I will call you! Is that too difficult a concept to get through your tiny pea brain?"

Deeply wounded, Tilly shook her head.

Lonnie glared at her a little while longer, just because
he was enjoying intimidating her, then he whipped around
and stormed out of the doctor's office, his shoulder banging the doorframe as he lost his balance again. He stopped
briefly, gripping the frame with his long bony fingers until
he was satisfied he wouldn't topple over, and then he continued out, slamming the door loudly behind him.

There was an uncomfortable silence.

Then Tilly disappeared from behind the reception desk
and opened the door leading to the examination rooms.
"Hayley?"

"Yes, I'm ready, thank you, Tilly," Hayley said, crossing over to the nurse, who led her inside to a large, metal,
old-fashioned weight scale.

"No, Tilly, you know how much I hate getting weighed
at the doctor's office. It's always so much more than
when I weigh myself at home."

"I understand, dear, but this is way more accurate than the one you have at home," Tilly said, before catching herself. "Um, I mean, would you like to empty your pockets before you step on the scale?"

Hayley wanted to refuse, but she knew Dr. Cormack would give her a hard time, so she decided to just get on with it, and accept the reality that the basket of garlic bread she had consumed after they closed the restaurant last night was probably already attached directly to her thighs. She began emptying her pockets of her phone, wallet, and loose change.

"What's going on with Lonnie Leighton?" Hayley asked casually.

Tilly stiffened. "What do you mean?"

"He doesn't look well," Hayley said.

"Has he ever?" Tilly whispered, still hurting from Lonnie calling her a pea brain.

Hayley smiled and shook off her shoes and removed her belt, hoping to shed another pound or two. "I know he's never been the healthiest person, not with the way he smokes and drinks, but he looks worse than I have ever seen him."

Tilly wagged an admonishing finger at Hayley. "You know I cannot discuss another patient's medical condition with anyone. That would be unethical and grounds for immediate dismissal, so I'm sorry, but you are not going to get anything out of me, Hayley Powell!"

"You're right, I'm sorry, Tilly, forget I even asked."

She was right.

Tilly would be fired if she told Hayley anything.

But she didn't have to.

Nurse Tilly had the most readable face of anyone Hayley had ever met. She could never hide her true feelings or what she was thinking. And it was painfully obvious at this moment just from Tilly's worried and somber expression that Lonnie Leighton was most likely gravely ill.

Just how ill remained a mystery.

But Hayley had a bad feeling. Even worse than the bad feeling she was already having about what her weight on that scale was going to be.

Tilly clutched her iPad impatiently, waiting for Hayley to finally get on the scale. With nothing left to discard from her body except her blouse and jeans, Hayley took a deep breath and stepped up on the rubber base as Tilly began to slowly move the slider weight farther down the scale.

The final number was far worse than she had even anticipated. Five and a half pounds heavier than she had been at home. She had been right to have a bad feeling.

And she was fairly certain she was also right about her other bad feeling when it came to Lonnie Leighton's health.

She just could not shake the unsettling thought that Lonnie's days left on earth were numbered.

Chapter 6

Hayley furrowed her brow as she stared slack jawed at Mona's son Dougie Barnes, who stood at the hostess station in the front of Hayley's restaurant. "Excuse me, you want to do what now, Dougie?"

"Propose."

"To whom?"

"Your hostess, Betty," he joked, snorting, startling Betty, who stood nearby. "I'm kidding! No, Olive. Olive Leighton. My girlfriend. And hopefully soon-to-be bride."

Hayley glanced around, panic rising in her throat. She could hardly speak. "You want to do it *here*?"

Dougie nodded his head. "I was wondering if you could seat us over there by the fireplace. That table for two looks really romantic." He then pulled a small red box out of his pants pocket and flipped it open. Inside, embedded in black velvet was a sparkling diamond ring. Maybe one or even two carats. Which on the low end might set Dougie back five grand. He was sparing no expense for his one true love.

Hayley had been in the kitchen running down the

night's specials with Kelton when Betty had summoned her to the front of the restaurant where Dougie was waiting for her. Olive had gone to the ladies' room and so Dougie alerted Hayley that they had to make a plan quickly before she returned.

Hayley could not help herself. "Oh, Dougie, it's gorgeous!"

"I know, Liddy helped me pick it out."

"Liddy?"

Liddy loved all the romance of a wedding, not to mention the accoutrements included in the planning, especially expensive engagement rings. Of course, she had had a spotty track record when it came to her own wedding, ditched at the altar, but that was another story. So she was happy to just horn her way into another couple's happy day, and luckily in Dougie's case, her interference was not just tolerated, it was welcome.

"She suggested you hide the ring in a clam shell since I know Olive is planning to order your risotto and clam special tonight so when she opens it to dig out the clam she'll be totally surprised."

Hayley's risotto clam special had been so popular, she had decided to leave it on the specials board for at least the rest of the week.

Hayley was fidgeting with her fingers. "Dougie, does Mona know what you're planning to do tonight?"

Dougie shook his head vigorously. "No, and please don't say anything, she'll just melt down like Chernobyl! She may even have a heart attack so it's best she not know, at least for a while. She just needs time to come around to the idea that, like it or not, a Leighton is going to be part of our family."

"Dougie, I really think you should tell her."

"Please, Aunt Hayley, I want this night to be perfect. I can't think of a better place than your restaurant to start a whole new chapter of my life. You've always been such a huge part of my childhood, my happiest memories have always involved you and my cousins Gemma and Dustin, and it just seems fitting that I do this here, with you."

There it was.

The Dougie charm.

He had charisma in spades.

So much more than his older brothers.

Or his younger sibling Chet, for that matter.

Hayley had always had a soft spot for Dougie.

She was not his real aunt.

He had just called her Aunt Hayley ever since he had learned to talk.

He had also always considered Hayley's children from her first marriage, Gemma and Dustin, as his real cousins, even though they were not.

But doing this behind Mona's back, there would be consequences, how severe remained to be seen. She was still on the fence. Would Mona see this as some kind of betrayal? On the other hand, Dougie was an adult. He was old enough to make his own decisions. And it was obvious this kid was head over heels in love. It was not up to her to stop him.

"Aunt Hayley, please, Olive will be back any second!"

Hayley sighed and held out her hand. "Give me the ring."

Dougie gleefully snapped the box shut and pressed it into the palm of her hand, which she quickly closed as Olive returned from the ladies' room with a tentative smile on her face. She knew Hayley was Mona's best friend and was not sure how she would be received.

Hayley offered her a warm smile. "Hello, Olive, you're looking very pretty tonight. That's a lovely dress."

Olive looked away shyly and muttered, "Thank you."

Betty stepped forward and picked up two menus from the pile next to her so she could seat the happy couple.

"Betty, why don't you show Dougie and Olive to that table for two by the fireplace."

"Sure thing," Betty said, ushering them along. "This way, lovebirds."

They dutifully followed behind her.

Hayley was still worrying about Mona's reaction to the news that her boy Dougie had become engaged to Olive Leighton at Hayley's Kitchen. She prayed that she would manage to talk Mona off the ledge.

Hayley made a beeline for the kitchen where she gave the ring to Kelton and instructed him to slip it in one of the clam shells when Olive's order came through. Kelton, usually not a demonstrative sort of guy, was unusually touched by the romantic nature of the moment. Hayley thought he might even cry. Who knew?

When she returned to the dining room, Hayley stopped cold. Standing at the hostess station chatting with Betty, who had just moments before seated Dougie and Olive, was Lonnie Leighton and his girlfriend, Abby Weston, a sweet, unassuming retired middle school teacher.

What were they doing here?

Hayley had never seen Lonnie Leighton set foot in her restaurant. Ever. And now, here he was, on a date with Abby, the same night as Dougie Barnes was planning to propose to his precious youngest daughter.

This was a disaster in the making.

Hayley raced over to Betty, who was scanning her iPad. Her face was pale and she attempted to block their view of the fireplace with her whole body. "Lonnie! What a nice surprise! Hi, Abby! I am so sorry, I wish you had given me more notice. I would have reserved a special table for you, but unfortunately we are *completely* booked for tonight."

"Well, then I guess it's a good thing I made a reservation," Lonnie growled.

Hayley's face fell. "You did?"

Betty finished scanning her iPad. "Here it is. Leighton. For two. Seven o'clock." She smiled brightly. "Right on time. I have a nice table by the fireplace."

"No!" Hayley found herself screaming.

They all froze.

"I've been receiving some complaints from a few customers that it's too hot by the fireplace. I don't want you to get sweaty and uncomfortable."

"It's summer. You don't even have a fire going."

Hayley glanced over.

He was right.

She paused, then turned back to Lonnie. "It's probably the heat from the kitchen."

Before Lonnie could note that the kitchen was on the opposite side of the dining room, Hayley quickly suggested, "Betty, why don't you seat them on the opposite side by the bay window?"

"I don't mind a little heat. It's very chilly out tonight," Abby said.

Hayley fought the urge to glare at Abby.

She liked Abby.

A lot.

In fact, her only issue with Abby Weston was what she could possibly see in Lonnie Leighton. But they seemed happy enough together so frankly it was none of her business.

"Trust me, Abby, it's too hot," Hayley insisted.

Not wanting to get into an argument with the restaurant's owner, sweet and luckily nonconfrontational Abby immediately backed down. "Sure, we can sit wherever. The food will taste the same, right?" Hayley laughed a little too hard.

She plucked two menus off the pile and shoved them at Betty, who now knew something was definitely up.

"Enjoy," Hayley purred. "I will send over some fried calamari on the house."

"Thank you, Hayley, that's very sweet of you," Abby cooed.

Abby followed Betty and Lonnie brought up the rear until he suddenly stopped and spun back around toward Hayley. He had a clear view of Dougie and Olive, but thankfully was focused on Hayley at the moment and did not notice them.

"By the way, you tell that brother-in-law of yours I'm coming down to the station tomorrow to see him."

Hayley's brother Randy was married to Bar Harbor's Chief of Police, Sergio Alvares.

"Oh?" Hayley croaked. "Did something happen?"

"That Mona Barnes viciously attacked my eldest daughter Vera in the clam flats yesterday, in broad daylight. I want her charged with assault!"

Hayley cleared her throat. "Um, I was there Lonnie, Vera was no victim, they were both—"

"I don't care what you saw, Hayley! I am making it my life's mission to put that awful, spiteful, vile woman out of business for good!"

And then he stalked off after Betty and Abby.

Hayley's only thought in that moment was to make it her own life's mission to make sure Lonnie Leighton did not witness Dougie Barnes propose to his youngest daughter Olive at a table barely thirty feet away.

Chapter 7

Hayley hurled herself in front of Lonnie after he sat down at a table for two with Abby, blocking his line of vision. "Can I offer you a cocktail or wine on the house, Lonnie?"

Lonnie studied her suspiciously, keyed into the fact that Hayley was acting mighty strange.

Abby answered for him. "That would be wonderful. Thank you, Hayley. I'll take a Rose Kennedy."

"Whiskey, straight up," Lonnie snorted.

"I'll bring some stuffed mushrooms too, along with the calamari."

"Oh, Hayley, you're spoiling us," Abby giggled.

"We have a very popular special tonight, folks seem to love it, it's a Clam Risotto. We also have a full lobster dinner, a flat iron steak with mashed potatoes and buttered asparagus, oh, and the fish tonight is a garlic butter baked salmon."

She noticed Lonnie trying to peer around her to see if he knew anyone dining at the restaurant this evening. Hayley opened up one of the menus she was holding and thrust it in front of his face. "We also have our regular menu items. Although we may be out of the veal scallopini, I'll have to check."

Lonnie gave her a curious look, then started perusing the menu as Abby offered up a pleasant yet vacant smile.

"I'll be right back with your drinks," Hayley chirped, scurrying away, sweat pouring down her brow. Her face was almost as wet as her chef Kelton's got from all the heat in the kitchen. She scooted over to the bar where one of her waitresses was mixing a Cosmo. "Rose Kennedy and whiskey straight up for table six. And keep them coming. The less lucid Lonnie Leighton becomes, the better chance we have of getting through this night without a disaster of epic proportions."

"I have no idea what you are talking about," the beautiful, raven-haired Christina said, giving her boss a blank stare.

"It's probably best you don't," Hayley muttered, bounding back to Lonnie and Abby's table to keep them occupied with small talk after noticing Olive eagerly diving into her Clam Risotto. It was now only a matter of minutes, seconds even, before she stumbled upon her secret surprise.

"Do you miss teaching, Abby?" Hayley asked casually, standing directly in front of Lonnie.

"I miss the kids, most of them anyway, but I don't miss the politics at the school, all the rules and regulations and paperwork, it was just getting to be too much. I was finally ready to call it quits."

"Well, you were a terrific teacher. Both Gemma and Dustin *loved* being in your class."

"That's so nice to hear," Abby said.

Christina arrived with their drinks.

Abby raised her glass. "Here's to retirement."

Lonnie begrudgingly clinked glasses with her before downing his whiskey in one gulp. "The day I retire is the day they bury me six feet under. And that's the God's honest truth!"

"Oh, I know, Lonnie, hard work is what's always kept you alive and kicking," Hayley said, instantly regretting it.

Both Lonnie and Abby went quiet, staring down at the white tablecloth, the melted wax candle in the middle flickering.

Hayley knew she had just put her foot in her mouth.

Seeing him so pale and gaunt at Dr. Cormack's office.

There was definitely something wrong with him.

And she had stupidly just made things very awkward.

After an agonizingly long pause, Lonnie barked, "You're right. It gives me purpose. I'll never be the guy to just lie around on the couch all day watching sports or Fox News." He thrust his empty glass toward Hayley. "Mind if I have another?"

"No, not at all," she said, taking the glass.

They suddenly heard people applauding.

Hayley's stomach dropped.

Her customers usually only applauded when the staff sang "Happy Birthday" while delivering a piece of chocolate cake with a sparkling candle, or something even more significant had just happened in the restaurant, like a marriage proposal.

She took a deep breath.

At that moment, Betty, who was helping out the waiters, brought a plate of stuffed mushrooms for Lonnie and Abby.

"These are quite good, if I do say so myself. The secret

ingredient is I use chicken-flavored dry stuffing mix," Hayley blurted out nervously.

Abby nodded politely.

Lonnie was too distracted by the applause. "What's going on over there?" He moved his head from side to side, but Hayley deliberately stood in his way. Finally, frustrated, Lonnie bolted up from his chair and leaned to the right so he could see past Hayley.

That's when his mouth dropped open in shock, his jaw nearly hitting the floor.

Hayley slowly turned around to see Olive in her chair at the table, eyes dancing, tears running down her cherubic cheeks, hands to her mouth as Dougie was down on one knee in front of her, the clam shell in one hand as he extracted the engagement ring from it with the other. He slipped it on Olive's finger as the entire restaurant continued clapping and cheering them on.

Lonnie angrily pushed past Hayley, knocking into a passing busboy who dropped a pitcher of water, which splashed all over the floor. Lonnie stomped over to the table by the fireplace, screaming into Dougie's face. "What the hell do you think you're doing, boy?"

Dougie's eyes nearly popped out of their sockets at the sight of Olive's father. But he remained resolute, and slowly climbed to his feet until he was eye to eye with Lonnie. "I have asked . . ." There seemed to be a frog caught in his throat so he took time to clear it, then continued. "I have asked Olive to marry me, and she said yes."

Lonnie took this in, his whole head reddening with rage. "Over my dead body!"

Olive was shrinking in her seat. "Daddy, please—"

"Don't you say a word! I will deal with you later! I

want you to get up from this table and go home right
now!" Lonnie screeched.

Olive, in a flood of tears, covered her face with her
trembling hands, jumped up, and fled the restaurant.

Lonnie fixed his furious gaze on Dougie for a moment,
who was bravely standing his ground.

Hayley then noticed Lonnie glance down at a steak
knife sitting on a neighboring table. She feared he might
snatch it up and drive it right through Dougie's chest.

She turned to Dougie. "Dougie, go to the kitchen and
wait for me. I will handle this."

"No, Aunt Hayley, this is my problem and I'm going
to deal with it—"

Hayley held up a hand. "Trust me. It will be better if
you go . . . *now*."

Dougie flicked his eyes from Hayley to a murderous
Lonnie, whose fingers were dangerously close to the handle of that seriously sharp steak knife. He sighed, then
nodded slightly and retreated to the kitchen.

Abby suddenly appeared at Lonnie's right shoulder.
"Lonnie, you're causing a scene. I think it's best if we
just go home."

"If I ever see that no-good punk anywhere near my
daughter again, I swear—"

"Noted, Lonnie. Now leave," Hayley insisted.

"But we haven't eaten our dinner yet," Lonnie barked.

"Please, let's just go," Abby begged, tugging on Lonnie's shirt sleeve.

Lonnie didn't budge.

"Lonnie, it's within my rights to refuse service to anyone, which means, I can ask you to leave. If you don't,
then you'll leave me no choice but to call the police and
have you removed."

"You wouldn't dare!" Lonnie scoffed.

"Try me."

He glared at her, but then realized she probably was not bluffing, so he spun around, shaking Abby's hand off his arm, and banged out of the restaurant, screaming, "I hope you all get food poisoning!"

Betty slid in next to Hayley. "I can't wait to read his Yelp review."

Hayley wanted to laugh, but nothing about this was even remotely funny.

There was no telling what lengths Lonnie Leighton would go to destroy his daughter's happiness, not to mention Mona's business. But right now, it was about repairing the damage Lonnie had caused to her customers' dining experience.

She knew what she had to do.

"Sorry you had to live through all that drama, folks. I hope I can make it up to you by offering everyone a free dessert tonight!"

This time there wasn't just polite applause.

It was downright thunderous.

Chapter 8

Dougie was slumped down in the passenger seat of Hayley's car, despondent and inconsolable as she drove him home after closing up the restaurant for the night. Dougie had walked into town earlier that evening and met Olive on the street corner just down from Hayley's Kitchen so neither of their families would see them leaving to go on their date together. What they had not counted on was Olive's volatile, short-tempered father Lonnie deciding to dine out on the same night at the same restaurant.

"I planned this proposal for so long, I went over every detail again and again. I wanted it to be so special, a night we would remember for the rest of our lives."

Well, in that regard, the night was a resounding success. They all would certainly remember it for the rest of their lives.

"This was going to be the start of our whole new life together, Aunt Hayley. But now I've gone and made a big mess of everything!" Dougie wailed.

"Dougie, this is *not* your fault," Hayley insisted, glancing over at him as she turned off the main road out of town toward Mona's house. "Nothing ever turns out the way we plan it, but I can plainly see how much you and Olive love each other, and nobody, not Lonnie, not even your mother, should ever try and interfere with that."

"Do you really mean that?"

"Of course I do," Hayley said firmly, although she knew she would be on very shaky ground with Mona. "You can't help who you love, and if that love is strong enough, then nothing will ever be able to break it."

"Thank you, you've made me feel a whole lot better."

When Hayley pulled up in front of Mona's house, she was relieved to see all the lights in the house off, which meant Mona had already gone to bed, sparing her from having to explain what had happened at the restaurant and why she was driving Dougie home.

"Good night, Aunt Hayley," Dougie said, leaning across the seat and bussing Hayley on the cheek. "Thanks for the ride."

"My pleasure, Dougie. You hang in there. Things will look clearer in the morning."

"I sure hope so," Dougie said, opening the car door and hopping out.

Hayley was just reaching for the gear to shift the car in reverse when suddenly she was startled by a loud crack. Dougie, who was walking toward the house, illuminated by her car's headlights, dropped to the ground.

Hayley cranked her head around.

Through the back window, she could just make out a figure in the dark aiming what looked like a shotgun.

Hayley rolled down the window. "Dougie! Dougie! Are you all right?"

"I'm fine!"

"What just happened?"

"I think someone's shooting at me!"

"Stay where you are!"

Dougie stayed flat on the ground, protected by the front of the car. Hayley sank down in her seat, waiting for the shooter to make his next move. She rolled down the driver's side window.

"Who's out there? Who's shooting at us!" Hayley cried.

She heard the shooter cock his gun, ready to fire another round. "I'm not going to warn you again, Barnes! You stay away from my daughter or the next one goes right between your eyes!"

Of course, it was Lonnie Leighton.

Out with his hunting rifle, stirring up trouble.

Probably drunk on one too many whiskey shots.

"Lonnie, you better get out of here before I call the police, for real this time!" Hayley shouted.

Another blast of gunfire.

"You hear me, Barnes?" Lonnie bellowed.

Dougie didn't dare move or say anything.

Lights began popping on inside Mona's house.

Everyone had now been alerted to the scene unfolding outside in the driveway.

"Go home, Lonnie! Now!" Hayley shouted through the open window.

"Not until he promises me he won't be chasing after my Olive anymore!"

The front door of the house flew open and Mona barreled out, wearing a light-blue nightgown, surprisingly feminine for Mona, and wielding her own shotgun. She cocked it and aimed it at Lonnie, who ducked behind

Hayley's back bumper as Dougie was sprawled out on the ground in front of her hood.

"Who the hell is taking potshots at my kid?" Mona roared.

"Lonnie Leighton!" Hayley yelled, ducking down in her seat as far as she possibly could.

Hayley could see Mona lower her rifle and rush over to Dougie to make sure he was not hurt, then raise it again and take direct aim in the direction where Lonnie was hiding. "Lonnie, you have thirty seconds to get off my property before I start shooting like it's the gunfight at the O.K. Corral!"

"I ain't going nowhere until your kid agrees to stop hounding my youngest, Olive!"

"I don't know what the hell you're talking about, Lonnie! How much have you been drinking tonight?" Mona cried.

Suddenly Mona's son Digger came bursting out of the house brandishing his own firearm, a Glock pistol. That's when Lonnie, still drunk as a skunk, was finally lucid enough to realize he was now hopelessly outnumbered. He sprang to his feet and made a run for it into the woods. After waiting a few minutes to make sure he was not going to try and circle back and start firing at them, Mona lowered her own rifle and Dougie crawled to his feet.

Mona rushed over to her son and brushed the dirt off his dress shirt. "Dougie, what was that crazy old bugger squawking about? You're not still seeing Olive Leighton, are you? You told me it was over!"

Hayley furrowed her brow.

Clearly poor Dougie had lied to his mother in order to keep the peace.

Dougie stared guiltily at the ground.

Mona gripped his arm tight. "Dougie?"

Deeply upset, he shook her hand away and ran past his brother Digger and hurried inside the house and upstairs to his room.

Digger stuffed his pistol in his pants. "I'm gonna go talk to him, make sure he's okay."

Digger disappeared back inside the house leaving Mona standing in the headlights of Hayley's car, squinting at her. "Why do I get the feeling you know more than you've told me?"

Hayley tried sinking in the seat even farther, but there was just nowhere to go.

Island Food & Spirits
BY
HAYLEY POWELL

When I was about eight years old, I remember my mother Sheila called up her two lifelong best friends, Jane and Celeste, and suggested they all take their daughters to Bangor for a day of shopping at the mall and to dinner at a new restaurant she had been dying to try. As it happened, Jane and Celeste were mothers to my own pair of BFFs, Mona and Liddy respectively, so it promised to be a really fun day!

So, after a whirlwind of shopping at our favorite stores, spending every last dime of our allowance, plus a few extra dollars Mom had slipped me when we pulled into the mall parking lot, we then all loaded into Jane's van and headed off to the new restaurant that all the locals had been buzzing about, which was known for its fresh locally sourced seafood and homemade pasta, two of my favorite foods! Well, to be perfectly honest, the list of my favorite foods could fill a phone book, but seafood and pasta are definitely way up there!

Our moms told us we could order anything we wanted, but they also insisted we order something we had never tried before just so we could enjoy a new experience. I excitedly opened my menu and immediately searched for the appetizers because even at that young age I already knew a thing or two about a yummy starter before the main course. I can't tell you how many deliciously breaded mozzarella sticks I had consumed in my very short life! But since I was encouraged to try something new, I pointed at the Baked Clams. That was it! That's what I wanted to try!

I had always been curious about clams, but the reason I had never tried them was because my mother hated them. She refused to bring any into our house. Whenever we ate at Jane's or Celeste's house they knew well enough not to serve clams. I asked her why she didn't like them but she didn't really have a good reason. She would just crinkle her nose and say, "They're just so rubbery and gross and they smell awful!"

When the waitress arrived, I was the first one up and I ordered the Baked Clams. My mother immediately tried talking me out of it. Luckily Jane and Celeste reminded her of the rule, and clams were something I had never tried. She had no choice but to go along with it, warning me that I would have to eat every last one, even if I didn't like them, so they would not go to waste.

When the waitress arrived with the plate of baked clams, my eyes lit up and I dove right in, surprising everyone, especially my mother. I was in heaven, devouring those little bits of yummy clams in a stuffing mixture baked in a clam shell. I took my last bite in record time, practically licking the bottoms of the shells clean, and then I turned to my mother and asked if I could order some more.

Jane and Celeste both laughed and ordered another plate. My mother just sat there, looking disgusted by the clams as the second helping arrived. Soon I was ready for a third.

Mona and Liddy started banging their forks on the table and chanting, "Do it! Do it! Do it!" Even their mothers joined in. Everyone was howling and cheering me on. My mother, who would have certainly put her foot down if we had not had an audience, finally just shrugged and flagged down the waitress for a third plate.

Well, I was just eight years old. My body could only take so much and I finally had to surrender before finishing my third full order of baked clams. Jane and Mona both helped me by eating the last few clams and everyone clapped and cheered, the adults toasting me with their wine. I held my grape soda up high in the air, stood up from my chair, and took a triumphant bow.

I was amazed that Mom wasn't even mad at me when I gave up on my homemade Fettuccini Alfredo after just two bites. She said we could wrap it up and give it to my brother Randy when we picked him up from his friend's house. Randy was basically a walking garbage disposal.

On the drive home, we had not even left the city limits of Bangor when I began to feel hot and uncomfortable. The air conditioner was on in the van but I kept feeling warmer and warmer. Then I began to get itchy and started scratching at my face. My eyes were watering and I was really feeling so awful that finally I called to my mother, who was sitting in the front passenger seat, and told her I wasn't feeling very good and that I couldn't stop itching.

My mother turned around and Jane flipped on the inside light to the van, and through my watery eyes, which now felt like they were closing up on me, I could see my mother's eyes grow wide and she clasped her hand to her mouth. She quickly unbuckled her seat belt and crawled over the seats to where I was sitting. Her horrified expression scared me so much I burst into tears, which of course just made me scratch my itchy face harder and harder. My mother instructed Jane to get us to the closest hospital as fast as she could because she thought I might be having a bad reaction to all the clams I had scarfed down! I kept thinking to myself, "How could something so good be so bad for me?"

Jane was always good in a crisis. She put the pedal to the metal, as they like to say, and we flew well over the speed limit heading to the Ellsworth hospital, which was probably about twenty minutes away. NASCAR Jane made it in a record ten minutes. We came to a screeching halt in front of the emergency room entrance and everyone began to move fast just like in the movies. Celeste slid open the van's side door, as my mother jumped out and carried me through the emergency room doors, screaming at the top of her lungs, "I have a dying child here!"

I remember wondering to myself, "Oh no! Who's dying?" But as I looked at Mona and Liddy's terrified expressions as they ran alongside me, I realized she was talking about *me*! Well, that just made me cry even louder as the ER nurses rushed over to us with a gurney. My mother practically threw me on top of it like a sack of potatoes even before they had a chance to come to a complete stop. They rushed me down a long hallway, with all three mothers racing alongside the gurney, assuring me that everything would be all right, even as tears poured down my mother's cheeks, and she kept wailing over and over, "I knew I never should have let her eat all those clams! Nothing good was ever going to come from eating those nasty things!" That's about the time I passed out.

Well, as you know, thankfully I did not die. And when I came to, I was feeling much better after a round of medicine for the hives, and everything was winding down back to normal.

I was released from the hospital but not without a warning to not eat clams or any shellfish until I had an allergy test. I remember feeling enormously disappointed. Yes, I got horribly sick. But going through life without eating clams? That was going to be an impossible challenge.

However, after a lot of allergy testing a few weeks later, it turned out that it was not the clams that made me sick at all. It was the green

pepper in the recipe. So, much to my delight—
and my mother's absolute horror—Jane invited
us over to her house to celebrate and served us
baked clams. My mother spent the whole evening on high alert, ready to rush to the hospital
at a moment's notice. But even after stuffing
myself once again with about thirty clams, all was
well. I had no reaction.

I also outgrew the green pepper allergy which
was never really going to affect me much because, frankly, I have never been a huge fan of
them anyway.

I bet you have already guessed today's recipe
that I will be sharing with you, and you would
be right! This is one of my all-time favorites—
Baked Stuffed Clams! But first, a cocktail that I
always love to serve alongside them. A simple
Cranberry Orange Cocktail which I just know
will send you right over the moon!

CRANBERRY ORANGE COCKTAIL

INGREDIENTS:
1½ ounces mandarin vodka
1½ ounces raspberry vodka
4 ounces cranberry juice
2 ounces orange juice

Fill your cocktail shaker with ice. Pour all the ingredients into the shaker with the ice.

Shake until well blended and pour into a rocks glass filled with ice.

If you are feeling fancy, you can garnish with a few cranberries and an orange slice.

BAKED STUFFED CLAMS

INGREDIENTS:
$1\frac{1}{2}$ cups fresh steamed chopped clams (you can
    also use canned chopped clams, but fresh is al-
    ways best)
$1\frac{1}{4}$ cup plain panko crumbs
$1\frac{1}{4}$ cup seasoned breadcrumbs
1 small onion diced
$\frac{1}{2}$ pepper diced
2 tablespoons butter
2 tablespoons chopped fresh parsley
$\frac{1}{2}$ cup clam broth
18 clam shells
1 lemon
Extra butter

In a large saucepan, sauté your onion and pepper in
the butter until soft. Add the rest of the ingredients
except the lemon and extra butter. Mix until well
combined.

Spoon your mixture evenly into the clam shells, add
a dollop of butter on top of each clam, and squeeze
a little lemon juice on each one.

Bake in a 350 degree preheated oven for 15 to 20
minutes.

Remove, serve, and enjoy!

Chapter 9

The following afternoon Mona called an emergency summit meeting with Hayley at Drinks Like A Fish to discuss the Dougie-Olive situation. Hayley had tried to calmly explain that there was no point in strategizing how to handle something they simply had no control over, but Mona was insistent. They sat atop two stools near the far end of the bar so they could have a little privacy, although except for Lyle Googins, a local tour boat operator, nursing an Irish whiskey with eyes half-mast, the bar was otherwise empty. Randy was in the kitchen frying up some onion rings, a favorite of Mona's, hoping it might help calm her frayed nerves.

"Mona, you need to call the police and report what happened last night," Hayley said.

Mona shook her head. "I don't want to drag the cops into this. It's my business and I will handle it the way I see fit. The boys and I are perfectly capable of defending our property."

"That's only going to lead to more trouble," Hayley warned.

"Then I will deal with it when it happens. That drunk doofus Lonnie showing up with a shotgun is not why I asked you to meet me here. Hayley. This is about Dougie. We need a plan!"

"No, Mona, we don't. You do not have a say in this," Hayley firmly reminded her.

"Of course I have a say. Dougie is my son."

"Who is of legal age. He can make his own decisions now."

"Not as long as he's living under my roof!"

"So what are you going to do, kick him out? Driving him away will only make things worse, for you especially. Listen to me, Mona. Dougie and Olive are in love . . ."

Mona flinched, as if it was painful just hearing the words, but she decided to keep mum.

"You should respect that, and leave them alone to be happy together," Hayley pleaded.

Mona could not keep quiet anymore.

"Olive Leighton is just using poor Dougie and she's going to wind up breaking his heart. As a mother, I can't just stand by and watch it happen without doing *something*!"

"Dougie has a good head on his shoulders, Mona. He always has. He knows what he's doing."

"What the hell are you talking about? Dougie has his father's DNA. That's proof right there he has no idea what he's doing!"

"I beg to differ. Of all your kids, he's the most circumspect and responsible. I trust him to make the right decisions for himself. And in the end, if it doesn't work out, well, life isn't always easy. He'll get through it."

"But of all the girls he could pick, why Olive Leighton? Why the offspring of the devil himself? He might as well propose to Rosemary's Baby!"

"Mona, I will admit, Lonnie can be, shall we say, challenging . . ."

"He showed up at my house firing a shotgun, Hayley! I'd say he's a bit more than just challenging!"

"Duly noted. But from what I know about Olive, she's a nice girl, with a good heart."

"It's all an act! You know the saying, the apple never falls far from the tree?"

"Yes, but in this case, I believe Olive may be the exception. I saw the two of them together at my restaurant. I'm sorry, Mona, I am keenly aware of how you feel, but from where I'm standing, those two kids seem to belong together."

Randy showed up just in time with a heaping plate of onion rings, the thin stringy kind Mona was always craving, not the thick round ones she detested. Mona grabbed a fistful off the top of the pile and shoveled it into her mouth, chewing loudly, eyes darting back and forth as she rolled Hayley's words around in her head.

Hayley noticed Nurse Tilly and her boyfriend, Lieutenant Donnie, enter the bar and sit down at a round table by the window. Randy's manager Michelle ambled over to welcome them and take their drink order before disappearing back into the kitchen.

"Excuse me, Mona, I will be right back," Hayley said, sliding off her barstool and walking over to them. "Hi, Tilly. Hi, Donnie. Date night tonight?"

"Every night's a date night with this angel," Donnie cooed, googly-eyed, squeezing Tilly's hand.

Tilly giggled, embarrassed, playfully rolling her eyes. "Donnie, dear, sometimes you are just too much!"

"She works so hard, I love to get her out of her nurse's uniform every chance I get," Donnie said, chuckling.

There was a pause.

"Wait, that didn't come out right," Donnie snorted and the two erupted in gales of laughter.

Hayley played along, snickering. Then she casually dropped into the conversation, "It must feel good to laugh and let off a little steam with all you have to deal with during the day, Tilly, helping all those sick people, comforting those coping with bad diagnoses. It must be so tough."

Tilly's eyes narrowed as she stared at Hayley. "I know what you're doing, Hayley. You're going to try and pump me for information about Lonnie Leighton."

"What? No! I would never . . . Frankly, I had forgotten all about that!"

It was a little white lie.

Well, a lie.

Maybe not so little.

Of course that's exactly what she was doing.

"I told you, a patient's medical condition is strictly confidential."

"Of course, Tilly, I know that—"

Donnie wagged a scolding finger in Hayley's direction. "Tilly's right, Hayley! This is none of your business. I mean, the poor man is going through enough trying to put his affairs in order with only six months—"

"Donnie!" Tilly shrieked.

Donnie looked at her densely. "What? What did I say?"

She waited for him to realize his mistake.

It took nearly thirty seconds before it finally seeped

down into his brain and his eyes widened. He wanted to kick himself. "Oh, man, I can be so stupid!"

"You promised not to say anything!" Tilly wailed.

Hayley supposed that the strict patient confidentiality rules did not apply to Tilly's hot, cop boyfriend, especially during pillow talk.

Tilly was still angrily focused on a contrite Donnie. "This kind of breach could cost me my job!"

In an attempt to defuse the situation, Donnie slipped an arm around Tilly's shoulders and said softly in her ear, "No worries, babe, I'm a lieutenant now. I'm making enough money to support the both of us."

She slapped his arm away. "That's not the point. I love my job and I want to keep it." She whirled back around to Hayley. "Please, please, you did not hear this from me!"

Hayley mimed locking her lips and tossing away the key. "I swear to you, Tilly, I would never gossip about anyone's private health issues."

Tilly eyed her warily, not entirely sure she could trust Hayley, but having no choice, she simply nodded and whispered, "Thank you."

As Hayley walked back to Mona who had polished off most of the onion rings at this point, she could not believe her instincts had been so spot-on.

It was true.

Lonnie Leighton was dying.

Chapter 10

As Hayley and Mona strolled out of Drinks Like A Fish, the sun had already set and it was nearly dark. Hayley checked the time on her phone and gasped.

"It's almost eight o'clock! I had no idea how late it was."

"Will you come by the house while I sit Dougie down and have a talk with him?"

"No, Mona, I'm sorry, I can't."

"I need you to be there, Hayley. One, you're my best friend. Two, you will be neutral. Three, if you're not there and Dougie gives me any back talk, I will rip his face off."

"Mona, please!"

Mona threw her hands up in surrender. "Okay, I promise to remain calm. But I'm going to need some kind of moral support."

"I wish I could, but I really have to get home. Bruce is probably worried sick I haven't checked in."

"I doubt that."

Hayley cocked an eyebrow. "I know you're a little sensitive right now, Mona, but that was uncalled for."

"No, I mean he's not home. He's right over there."

She pointed across the street.

Hayley turned and was surprised to see Bruce standing on the street corner, leaning up against a lamppost, chatting with a woman whose back was to them. In the light that illuminated his face, she could see him chuckling over something the woman had just said.

Hayley's guard immediately went up. "Mona, are his eyes sparkling?"

Mona squinted to get a better look. "I can't tell from here."

"It looks to me like his eyes are sparkling. Bruce's eyes have *never* sparkled. At least around me. Who is that he's talking to?"

Mona shrugged. "Beats me. We're just going to have to wait until she turns around so we can see her face."

The woman touched Bruce's hand flirtatiously and threw her head back and laughed.

Bruce seemed to revel in the attention and made no move to withdraw the woman's hand from his hand as his shoulders shook from guffawing.

"They certainly seem to be cracking each other up," Hayley said. "He never laughs that hard at my jokes."

Finally, as a car rolled by them, the woman turned her head toward them so they could both get a good look at her face.

Hayley was stunned.

"Never seen her before," Mona shrugged.

"I have. At my restaurant."

It was Tabitha Collins.

The CEO of the Boston Common Seafood.

"She gave me her card. She wants to help me expand my business."

"What's she doing with Bruce?"

"I have absolutely no idea."

"Well, let's go find out."

Hayley reached out and grabbed a fistful of Mona's sweatshirt. "No, Mona."

"You need to find out how they know each other. And I will be there with you because one, I'm your friend, two, I will remain neutral, and three—"

"Mona, I have no intention of ripping her face off."

"No, but if there's any hanky-panky going on, I will be more than happy to do it myself."

"I trust Bruce, Mona."

Tabitha then threw her arms around Bruce and bussed him on the cheek. He drew her in for a hug, which lasted a bit longer than Hayley was comfortable with.

Mona could not take it anymore. "That's it, I'm going in."

She started to march off the curb and across the street.

"Mona, hold on a sec."

Mona stopped and turned back around.

Hayley raised her phone and called Bruce.

"I thought you trusted him."

"I do."

They glanced over to where Bruce and Tabitha continued chatting. Tabitha was in the middle of another funny story when Bruce's phone buzzed in his back pocket. He reached for it, took a cursory glance at the screen, and then put it back as he continued smiling while listening to Tabitha prattle on.

Hayley got his voice mail.

"Hi, this is Bruce, you know what to do."

Mona grimaced. "Why that son of a—"

"It doesn't mean anything!" Hayley tried convincing herself.

"Come on, are you really not going to walk over there to find out what the hell is going on?"

"For the last time, Mona, I trust Bruce. I'm sure he'll tell me all about it when he gets home."

But Hayley would be lying to herself if she denied that her suspicious nature was suddenly on high alert.

Bruce definitely had some serious explaining to do.

Chapter 11

Hayley was already in bed by the time Bruce rolled in an hour later. She heard him downstairs rummaging through the fridge for a quick bite to eat, and after a few minutes, he was stomping up the steps and appeared in the doorway to their bedroom, a surprised look on his face. "You turned in awfully early. I thought I'd find you downstairs binging one of your TV shows."

"I'm tired," Hayley said.

Bruce nodded, satisfied, then he began unbuttoning his shirt. "Great. I'll join you."

She folded her arms, eyes narrowing, and asked pointedly, "So where have you been?"

Without missing a beat, Bruce casually answered, "With an old girlfriend."

This stumped Hayley.

She had been expecting to catch him in a lie.

But here he was, coming right out with it.

He was so blasé about it, as if he had just told her he had stopped by the Big Apple convenience store to buy a pack of chewing gum.

It did little to calm Hayley's frazzled nerves. "Does this girlfriend have a name?"

"Tabitha Collins."

"I know. I saw the two of you together when Mona and I were leaving Drinks Like A Fish tonight."

Bruce gave her a curious look. "You saw us?"

"Yes."

"Then why did you ask where I was? Were you testing me?"

"No, I was not testing you."

"You were testing me."

"No, Bruce, I trust you," Hayley wailed defensively.

"To a point."

Hayley sighed, frustrated. More with herself for being exposed as the maddening cliché—the jealous wife. But she certainly was not ready to let this go entirely.

"How come I've never heard of her?"

Bruce shrugged. "I don't know. It was a long time ago. We dated for a while when I was writing for the *Globe* down in Boston before I moved back up to Maine to work at the *Island Times*."

"I'm just surprised you have never mentioned her. I mean, she's kind of a big deal, a CEO of a major company. She must be loaded."

Now it was Bruce's turn to fold his arms and narrow his eyes. "How do you know about all that?"

It was time for her to come clean. She recounted meeting Tabitha at her restaurant, how much Tabitha had loved Hayley's cooking, and the serious offer from her to help Hayley expand her business.

Bruce's mouth dropped open. "Wait, what? How could you not tell me about this?"

"Because I wasn't planning on pursuing it. It's just too much for me to take on right now."

Bruce nodded. "Fair enough. But I wish you had told me."

"I'm sorry. Wait? Why am I apologizing? You're the one who failed to mention you had a millionaire ex-girl-friend."

"She wasn't a millionaire when we met. She was at the bottom rung of the ladder, just a temp at the company when we lived together."

Hayley's eyes nearly popped out of her head. "You *lived* together? For how long?"

"Three years."

Hayley gasped. "Three *years*?"

Hayley's head was spinning.

This had not been some brief romance, or casual encounter, or even short-term relationship. Three years was a substantial amount of time. The two had obvious shared a life together.

Bruce studied Hayley as her mind raced.

"You're spiraling right now, aren't you?" Bruce sighed.

"No, I'm not!" Hayley barked, clearly spiraling.

"I think you are. Look, like I said, it was ages ago. We both knew shortly after we moved in together that we just weren't a right fit. But we decided not to physically split because we had a pricey apartment in Back Bay. She was a secretary and I was a freelancer. We stuck together out of convenience. Neither of us could afford to move and cough up a down payment on a new place. We were essentially roommates for the last ten months we lived together. She was actually dating someone else by the time I finally packed up my Pinto and left Boston to move back to Maine."

"How did you know she was in town?"

"She called me at the paper. We're probably Facebook friends, I don't even know. She said she was up here on business and would like to see me, for old times' sake. I knew you were with Mona tonight so I met up with her to say hello. I was just saying good night when you called me. I called you right back on my way home."

Hayley snatched up her phone and checked her voice mail.

"You didn't get it?"

"No, I got it. My ringer was off."

Bruce flashed her a self-satisfied smile. "We good?"

Hayley set her phone down on the night table and said sheepishly, "We're good."

Bruce slid out of his pants and crawled into bed next to Hayley, snuggling with her. "Need I remind you that I dated a number of women, just like you have been with a lot of men—"

"Hold on! I wouldn't say *a lot*!"

"Some." He glanced at her stewing expression. "A few."

She nodded, satisfied.

"My point is, we both have a past. And it's taken me a long time to work through my mistakes before settling down with my one true love."

Hayley smirked. "And who is that, may I ask?"

He didn't bother to answer her question. He just shut her up with a kiss.

Chapter 12

Hayley's stomach flip-flopped when she saw the restaurant's reservations list for tonight on Betty's iPad at the hostess station.

Leighton, Party of Five, 6:30 PM.

There was only one Leighton family she knew of in this town. And that was Lonnie, his three daughters, and most likely his girlfriend Abby. What nerve he had showing up at her restaurant after his dangerous drunken escapade the other night, firing his shotgun at poor Dougie, not to mention Hayley herself.

No, she was not going to stand for this.

There had to be consequences for his actions.

The restaurant filled up pretty quickly after they opened their doors at five o'clock. Hayley scooted between the kitchen to check to see if her chef, Kelton, needed anything and the dining room where she greeted her arriving customers. She kept one eye on the door, waiting anxiously for the Leightons and sure enough, at six thirty on the dot, the whole family rolled in. Lonnie looked sicker and more gaunt than ever before. He was sulking and complaining about something. Vera looked her usual angry and tense self, as if she were wishing she was anywhere else. Ruth, the middle daughter, had an absent expression on her face, as if she had already checked out for the evening. And the youngest Olive just looked miserable and distraught. As for Abby, she had done herself up nice tonight with a touch of makeup and a flattering lipstick shade. Her hair was curled and she wore a slimming navy Capri pant set. Lonnie's three daughters, however, were dressed down in jeans and t-shirts, barely making an effort.

Betty greeted them with a warm smile and checked their name off her reservation list. Hayley made a beeline over to the hostess station and snatched the iPad out of Betty's hand. "Thank you, Betty, I will handle this."

"But I have their table ready for them," Betty said, still smiling, but utterly confused.

"I'm afraid Lonnie is no longer welcome to dine here."

Lonnie glared at her. "What are you talking about? My money's just as good as anybody else's in this town."

"This has nothing to do with money and you know it. This has to do with the stunt you pulled at Mona's house the other night. You're lucky you're not in jail right now. You could have killed somebody."

"I never aimed at anybody!" Lonnie protested. "I just fired into the air to scare that little creep so he'd stop chasing after Olive."

Vera stepped forward. "You can't ban my father from eating here. He is a respected businessman in Bar Harbor."

Hayley wanted to laugh but wisely refrained.

Olive kept her eyes glued to the floor, supremely embarrassed.

Ruth stared vacantly out the window as if she wasn't exactly sure where she even was.

The vein on Lonnie's temple throbbed as he got madder and sputtered, "This is ridiculous! You can't just . . . I mean . . ." He turned to Abby. "How can she . . . ?"

Abby suddenly took charge. "Hayley, may I have a word?"

"Of course, Abby."

She was more than willing to calmly discuss the situation with the one rational person in the group. They stepped to the side as Vera tried to comfort her increasingly agitated father.

"He knows what he did was wrong and he has promised me he won't do anything stupid like that ever again," Abby whispered.

"I'm glad to hear that, Abby, but I can't ignore the fact that he—"

"It's his birthday."

This stopped Hayley. "Oh . . ."

"Lonnie's been having a really tough time lately. It's not just what's been going on with Olive, it's everything, and he's been dealing with some serious health challenges."

Hayley glanced over at Lonnie, who seemed to hold onto Vera's arm to keep himself steady, his face pale, his cheeks drawn, his eyes almost yellow.

"We were just hoping to have a nice family dinner out and forget about all the troubles we've been going through, and although he'd never admit it, Lonnie just loves your cooking. He's been talking about your Linguini with Clam Sauce all day," Abby said. "He doesn't even care that you bought the clams from Mona."

This made Hayley chuckle.

She could feel her steely resolve slowly start to melt away. Lonnie was clearly dying. And on top of that, it was his birthday.

Finally, she sighed. "Do you promise to personally keep him in line?"

Abby gave her a vigorous nod. "Yes, of course. Absolutely."

Hayley turned back to Betty, who stood awkwardly at the hostess station desperately trying to make small talk with Lonnie's three daughters, none of whom were remotely interested in engaging in any sort of conversation. "Betty, would you show the Leightons to their table?"

Betty, relieved that an ugly scene had been mercifully averted, grabbed a stack of menus and said brightly, "Right this way, folks."

She led them to the large table in the back that had been reserved for them. Once they were seated, Hayley focused on the other tables, making sure their wine glasses were filled and their food was coming out in a timely fashion. Her superstar-server Christina, an immigrant from Honduras, was juggling nine tables at once and doing a bang-up job keeping them all straight. Between her trips to the kitchen and the dining room Hayley managed to check up on the Leightons every so often. She noticed Christina delivering whiskey after whiskey to Lonnie and prayed he wouldn't get drunk and belligerent. She spotted Olive picking at her food, sniffling and despondent. At another point, she spotted Vera wagging a finger in Abby's face, berating her about something. Lonnie just let it happen as he downed his fourth whiskey at last count. Then, just as Christina delivered the dessert menus for them to peruse, Hayley saw Abby throw down her napkin in disgust, pop up to her feet, and storm out of the restaurant, leaving the Leightons stunned.

Hayley did not have time to find out what had happened because she had to return to the kitchen to make sure there wasn't a backup on the orders. Once Kelton assured her he had everything under control, Hayley turned to find Betty standing behind her.

"Everything okay?" Hayley asked.

"Oh, yes. Everything's fine. I just wanted to let you know Mona's here in case you wanted to go out and say hello."

Hayley stared at Betty, dumbfounded. "Mona's not coming tonight."

"Yes, she's here with her kids. She called earlier, and as luck would have it, we just happened to have a cancellation so I was able to squeeze her in at the last minute."

"That's not luck, Betty, that's a disaster in the making!"

Betty looked confused again.

"Where did you seat them?"

"Table nine. In the back."

"Right next to the Leightons!"

Hayley flew out of the kitchen and into the dining room, but she was too late. She had a clear view of the Leighton family hurling barbs back and forth with the Barnes family, which included Mona, Dennis Jr., Digger, Dougie, and the two youngest, Chet and Jody.

Hayley could not hear what anyone was saying, but the shouting continued to grow in volume over the din of the other diners. She saw Dougie and Olive both stand up and try to defuse the tension, but it was too late. Mona barked something obviously rude at Vera, who in retaliation, scooped up her glass of the house Burgundy and viciously flung it at Mona, the red wine drenching her face. Mona erupted in a battle cry and then all hell broke loose.

Chapter 13

Hayley watched helplessly as Mona lunged at Vera, grabbing her by her collar and screaming obscenities into her face as Vera grabbed Mona by both arms and tried to violently shove her back. Meanwhile, Lonnie had managed to climb to his feet and head straight for Dougie, but fortunately his two older and much beefier brothers, Donnie Jr. and Digger, jumped up from their table and muscled their way in front of Dougie to form a barricade and keep Lonnie at bay. Although, given how frail and weak he was, Hayley was fairly certain he would not have been able to do much damage to Dougie even without the protective shield of his professional wrestler-sized siblings.

The rest of the people in the restaurant, both customers and servers, were glued to the increasingly chaotic floor show. Hayley predicted another round of free desserts for everyone would soon be in order.

Lonnie, unintimidated by the bulky Barnes boys, kept trying to charge toward Dougie, screaming at him to stay away from his daughter, as Donnie Jr. and Digger thrust their massive chests out in a show of force.

Ruth, finally snapping out of her personal daydreams, came to the realization that she could no longer stay silent and, as the most neutral Leighton family member, needed to intervene and do something. She tried inserting herself between Mona and Vera and split them apart but to no avail. She turned to Mona. "Please, Mona, Vera didn't mean to spill her wine on you. It was an accident."

Still grappling with Vera, Mona let out an exasperated groan. "Oh, wake up, Ruth, that was no accident and you know it!"

Even Vera snickered at the idea that tossing her wine in Mona's face had been an unintentional act.

Ruth turned to Hayley for some help.

Hayley knew the Leightons would never listen to her, her only calling card was to get through to Mona. "Listen to me, Mona, if you force me to call Sergio, you may think you have pull with him and not get arrested, but there is a room full of witnesses here who saw you attack Vera first, and I won't be able to get you out of this one."

"What? She started it! She threw her wine in my face!" Mona wailed, still gripping Vera by the shirt collar.

"And I would have asked her to leave, but you took it too far by going for the jugular. If you let go of her now, we may be able to resolve this without involving the police."

Reluctantly, Mona released Vera from her grip and took a wide step back.

Vera sneered at her. "You're just surrendering because you know I can take you in a fight."

Mona's nostrils flared.

Hayley jumped between them before Mona had a chance to attack again. She glared at a smirking Vera. "Vera, I think it's time for you to go."

"But I was going to order dessert. The crème brûlée sounds divine," Vera said, her words dripping with sarcasm.

Hayley stood her ground. "Good night, Vera!"

Vera threw Mona one last infuriatingly smug smile and then sashayed away, right out of the restaurant.

Lonnie pointed a bony finger at Dougie, who was peering through the thick shoulders of his older brothers. "I know what you're up to, you little punk! You're just dating Olive in order to get your grubby little hands on the Leighton family's corporate secrets!"

Mona guffawed. "You really are one crazy loon, Lonnie! Like I would ever want to adopt the business practices of a bunch of backwoods redneck idiots!"

Donnie weakly called out from behind his brothers. "I love your daughter, Mr. Leighton!"

"You stay away from her! I swear, I will get a restraining order to keep you from—"

"Lonnie, out!" Hayley cried.

This stopped Lonnie. He had never seen Hayley so angry. Nobody watching the lunacy unfolding in the dining room had either, but Hayley had had enough of this nonsense.

"But I still have to tip our waitress," Lonnie said.

Hayley pointed to the door. "I will cover it. Now go, get out of here!"

Lonnie sniffed, and shakily made his way out of the restaurant. "Come on, Olive! We're leaving!"

Olive lagged behind, hoping to talk to Dougie, but Ruth quickly took her by the arm and forcefully ushered her out. "Come on, Olive, you know Daddy doesn't like to be kept waiting."

Once the Leighton family was mercifully gone, people returned to their meals, most likely discussing the dramatic events they had just witnessed. A few had been recording everything on their phones and were posting the videos to social media, which Hayley knew would cause quite a stir, at least in local circles.

Dennis Jr. and Digger spun around to confront their little brother.

"Okay, kid, you've had your fun, it's time to end this thing with Olive Leighton right now," Digger said.

"What? No . . . I won't . . . She . . . No," Dougie sputtered, upset.

"Can't you see it's killing Mom?" Dennis Jr. shouted. "For the sake of the family, Dougie, you don't have a choice."

Dougie took a deep breath and turned to his mother. "I love you, Mom, and you know I would never do anything to intentionally hurt you. You've been the best mother in the world. I had a really happy childhood." He glanced over at his brothers. "Except for those two lumberjacks picking on me and giving me wedgies all the time, but mostly it was good." He turned back and locked eyes with Mona. "But I'm a man now, and I have to find my own path in life, and that path has led me to Olive Leighton, and I'm sorry you hate her family, but I love her, Mom. She's the one for me, I feel it in my heart, my bones, and I can't imagine my life without her. I don't want to be a lobsterman like Dennis and Digger here. I want to be a writer, and Olive is the only one who seems to support me in that dream. She gets me. I understand how you feel, but I can't give her up. I just can't."

Mona stood staring at her son silently as Hayley quietly asked Christina to bring two bowls of ice cream for Mona's youngest, Chet and Jody, who sat frozen at the table, not sure what to make of any of this.

Mona nodded slightly and mumbled, "I hear you."

Dougie took a step closer. "What?"

"I said I hear you."

Dougie had a confused expression on his face. "What does that mean exactly?"

Hayley could tell this was hard for Mona, but she knew in her gut, her friend would eventually do the right thing, after exhausting all other possibilities, of course. "Do what you want. I just want you to be happy."

Dougie broke out into a bright, electric smile and grabbed his mother in a big bear hug and kissed her left cheek. "Thank you, Mom! Thank you! I love you!"

Mona, never one to be comfortable with public displays of affection, especially in front of a room full of eyes gaping at her, wiggled uncomfortably in his grasp. "All right, Dougie, that's enough. People are watching." She extricated herself from her beaming son and said to Hayley, "We'd like to order our dinner now if that's okay with you."

"Of course, Christina will be right over to tell you about tonight's specials," Hayley said with a wink toward a beaming Dougie.

Chapter 14

When Hayley breezed into Mona's shop to pick up her fresh seafood order for the restaurant that evening, the last person she expected to see standing at the counter was Ruth Leighton, Lonnie's middle daughter, in a billowy, sky-blue sundress, her hair pulled back in a ponytail, her face full of apprehension, as if she was suddenly second-guessing her decision to show up unannounced.

"Hello, Ruth," Hayley said, eyes darting to Mona behind the counter, who was staring grimly at her unexpected customer.

"Nice to see you, Hayley. Dinner at your place was lovely last night . . ."

"Until it wasn't," Mona growled.

"Yes, that was an unfortunate scene," Ruth muttered in Mona's direction before turning back to Hayley. "But the food was scrumptious. I would love to get my hands on the recipe for your Clam—"

"How can I help you, Ruth?" Mona interjected, quickly losing patience.

"I am obviously not here to buy seafood, we have plenty of our own back at our shop," Ruth said softly with a forced smile.

"Obviously," Mona growled.

Digger suddenly appeared from out back carrying a large sealed styrofoam box in his muscled arms. Inside was Hayley's daily order of shellfish packed tightly with icy cold gel packs. "Morning, Hayley, if you pop the trunk, I'll put this in your car." He stopped in his tracks at the sight of Ruth Leighton in the shop. "Well, well, well, look who's stepped behind enemy lines. What do you want?"

"I came to ask for a truce," Ruth said.

Mona and Digger exchanged skeptical looks.

"A truce, huh? Does Lonnie even know you're here?" Mona pressed, suspicious.

"Actually, no, and neither does Vera. But no one in the family wants a repeat of last night. Scenes like that are bad for both our businesses."

Mona snorted, but Hayley could tell that deep down Mona knew Ruth was right.

"Well, a truce has to be from both sides, and if your daddy and crazy loon of a sister won't come to the table, then there is really no point—"

"That's just it. They will. Once I speak with them about why we need to lower the temperature on this ridiculous feud."

"No offense, Ruth," Digger said. "But I've known your family for as long as I can remember, way back when I was like four or five years old, and in all that time, I have never, ever seen Lonnie or Vera listen to anyone, especially the shy, quiet, pretty one in the family."

She perked up at the word "pretty" but then said defensively, "I'm not shy, just introverted."

Digger set the styrofoam box down on top of the counter and glanced over at his mother.

"Look," Ruth continued, undeterred. "You may or may not know this, but my daddy is dying."

There was a long silence.

Both Mona and Digger were stunned.

Hayley cleared her throat. "Yes, I heard he's not been doing well."

"He's got about three months, tops."

"Oh, Ruth, I'm so sorry," Hayley whispered.

Less time than even Nurse Tilly had thought.

"Our families fighting like this seems pointless, especially since Daddy has so little time left. I just want us to get along and not go on the attack whenever we're in the same room. If I can go back and tell Daddy that you, Mona, and your boys want to find a way for our two families to co-exist peacefully, then I know he will agree to dial back the rhetoric and accusations and maybe we'll all be able to find a new normal without this constant battling."

"I think that's a wonderful goal," Hayley piped in, although she could still see the healthy dose of skepticism coming from both Mona and Digger. "Mona, what do you think?"

Mona took a while to respond.

Digger folded his arms. "This could be some kind of trick, Mom. I wouldn't put something like that past the Leightons."

Ruth looked visibly hurt.

Digger noticed and softened a bit. "I didn't mean you, Ruth. You've always been the nice one."

She smiled tentatively.

Mona studied Ruth for a bit. "I trust you, Ruth."

"Thank you, Mona," Ruth said, relieved.

"But I don't trust your daddy. Or your sister for that matter. So if we call this truce, and it goes sideways, it's on you! And you will regret ever stepping foot into my shop!"

"Let me talk to them and see how far I get."

"And Lonnie better lay off my Dougie," Mona insisted. "I already told my son if he is truly in love with your baby sister Olive, then I won't stand in the way. But if Lonnie insists on harassing him, then it's going to be all-out war."

Ruth raised a hand. "No! He won't. I promise. Personally, I'm very happy to hear you've given your blessing to Olive and Dougie. I just hope I can get Daddy there too, before it's too late. Olive will never be able to live with herself if Daddy dies angry with her."

Mona impatiently tapped her foot on the hardwood floor. "Anything else, Ruth?"

Realizing she had probably overstayed her welcome, Ruth took a step toward the door. "No, that's it. Thank you for listening, Mona, thank you, Digger, Hayley."

"One more thing before you go," Mona barked.

Ruth stopped and looked nervously at Mona. "Yes?"

"If this truce is ever going to work, you're going to have to keep your sister Vera in line too! That one's got one hell of a mean streak, and I will not put up with it anymore, do you hear me?"

"Loud and clear," Ruth promised before hurrying out the door before Mona changed her mind.

Mona glanced at Hayley. "I mean, she's short-tempered,

bull-headed, always mad about something. Who can put up with someone like that?"

Both Hayley and Digger marveled at the lack of self-awareness coming out of Mona Barnes. She might as well have been describing herself. Mona and Vera Leighton were like oil and water because in actuality they were both so much alike.

"Come on, Hayley, let's go load up your car," Digger said, lifting the styrofoam box off the counter and following Hayley out of the shop. When the door closed behind them and Mona was inside and out of earshot, Digger joked to Hayley, "Pot, meet Kettle."

Chapter 15

Mona launched the grimy yellow tennis ball with teeth marks high into the air and Hayley's dog Leroy and Mona's golden retriever Sadie automatically sprang into action, chasing after as it bounced on the grass in Agamont Park adjacent to the town pier as Hayley and Mona strolled along the shore path. Leroy raced as fast as his tiny legs could carry him, actually believing that maybe this time, just once, he might fetch it before Sadie. But like Charlie Brown hoping this time might be different with Lucy and the football, it was never meant to be. Sadie sailed past Leroy and snatched the rolling tennis ball up into her mouth, preening proudly as she trotted back to deliver the ball to Mona. Leroy, tail wagging excitedly as he skidded through some mud, spun around, and panting heavily, ran back to catch up to Sadie.

Hayley watched her little dog trying his best. "He's getting up there in years, but thankfully he still has a lot of energy still left."

"That's because my Sadie keeps him young," Mona remarked.

Sadie stopped in front of Mona, the ball still lodged between her teeth. She tried to take it out, but she playfully bit down on the ball harder, resisting. "Come on, Sadie, do you want to play or not?" She yanked on it again, but Sadie was not about to give up her prize.

"Fine," Mona sighed, reaching into her coat pocket and extracting another clean yellow tennis ball. Like a pitcher on the mound, Mona reared back and hurled the ball forward. "There you go, Leroy, it's all yours!"

The ball sailed through the air.

Surprised, Leroy did another about-turn and followed the ball with his eyes to keep track of it as he ran as fast as he could. Confused, Sadie dropped the ball in her mouth at Mona's feet and skittered off to catch up to Leroy and the new ball.

Mona bent down and picked up the dirty tennis ball and carried it in her hand as she and Hayley continued walking along the path. All was quiet this cloudy day except for the calls of a few seagulls nearby. The ocean was at low tide so there was not even the typical sound of waves crashing against the rocks.

Finally, Mona broke the silence.

"I've been thinking of baking a cake and taking it over to Lonnie Leighton as kind of a peace offering."

"Mona, you've never baked a cake in your life."

"That's why I'm telling you. I was hoping you'd volunteer to do it for me."

"What kind of cake?"

Mona shrugged. "I'll get Dougie to ask Olive. She'll know what he likes."

"I think that's a lovely idea, Mona."

"Well, I thought about it, and Ruth is right, life is too short. You never know when your time's up, so you should make the most of it while you're still here. I remember reading when that teen idol from the seventies, David Cassidy, died, his last words were, 'So much wasted time.' That kind of stuck with me. I figure when it comes to the Leightons, there is plenty of room for two seafood businesses in town. What's the point of constantly fighting?"

Much to Hayley and Mona's surprise, Leroy suddenly scurried up to them, the fresh tennis ball in his mouth. He could not have looked more proud or gratified.

"I can't believe it, Leroy, you finally did it! You beat Sadie!" Hayley cooed, bending down to scratch the top of his head. Tail still wagging vigorously, his head held high, Leroy opened his mouth to allow Hayley to pluck out the tennis ball. He was eager to go again and prove this wasn't just a fluke. Hayley pitched the ball but it only flew a few feet before bouncing off the stone edge of the shore path and disappearing into the low tide clam flats. Leroy and Sadie still chased after it but stopped at the path's edge, unable to climb down to retrieve it.

"I can't believe you were ever on the high school softball team with a throw like that," Mona scoffed, shaking her head.

"I only joined the team because I had a crush on Marcus Miller on the boys' baseball team and wanted to sit next to him on the bus both teams took to all the away games. He showed me how to French kiss when we played Dover Foxcroft. I was so naive, I looked at him and said, 'But Marcus, you told me you moved here from New Jersey.'"

Mona chuckled. "So will you help me out?"

"Of course, Mona. I'd be happy to bake you a cake to give Lonnie."

"I don't have a lot of regrets in my life, don't see the point of them. But this time, I do feel bad for stoking this feud between the Barnes and the Leighton families. Honestly, I feel terrible that Lonnie is so ill. I don't want his final days to be filled with all this drama and tension."

"I'm happy to hear that, Mona."

"Actually, the cake is just an excuse. What I really want to do when I go to his house is apologize for my own bad behavior all these years."

"That's very big of you, but Lonnie has certainly been no angel."

"Oh, I know, but someone's got to make the first move."

Hayley patted Mona's back.

She was immensely proud of her.

It was a rare occasion when Mona Barnes admitted any wrongdoing, let alone show up at her enemy's house with a cake.

This was a huge deal.

The dogs barking wildly interrupted them.

They glanced over to see Leroy and Sadie, side by side, at the edge of the path, staring down at the flats, presumably at their great prize tennis ball slowly sinking in the mud.

Mona snatched the dirty tennis ball from her coat pocket and held it high up in the air. "Here you go! Fetch this one!" She hurled it hard and it zipped through the air, right past the two dogs, who didn't pay any attention to it. It bounced on the gravel, rolling down the path.

"Hey, you knuckleheads! It's straight ahead! Go get it!" Mona called out.

But the dogs didn't move.

They were both on all fours, heads lowered over the edge of the path, distracted by something, still barking.

"What's got them so riled up?"

When Hayley and Mona reached their two dogs, they stopped suddenly in their tracks, stunned.

The dogs were barking at a man lying face down in the clam flats, near the exact same spot where Mona had her mud-wrestling match with Vera Leighton.

"Omigod!" Hayley gasped.

Mona leaped over the side of the shore path down to the protruding rocks along the edge, slipping and sliding on seaweed until she managed to get her footing in the muddy flats. Hayley followed close behind, gingerly, trying to maintain her balance. Mona reached the man first. She bent down and grabbed a fistful of his plaid flannel shirt and tugged on it with all her might. The man's body slowly turned over, and the shock caused Mona to stumble back and fall flat on her butt. By now, Hayley had caught up to her and could plainly see the man's face. Although it was covered in mud, she instantly recognized him.

It was Lonnie Leighton.

And he wasn't breathing.

He was, Hayley feared, very much dead.

Island Food & Spirits
BY
HAYLEY POWELL

"Little Miss Steamer" is a title every little girl from Mount Desert Island between the ages of ten and thirteen dreamed about every Fourth of July. That is, every girl with the notable exception of Mona Butler (her maiden name), who just shook her head in disgust whenever Liddy and I got caught up in the excitement of discussing it, which was quite a bit during the summer all three of us were ten years old. "Little Miss Steamer" was, for lack of a better description, Bar Harbor's local version of Miss Pre-Teen America. All of us pre-adolescent girls who entered this beloved annual pageant believed it was on the same grand scale as Miss America or Miss Universe, hosted by famous former game show hosts or aging pop singers, not the Chief Home Loan Officer at Bar Harbor Banking and Trust, who had once appeared as a contestant on *Match Game '78* when he was in college. He was the closest person we had to a celebrity, even though he had lost after the first round despite guessing the same answer as Charles Nelson Reilly and Brett Somers.

All of us pre-teen entrants hardly knew the difference between a real celebrity and a local one, so to us, everything about the "Little Miss Steamer" pageant was pure magic.

Every July 4th, the Bar Harbor Rotary put on a blueberry pancake breakfast before the big Fourth of July Parade, and then after the parade, they hosted a huge picnic with steamed lobsters, clams, mussels, corn on the cob, and strawberry shortcake, along with games, lobster races, and of course, the main attraction, at least for all the middle school girls, the "Little Miss Steamer" contest where one lucky girl would be awarded the coveted title of "Little Miss Steamer" (for those who may not know, steamer is short for a steamed clam).

Every little girl could not wait to turn ten, the starting age to participate. The winner won a cash prize of $100, a $25 gift certificate to Bee's Candy store, four complimentary tickets to the Bangor State Fair, and most importantly, their picture taken wearing the "Little Miss Steamer" sash, which would be splashed on the front page of the *Island Times*! All those prizes and publicity made the winner feel like royalty. Well-wishers would stop her in the street or at the grocery store, congratulating her, while she basked in the attention that came with her fifteen minutes of fame.

Mona, even at ten years old, thought the entire enterprise was utterly ridiculous and just laughed at Liddy and me for getting so worked up over a stupid sash, one we both secretly prayed we would win. Mona adamantly refused to waste her time on such foolishness and would not be caught dead dressing up and acting silly in front of a crowd.

No, not in a million years.

Of course, that was before her mother Jane came storming home from the Shop 'n Save, boiling mad after a run-in with someone. Mona, Liddy, and I were sitting at the kitchen table having a snack when Jane ordered Mona to get in the car because they were going to drive to Ellsworth and buy Mona a dress.

Well, you can imagine our mouths dropping open in shock.

Mona had never worn a dress in her life!

When Mona started to protest, Jane shot her a hard look, which told Mona she probably should not argue this one. With her head down, Mona miserably shuffled to the car as Liddy and I scurried out of the house, both dying of curiosity as to why Jane was suddenly going to force Mona to wear a frilly dress.

Apparently, Jane had run into Lonnie Leighton at the store, and it was a well-known fact that the two families, the Butlers and the Leightons, both ran fresh seafood businesses and had been archrivals for years. The families were still touchy and angry that the Rotary had chosen both of them to supply the lobsters and clams for the upcoming Fourth of July Seafood Festival in order not to play favorites, but it just

made their raging animosity toward one another even worse.

Lonnie was already in one of his typically
foul moods when he ran into Jane and wrong-
fully decided to give her a little advice, suggesting she keep Mona out of the "Little Miss
Steamer" competition because the poor girl did
not stand a chance against his own precious
daughter Vera, the same age as Mona, who
would surely be crowned the winner. Jane just
shrugged and told him it did not matter because Mona had zero interest in those girly
types of things and started to walk away to the
produce section. Lonnie just snickered and
then in a sneering tone said, "Just like a Butler
to chicken out when a Leighton is involved because there is no way she would have won anyway going up against my Vera."

That's when Jane snapped. She spun back
around to Lonnie and shouted loud enough
for the check-out girls at the front registers to
hear, "Lonnie, no Butler has ever backed down
to a Leighton, so you better get ready to console that little brat of yours when my Mona wins
that friggin' contest!"

Poor Mona's fate was effectively sealed.

There was no way she was going to get out of
this one.

Mona begged and pleaded with her mother
to change her mind but Jane held fast. She was
intractable. The family honor was on the line
and it was Mona's duty to wipe that self-satisfied

smirk off Lonnie Leighton's ugly face by winning "Little Miss Steamer".

When the Fourth of July Lobster Festival finally rolled around, I have to admit, it was disconcerting to see Mona in a dress. The whole town did double takes as they passed by us, but we tried to ignore them, consuming plates of blueberry pancakes, watching the parade, and then heading to the ball park for a monstrous seafood lunch. My brother Randy ran off to play games with his friends, but Liddy, Mona and I were instructed to stay close by because they were about to begin the "Little Miss Steamer" contest.

Of course, Liddy and I were giddy with excitement and dreams of the prizes, but poor Mona just sat there on a folding chair at the table with a long face and her head hung low as if she were about to have all of her wisdom teeth extracted.

The rules were simple. After all the girls paraded past the judges and spectators in their best dresses, the host would then ask each girl a question that she had to answer on the spot. The judges would do an elimination round. Then there would be a second question and the judges would choose their three favorites, and finally, the third question would determine the ultimate winner.

The first question was a breeze, something about our favorite subject in school, and ten girls made the cut, including me, Liddy, and

Mona, even though Mona had tried to get herself eliminated by answering, "Recess."

Next question, role models. There were a lot of good answers. First Lady Nancy Reagan, astronaut Sally Ride, the first woman Supreme Court Justice Sandra Day O'Conner. Mona tried again to tank her chances by answering, "Madonna."

That one caused the whole audience to roar with laughter.

The judges chose the final three, calling up Kat Emerson, who was the smartest girl in our class, and then, Vera Leighton, whose father whooped and hollered with joy when her name was called, and finally, you guessed it, against all odds, Mona Butler. Mona looked absolutely horrified as we all had to practically shove her up onto the platform.

The last and final question which would determine the winner was, "What do you want to be when you grow up and why?"

Kat was first and said she wanted to be a nurse just like her mom and marry a doctor just like her mom did too. There were a few chuckles from some of the adults in the audience since half the town knew that Kat's mother had chased and hounded her poor doctor husband relentlessly until he finally gave up and agreed to marry her.

Then it was Vera's turn. She answered in a loud, clear voice while smiling at Lonnie, "I am going to work with my daddy because I want to be just like him!"

Of course Lonnie jumped out of his seat, cheering and clapping wildly for his little girl's perfect answer, although everyone else just clapped politely with tight smiles because they had known Lonnie Leighton most of their lives and the last thing Bar Harbor needed was someone just like him!

I saw Vera give Mona a smug smirk and whisper something in her ear which obviously irritated Mona. Suddenly Mona stood up straighter and gave the crowd a megawatt smile. Whatever Vera said had just made Mona want to try harder to win.

The host asked Mona the same question. "What do you want to be when you grow up and why?" Without missing a beat, Mona turned to the audience and said, "I want to be a lobsterman." She paused dramatically, as if she had forgotten what she was going to say next, but then, she smiled at her parents. Everyone expected her to say the same thing as Vera, that she wanted to be just like her dad. But instead, she announced, loud and proud, "Because I'm going to be the first female lobsterman on the island, and I don't just want to work with my daddy, I want to be the boss, and I'm going to own the best seafood business around!"

The audience erupted in thunderous applause and Mona gave a furious Vera a playful wink.

Mona Butler was crowned "Little Miss Steamer", and although she would never admit it to this day, we could all tell she enjoyed her reign.

This week, in honor of "Little Miss Steamer", I have one of Mona's favorite cocktails and an easy, delicious, steamed clam recipe for everyone to enjoy!

Mona always loves a good cold beer but this beer cocktail has become one of her go-to drinks with a nice bowl of steamers.

SUMMERTIME BEER COCKTAIL

INGREDIENTS:
3 ounces of a pale ale (light beer)
6 ounces Sparkling Ice Peach Nectarine
Fresh strawberry (optional)

Fill a glass with ice cubes and add your beer and
Sparkling Ice Peach Nectarine.

Give it a stir, garnish with a fresh strawberry, if you
like, and enjoy!

MONA'S EASY DELICIOUS STEAMED CLAMS

INGREDIENTS:
6 tablespoons butter (one stick)
1 tablespoon minced garlic (more if you're a garlic
   lover like I am)
1 cup white wine (use whatever you prefer drinking)
1 tablespoon fresh squeezed lemon juice
3 dozen little neck clams
Some chopped fresh parsley for sprinkling on top
   (optional)
Lemon wedges for squeezing (optional)

In a large saucepan (with a lid) add half of the butter and melt over medium heat. Add your garlic and
cook for about 30 seconds.

Add your wine and lemon juice and bring to a boil.

Add the clams and remaining butter. Cover the pan
with the lid and steam until all of the clams have
opened, 7 to 9 minutes, while shaking your pan occasionally.

Throw away any unopened clams; they are not good.

Ladle clams and the broth into bowls and serve with
some crusty bread to dip into the broth.

Chapter 16

Bar Harbor Police Chief Sergio Alvares, who happened to be Hayley's brother-in-law, along with his right-hand man, Lieutenant Donnie, were on the scene within minutes of Hayley calling 911. As Sergio inspected the body, Lieutenant Donnie blocked Hayley from joining him. Mona hung back, in a daze, staring at Lonnie, disconcerted by his glassy eyes that were still open and seemed to be fixated on her accusingly.

"Excuse me, Hayley, I'm going to have to ask you to steer clear of the body until forensics arrives to do a thorough investigation," Lieutenant Donnie said forcefully, physically backing Hayley up with his body.

Hayley sighed, frustrated. "I am fully aware of the protocol, Donnie. This is not the first time I have stumbled across a dead body."

"Man, you can sure say that again," Donnie snickered.

Hayley tossed him an annoyed look.

"Why do you need an investigation anyway?" Mona asked, suddenly snapping out of her state of shock and averting her eyes away from Lonnie. "In case you didn't know, Lonnie Leighton was dying. He didn't have much time left. It looks like his ticker just gave out sooner than expected."

"Well, we will let forensics make that determination, Mona, but I appreciate your input."

Mona bristled at the young man's obvious condescension.

Hayley had noticed that ever since Sergio promoted Donnie to lieutenant, his confidence as well as his arrogance had grown exponentially. Still, at the end of the day, no one could argue that he wasn't developing into a pretty good cop.

Sergio knelt down to examine the position of the body, then glanced over to Hayley and Mona. "Is this the way you found him?"

"Uh, no, we didn't know who it was at first so Mona turned him over, that's when we recognized Lonnie," Hayley said guiltily, knowing it was wrong to touch the body and inadvertently tamper with a potential crime scene. But she, like Mona, also believed that poor Lonnie simply expired from his long illness.

A thought suddenly popped into Hayley's head.

Someone needed to call Vera, Ruth, and Olive. They had to know about their father. Before word got around town.

Hayley stepped away, pulling her phone out of the back pocket of her jeans and was about to look up Vera's number when she glanced down at Lonnie's clam bucket and noticed something glistening in the midday sun. She reached down and picked the small object out of the bucket and looked it over.

Donnie noticed her studying something in the palm of

her hand and marched over to see for himself if it might be a clue. "What's that?"

Hayley held it up. "A class ring."

She turned it over so they could see the inscription on the inside, which she read aloud. "Mount Desert Island High School Class of 2019."

Donnie's face scrunched up. "Where did you find it?"

"It was in Lonnie's clam bucket."

Donnie fumed. "Hayley, I told you to stay back and let us do our job. You are not a police officer!"

"I am well aware of that, Donnie, I wasn't looking for it, I just saw it!"

Donnie snatched the ring out of her hand. "You never should have touched it. Now your fingerprints are all over it!"

Hayley's eyes narrowed. "And so are yours."

Realizing his error, Donnie huffed and stormed off, heading straight for Sergio. He held out the ring. "Look what I just found in Lonnie Leighton's clam bucket, boss. A class ring. Class of 2019. That's pretty recent so I don't imagine it belongs to Lonnie."

Sergio smirked, trying hard not to laugh at Captain Obvious's keen deduction. "You're right, Donnie. Good work. Now why don't you go put that in the evidence bag?"

"Sure thing, boss!" Donnie chirped, hustling off, proud of himself.

Maybe Donnie had more to learn about being a cop than she initially believed.

Hayley went back to finding Vera's number. She located it in her list of contacts and made the call, which went straight to voice mail.

"This is Vera. Make it brief after the beep. I'm very busy."

Always the charmer.

Beep.

"Hi, Vera, this is Hayley, Hayley Powell. I need you to call me back just as soon as you get this. It's very important. It's about your father . . ." She didn't want to go into detail on a voice mail. "I'll try Ruth." Then she ended the call.

Sergio, having finished his preliminary investigation, ambled over to Hayley, who was now trying to find Ruth's number. Mona stood a few feet away, still rattled by the discovery of Lonnie's corpse.

Hayley lowered her phone. "So?"

Sergio shrugged. "Mona might be right. I will need to speak to his doctor."

"Dr. Cormack. Donnie's girlfriend Tilly is his nurse."

Sergio nodded solemnly. "But still, even if he confirms a terminal illness, my gut is telling me to request a full autopsy."

Hayley peeked back over at Lonnie's body in the clam flats. "Mine is telling me the same thing."

Sergio turned to Mona. "I heard you had an alteration the other night."

Mona shot him a confused look. "What? When have I ever worn clothes that need altering? Just hand me a sweatshirt, size large, and I'm good to go."

Sergio's eyebrows rose. "What are you talking about?"

"What are *you* talking about?" Mona barked.

Hayley stepped forward to the rescue. "Altercation."

They both turned to her, confounded.

"He meant altercation, not alteration."

Sergio was from Brazil and English was his second language.

"At my restaurant. The altercation between your family and the Leightons," Hayley explained.

"Oh, that," Mona scoffed. "That was nothing."

Sergio slowly shook his head. "That's not what I heard. People all over town were talking about it. It came near turning into an all-out brawl. They were afraid I'd have to call in a SWAT team."

"Well, that's just ridiculous!" Mona scoffed. "I got over it. I was actually going to bake Lonnie a cake as a peace offering."

Sergio's eyebrows rose again. "*You* were going to bake a cake?"

"Okay! I was going to have Hayley do it! My God, what's with the third degree?"

Sergio spoke calmly, evenly, slow and steady. "Mona, you know I think the world of you, and personally it pains me to have to say this, but if this turns out to be more than just the sad end of a terminal illness, then you, your sons, your whole family are going to be suspects."

"*What?*" Mona wailed.

"I just want you to be prepared," Sergio warned.

This did not sit well with Mona.

She despised being the center of attention.

The only thing worse would be if she was smack-dab in the middle of a murder investigation.

And Hayley feared that was exactly what was about to happen.

Chapter 17

When Sabrina Merryweather opened the door to her sprawling hilltop home with an expansive ocean view to find Hayley standing on her doorstep, her eyes widened in surprise and a joyous smile spread across her porcelain, diamond-shaped face. "I can't believe it! After bugging you relentlessly for all these months, you actually decided to show up."

Hayley was totally confused.

She had just stopped by Sabrina's house to sweet talk her into divulging any information she had concluded about Lonnie Leighton's death, hoping that if she believed he expired from his illness, Hayley would be able to alert Mona and her family that they were in the clear and could rest easy.

So she was completely in the dark about what Sabrina could possibly be talking about.

"Come in, come in," Sabrina sang, grabbing her arm and pulling her inside. "You're the last to arrive! The others will be so happy to see you." She led Hayley down the hallway to the large, open living room where four women sat around in chairs and on couches, forming a semi-circle. All of them had worn paperback books on their laps or on the coffee table in front of them. "Look who has finally decided to join us, ladies!"

They all reacted with astonished looks, mouths agape.

One of the women, Carla McFarland, whom Hayley had known for years because their sons grew up close buddies, sat back in her chair and shook her head. "I see it, but I honestly don't believe it."

"Hi, Carla," Hayley said, nodding in her direction.

Hayley also recognized Dr. Mira Reddy, a physician from the Jackson Lab in biomedical research, whose daughter Pia was a classmate of Mona's youngest, Jody. Dr. Reddy was perched on top of one of Sabrina's barstools, scowling, clutching her book, staring at Hayley, obviously not a fan of surprise last-minute guests. The other two women were familiar to Hayley, but she could not place names with their faces. Luckily Sabrina was ready with introductions. "This is Lynn, an old college friend. She's renting a house in Seal Harbor with her husband this summer, and Cathy works at the bank in financing. She just moved to town in February."

"Nice to meet you both," Hayley said.

"Let me get you some wine, You're a Cabernet girl, am I right?" She didn't wait for Hayley to answer. "I assume since you're here, you read the book."

The book.

Of course.

This was Sabrina's monthly book club.

She had been hounding Hayley to join them. Sabrina would dutifully email Hayley the selection every month, optimistic that one evening Hayley might just show up. And she was now under the impression this was that night.

Hayley hated the idea of disappointing her.

Especially since she was in desperate need of confidential information.

Sabrina zipped back with a heavy pour in a large-stemmed glass for Hayley. "Why don't you sit next to Mira over there?"

Hayley nodded as she took the wine and crossed the room and sat up on a barstool next to Dr. Reddy, who barely acknowledged her, preferring to bury her face in the pages of her book.

Hayley gave a cursory glance at the book jacket.

The Notebook by Nicholas Sparks.

A classic contemporary romance novel.

One that Hayley had never read.

But luck was on her side tonight.

She had seen the movie with Rachel McAdams and Ryan Gosling, as well as Gena Rowlands and one of her mom's all-time favorite actors, Mr. *Rockford Files* himself, James Garner, playing the McAdams and Gosling characters as senior citizens decades later. Hayley had watched the film countless times and felt she could offer a few observations on the story, at least bluff her way through until she could corner Sabrina with what she really wanted.

After putting out some snacks and making sure everyone's wineglass was full, Sabrina plopped down on the couch next to Cathy and began moderating.

"As you know, after some really dark and heavy

books, I decided we should do a few lighter reads, but not too risqué like the *Fifty Shades* trilogy, which in my opinion, have been done to death in book clubs. Whips and chains, okay, I get it, enough! Big yawn."

Lynn chuckled appreciatively.

Sabrina held up her copy of *The Notebook*. "This is one of my absolute favorites. I read it in one sitting the day it first came out, so I thought it might be fun to discuss. Okay, thoughts? Who wants to start?"

Cathy chimed in. "I run hot and cold on Nicholas Sparks. I mean he can be so schmaltzy sometimes, but this was one of his best. A forever love story, so emotionally charged, and with such a satisfying ending."

"I hated it," Dr. Reddy spit out.

The other women waited for more.

But that was it.

"Would you care to elaborate, Mira?" Sabrina prodded.

"No, why would I want to talk about a boring, inconsequential book I despised? When can we get back to more substantive works?"

Sabrina moaned. "Okay, fine, Mira, next time, when it's your turn to choose the book, you can select another Russian classic, like Tolstoy or Dostoyevsky!"

Lynn popped an oatmeal cookie in her mouth. "Oh, please, don't. I hate when we have to read a book so thick it could also be used as a doorstop."

Sabrina turned to Hayley. "What about you, Hayley? Did the ending work for you?"

"Oh, yes," Hayley gushed. "I cried so hard when the old couple died in each other's arms. It was so romantic, after all they had been through, to go out together like that, I just sobbed and sobbed!"

There was an uncomfortable silence.

Hayley instantly knew she had put her foot in her mouth.

Yet again.

"That's not the ending of the book, that's the ending of the *movie*," Cathy said accusingly.

Hayley's stomach tightened. "Oh . . ."

Lynn grabbed another cookie off the plate and stuffed it in her mouth. "Actually, the author suggests that Noah and Allie are going to make love at the end."

"Which is just ridiculous!" Dr. Reddy scoffed. "I mean, seriously, with Allie's Alzheimer's and Noah's arthritis, tell me just how that would work!"

"We get it, Mira, you're not a fan of the book!" Sabrina snapped, insulted.

Cathy locked eyes with Hayley. "Did you actually *read* the book, Hayley?"

There was no point in continuing the charade any longer.

"No," Hayley muttered. "But I've seen the movie about a dozen times."

"Why come to our book club if you weren't even going to bother reading the selection?" Lynn asked, her mouth full, chewing.

"Well, um, actually," Hayley fumbled, eyeing Sabrina guiltily.

A sly smile crept across Sabrina's face. "Because she's not here for our little book club, she's here to pump me for information about the cause of Lonnie Leighton's death."

Cathy perked up, surprised. "The lobsterman? He died?"

Sabrina nodded. "Yes. Hayley here was one of the people who found the body."

"I am hardly surprised to hear that," Dr. Reddy snorted, well aware of Hayley's history with discovering dead bodies.

"He had three daughters, those poor girls," Cathy lamented.

Sabrina wagged an admonishing finger at Hayley. "The body's still warm and here you are already fishing for juicy tidbits of information."

Hayley bowed her head, ashamed of herself. "Sabrina, I am so sorry, I should have just been upfront—"

Sabrina raised a hand and cut her off. "Hayley, you know perfectly well it is department policy that I only share my findings and conclusions with the officers and detectives investigating the death. If I were to reveal any details to a civilian, someone not in any way connected to the case, that would be completely unethical and unprofessional."

"I understand," Hayley muttered, eyes downcast.

Sabrina erupted in laughter. "But since when have I worried about ethics and professionalism? Of course I'll spill whatever I know to one of my high school besties!"

Hayley bit her tongue. Sabrina had been the mean girl who tormented Hayley in high school but had over the years rewritten their history after they reconnected as adults.

Hayley was not about to argue with her assessment of their friendship, past or present.

Sabrina clasped her hands together. "Gather 'round, girls, this is the scoop!"

Lynn and Cathy leaned forward expectantly.

Dr. Reddy bristled, wanting no part of this.

"First of all, I have not conducted anything near a full autopsy yet, so what I'm going to tell you are just my initial impressions."

Like Lynn and Cathy, Hayley found herself leaning forward in anticipation, almost to the point where she was about to tumble off the barstool.

"But if I were to take an educated guess, I think Lonnie was probably disoriented from his medication. He was taking some pretty powerful stuff for his illness, pills with very strong side effects—dizziness, drowsiness, vertigo. When he went clamming, he somehow lost his balance and fell, perhaps suffocating in the low tide clam flats."

"How horrible," Lynn said with a waxy complexion.

It made perfect sense.

But Hayley had a distinct feeling there was more to it than that.

As if reading her mind, Sabrina added, "But I promise to call you when I complete the full autopsy report . . . After I notify Chief Sergio, of course."

Sabrina winked at Hayley as if to signal her that she was just saying that for Dr. Reddy's benefit, who was still perched on top of a barstool, listening with an obvious look of disdain and judgement.

Sabrina may have been an enemy during Hayley's adolescence, but now that they were grown-ups, she had matured into a key ally, for which Hayley was forever grateful.

If there was any foul play involved in Lonnie Leighton's death, Hayley would be among the first to hear about it, and that was definitely worth the embarrassment of crashing a book club meeting.

She promised to read *The Notebook* right away.

Cross her heart and hope to die.

Chapter 18

Hayley had not been home from Sabrina's house for five minutes when she received an urgent text from Mona.

Cops here. Dougie might be arrested. SOS!

Hayley quickly grabbed a store-bought pound cake, ripped open the packaging and carefully transferred it to one of her own Tupperware containers. Then she dashed out to her car and sped over to Mona's house, pulling up behind Sergio's police cruiser. She hopped out with her Tupperware, ran up the porch steps and pounded on the front door. After a few moments, Mona flung it open.

She was as white as a sheet.

"What took you so long? They're in the living room! They could be reading him his rights for all I know!"

Hayley pushed past Mona and marched down to her living room where she found Sergio and Lieutenant Donnie standing over a shaken Dougie, who sat scrunched up on the couch, as if he was wishing he could just shrink and disappear into the cushions.

Sergio held out a shiny object.

The class ring Hayley had found in Lonnie's clam bucket.

Sensing someone hovering behind him, Sergio turned and sighed at the sight of his sister-in-law. "Hayley, what are you doing here?"

Hayley held up the Tupperware. "Didn't Mona tell you? Her boy Chet finally passed a Biology exam today. First time this semester. Well, that's cause for celebration, so I brought over one of my homemade pound cakes. Where is our little Einstein?"

"Up in his room. He'll be down in a minute."

Sergio eyed Hayley suspiciously.

He could tell she was full of it.

"I love pound cake!" Lieutenant Donnie crowed.

"I will be sure to save you a piece then, Donnie," Hayley offered with a wan smile.

Hayley returned her attention to Sergio, who folded his muscled arms expectantly. "Any word on the cause of death yet?"

"No, Hayley, but we are not waiting around for Sabrina's results to start asking questions. And what I want to know is, what was this MDI class ring doing in Lonnie Leighton's clam bucket? It obviously did not belong to him."

Donnie raised his hand. "Right, because Lonnie is an old geezer and the year inscribed on the inside of the band—"

"Yes, we got it, Donnie! But thank you for reminding us!" Sergio said in a measured tone.

"What does that ring have to do with my Dougie?" Mona demanded to know.

Sergio kept his eyes glued to Dougie as he answered Mona. "I got my hands on a copy of the MDI Class of

2019 yearbook, and imagine my surprise when I noticed that Dougie was in that same graduating class."

"Big deal," Mona sniffed. "So were about a hundred and forty other kids."

"Yes, but how many of them were being threatened by Lonnie Leighton? That brings the number down quite a bit, wouldn't you say?" Sergio said.

Hayley flipped open the cover of her Tupperware. "Pound cake, Sergio?"

"No, not now," Sergio growled, still focused on a fidgety Dougie, who looked as if he was on the verge of a nervous breakdown.

"I would love some," Donnie piped in.

"Shut up, Donnie!" Sergio snapped.

Wounded, Donnie slowly backed himself into a corner and stared at the floor.

"Tell me, Dougie, does this ring belong to you?"

Dougie suddenly sprang to his feet and bolted up the stairs to his room.

"Dougie, come back!" Mona called after him.

"Hiding in his room is not going to make this go away," Sergio said solemnly.

"I know, Sergio, but Dougie can be a little high strung," Mona sighed. "He's been known to have panic attacks on a few occasions in the past, so please, tread lightly, pressuring him will only make things worse."

"He needs to answer my questions, Mona. Either here or down at the station."

Donnie had inched his way out of the corner and was now sniffing the pound cake Hayley was holding, so she lowered the lid and sealed it closed.

Donnie frowned, hungry and frustrated.

Suddenly Dougie came flying down the stairs, marched

over to Sergio and snapped, "Here." He held out his fist. When Sergio opened the palm of his hand, Dougie dropped a round object in the middle of it.

Sergio studied the object in his hand. "What's this?"

"My class ring. It was up in my room."

Sergio turned the ring over to inspect it and grimaced.

Mona folded her arms, triumphant. "See? The ring Hayley found in Lonnie's clam bucket does not belong to my Dougie so he's in the clear!"

Sergio raised an eyebrow. "*Hayley*? I thought Donnie found—"

Lieutenant Donnie angrily cleared his throat, perturbed that Mona had just busted him in front of the boss for lying about the fact that it had not been he who discovered the ring clue in the clam bucket.

But Chief Sergio let it go.

At least for the moment.

He turned back to Dougie. "Okay, son, I appreciate you clearing this up. Any idea who the other ring belongs to?"

Dougie shook his head.

His face flinched slightly.

Hayley had seen him do that before.

When he lied to his mother about not throwing a party at the house his junior year of high school when Mona had to go out of town for an uncle's funeral.

It apparently was a physical manifestation of guilt.

A built-in lie detector.

Which meant Dougie Barnes was probably lying right now. And lying to the police could get him into a whole lot of trouble.

Sergio, not knowing Dougie nearly as well as his Aunt Hayley did, appeared satisfied.

He nodded, thanked Dougie and Mona for their time, and headed out the door with his lieutenant scampering after him like an eager puppy being taken out for a walk, leaving Hayley with alarm bells going off in her head, wondering just who Dougie was protecting?

Before she even had a chance to ask him, Dougie was pounding back upstairs to his room.

He was done talking.

To anyone.

Chapter 19

As Hayley climbed out of the shower and toweled herself off, there was a knock on the bathroom door.

"Be out in a minute!"

"Can I come in?" Bruce asked from the other side.

"Only if it's an emergency."

The door opened a crack and Bruce peered in, leering as Hayley reached for her robe and slipped it on.

"It is. I have this burning desire to see my wife in all her natural beauty."

Hayley laughed and Bruce reached out and grabbed her left arm, passionately planting kisses up and down it. "So when did you start channeling Gomez Addams?"

"I'm just feeling extra amorous tonight. We haven't had a date night in such a long time because you've been so busy with the restaurant."

"Is someone feeling guilty?"

Bruce stopped kissing her arm and stood upright, perplexed. "Guilty? Why would I be feeling guilty?"

Hayley shot him a pointed look.

"Oh, you mean because I met up with my ex-girlfriend?

I told you, that was nothing. Are you still jealous about that?"

"No, I'm not jealous. Trust me, you'll know when I'm jealous. I will tell you I'm jealous."

Bruce wasn't sure how to respond so he just nodded. "Okay. I'll be waiting in the bedroom if you care to join me." He disappeared out the door. Hayley stared at herself in the mirror, patting her hair with the towel. She hung it on a rung and marched out of the bathroom and into the bedroom, stopping at the doorway. Bruce was on his side of the bed, unbuttoning his shirt.

"Bruce?"

"Yes?"

"I'm jealous."

He circled back around and took Hayley into his arms. "You have no reason to be."

"How can you say that? Tabitha is rich, successful, and very, very pretty."

"Yes, she is all those things. And so are you."

"Rich?"

"Okay, so you're two of those things. But there is one big difference between you and Tabitha."

"What?"

"I love *you*, with all my heart. And that love's something Tabitha will never have."

"I promised myself I would not bring up her name again."

"Guess that didn't work out so well, huh?"

Hayley shook her head. "No, it didn't. I'm sorry, Bruce. I'm usually not the jealous type. There's just something about that woman that scares me a little. I can't quite put my finger on it."

"Then you should face your fears. Let's have dinner

with her, show her just how happily married the two of us are."

Hayley frowned, skeptically. "A whole dinner? How about just a quick drink at Randy's?"

"Hayley, I assure you, there is nothing to fear from Tabitha Collins."

Bruce kissed Hayley softly on the lips.

She started feeling warm inside and he was about to guide her to the bed when there was loud pounding downstairs on the front door. Bruce checked the clock on his nightstand. "Who could that be? It's almost nine."

They paused.

Waiting to see if whoever was at the door might go away.

Seconds later, there was more pounding.

He knew Hayley's curiosity would get the best of her.

Bruce sighed. "Why does this always happen at the exact moment I'm about to get lucky?"

Hayley pulled out of Bruce's embrace and scurried out of the bedroom and down the stairs. "There might be a problem at the restaurant."

Bruce followed behind her.

When Hayley opened the door, she was surprised to find Sabrina on the front porch.

"I hope I'm not stopping by too late," Sabrina whispered.

Bruce landed behind his wife. "Actually—"

"No, not at all!" Hayley interrupted. "Come in."

"I just wanted to give you this," Sabrina said, fishing through her Hermes bag and pulling out a paperback book, which she handed to Hayley.

Hayley glanced at the cover. "*Sense and Sensibility*?"

Sabrina rolled her eyes with a sigh. "I know, Jane

Austen? How cliché can we get? But you can guess whose pick it was."

She didn't have to.

It had to have been Dr. Reddy.

"You could have just called and told me. I would've picked up a copy at Sherman's."

"Well, if I did that, then I wouldn't have also been able to tell you the blood tests came back on Lonnie Leighton."

Hayley and Bruce exchanged expectant looks before Hayley swiveled her head back around toward Sabrina. "And?"

"See, I knew you were dying to know. I have already informed Chief Alvares so I don't feel as if I'm breaking any ethics rules. Wink, wink."

Hayley was reasonably sure Sabrina should not be sharing this information with her, but luckily, besides being a talented and meticulous county coroner, Sabrina Merryweather was also a hopeless gossip.

"There were prescribed sleeping pills in his system, which would bolster my initial theory that Lonnie was groggy and disoriented and that may have been what caused him to accidentally fall."

"Sleeping pills? In the middle of the day? Doesn't that strike you as odd?"

Sabrina shrugged. "What do you mean?"

"I mean, you take sleeping pills at night. What if someone slipped them in his food or force-fed them to him?"

"To what end?"

"To make it easier to kill him."

Sabrina's eyes widened. "Gosh, Hayley, what a suspicious mind you have! The Chief spoke to his two oldest daughters, Vera and Ruth, who told him their father was an insomniac who popped those sleeping pills like they were Tic Tacs, day and night, in the hopes of catching a few hours of sleep whenever he could. The Chief had no reason to doubt their story, especially since Dr. Cormack also confirmed it."

"So you believe it was just an accident?" Bruce asked.

"Yes, based on all the information I have gathered. Lonnie's eyes were bloodshot, which is a telltale sign of suffocation. You and Mona found him face down in the clam flats."

"Is it really possible for someone to suffocate that way?" Hayley asked.

"Of course. If mud gets into your lungs, it's entirely possible," Sabrina explained. "But unfortunately, at the end of the day, I cannot be one hundred percent certain what exactly happened, so basically I had no choice but to rule the cause of death as inconclusive."

Hayley grimaced, still not entirely convinced they had all the answers. "What happens now?"

"My job is finished. According to county policy, once I issue my report, the body is immediately returned to the family, which is happening as we speak."

"Then it's over," Bruce said.

Sabrina tapped the paperback cover. "I expect you to read it cover to cover this time, Hayley. No cheating by watching the movie, no matter how good Emma Thompson and Kate Winslet are and how sexy Hugh Grant is in it! See you next month!"

Sabrina gave them a cursory wave and then hurried back out to her parked Audi in front of the house.

Bruce watched her hop in and pull away before he looked at Hayley, dubiously. "It *is* over, isn't it?"

"Yes, it's over," Hayley said matter-of-factly.

Bruce gave her a wan smile.

And even Hayley could tell her words were ringing hollow.

Because in her mind, the death of Lonnie Leighton was anything but over. There were too many questions still unresolved.

Inconclusive was a far cry from accidental.

Chapter 20

"I will have the Wild Maine Blueberry Pancakes, with the real Maine syrup and a side of bacon, extra crispy, okay, Pam?" Hayley said to the jolly waitress scribbling on her pad at their booth in Jordan's Restaurant, a Bar Harbor staple.

"You got it," Pam said, still writing.

"Someone's hungry," Bruce noted from across the table.

Hayley leaned forward, whispering, "Well, you made me work up quite an appetite when you woke me up so early this morning."

She winked at Bruce, causing Pam to smirk.

"What about you, Bruce?" Pam asked.

Bruce was still perusing the menu printed on the place mat in front of him. "How about the Feta Spinach and Tomato Omelet with a side of home fries?"

Pam continued scribbling. "Toast?"

"English muffin."

"Coming right up. I'll be back with more coffee for

you two lovebirds," Pam said, sliding her pen behind her ear and heading back toward the kitchen.

Hayley blanched. "How did she know? I never said exactly *what* worked up my appetite."

"Maybe it's because you're glowing."

"I am not!"

"Okay, maybe it's the lighting in here, but there is definitely a soft glow and I am going to take complete credit."

"You're incorrigible."

"That's one of the things you love about me. That and my mad skills I displayed earlier this morning in the bed—"

"That's enough, Bruce!" Hayley said, snickering. She noticed a woman standing at the counter ordering a coffee to go. Her back was to them, but Hayley immediately recognized her. "Hey, isn't that—?"

Bruce swiveled his head around. "Yeah, that's Tabitha." He nonchalantly turned back toward Hayley.

"Aren't you going to say hello?" Hayley asked.

Bruce shook his head. "No. She probably won't see us all the way over here in the corner."

Hayley knew exactly what he was doing.

He was avoiding his ex-girlfriend to keep the peace with his current wife, and that made Hayley feel bad. She certainly did not want Bruce walking on eggshells, worried about maintaining a friendship with his ex just because Hayley could have a jealous streak.

Hayley raised her hand. "Tabitha!"

Bruce shrank in his seat. "What are you doing?"

"I'm just being polite," Hayley answered.

Tabitha turned around to see who was calling her

name. She lit up at the sight of Bruce. She picked up her paper cup of coffee and ambled over. "Good morning."

"Hi, Tabitha, are you not eating breakfast?" Hayley asked.

"I thought about sitting at the counter, but then I decided to just get a coffee to go."

"This place is known for their world-famous blueberry pancakes," Hayley said. "Why don't you join us?"

Bruce's eyes nearly popped out of his head.

He could not understand what was happening.

But Hayley was on a mission to prove to her husband that she was not threatened in any way by his stunningly gorgeous, uber-rich ex-girlfriend.

Tabitha hesitated, not sure this was such a good idea.

But Hayley slid over in the booth allowing her room to sit down next to her. "Please."

Tabitha shrugged and sat down. "All right. Thank you. That's very sweet of you."

Bruce had a smile frozen on his face.

He wasn't sure how he should react to all of this.

"How long are you in town for?" Hayley asked.

"A few more days. I was hoping you might change your mind about expanding your business before I leave," Tabitha said.

Pam appeared with their order and set Bruce's omelet down in front of him. Then she began serving Hayley, feeling the need to tick off all the food she ordered. "Here we go, Hungry Hayley. Stack of blueberry pancakes, extra syrup because I know how much you love it, side of bacon, extra crispy."

Hayley suddenly felt embarrassed for ordering so much food in front of the svelte Tabitha.

"Can I get you something, honey?" Pam asked her.

"Just a low-fat yogurt, maybe with a few of those world-famous blueberries I have been hearing so much about?"

"Sure thing, love," Pam said before skittering away.

Low fat yogurt?

Hayley stared at her plate of food.

The syrup alone was probably over a thousand calories.

Why was she suddenly feeling so insecure?

"It's not just the blueberries, it's also the delicious pancakes that are famous," Hayley felt the need to explain again.

"Well, if I eat a whole stack of pancakes, I will bloat so much, people might think I'm expecting," Tabitha joked.

Hayley put down her fork.

She had just lost her appetite.

Bruce nervously dove into his omelet.

There was an awkward pause.

"I had a dream about you last night, Bruce," Tabitha said out of the blue.

Bruce kept his eyes trained on a stray piece of feta cheese on his plate that he was trying to stab with his fork. "Oh?"

"We were still living in our tiny apartment in Back Bay," she said, laughing, as she turned to Hayley. "I insisted we live in a nice neighborhood in Boston, but to do that, we had to rent a place the size of a broom closet. Anyway, you know how claustrophobic Bruce can get . . ."

"Um, no, I did not know that," Hayley said, stupefied.

"I used to be. I've been able to get it under control as I've gotten older," Bruce said.

"Anyway, in the dream, Bruce and I were taking the

elevator down to the lobby and it started jerking like it was going to fall and there was hardly room to move and Bruce started hyperventilating and I was hugging him to calm him down and then all of a sudden, the top of the elevator popped open and Dwayne Johnson was suddenly there, and he reached down and pulled us out to safety. Isn't that crazy? Only then did I realize I had fallen asleep watching one of his movies on cable. *Skyscraper*, I think it was called."

Bruce remained silent, not daring to utter a word.

"I had a celebrity dream once where I was in a hot dog eating contest with Harry Styles," Hayley interjected.

"Who won?" Tabitha asked.

"I did," Hayley said. "I mean, have you seen him? He's so tiny. He never stood a chance."

Where on earth did that come from?

And why did she have to mention her dream was about eating food?

The fact was, most of her dreams involved food.

Tabitha threw her head back and guffawed. "Hayley, you are too funny."

They suddenly heard music coming from somewhere.

It was Fleetwood Mac.

Tabitha rummaged in her purse for her phone. "That's me." She checked the screen. "I need to take this. It's my office in Boston. Excuse me." She jumped up and headed outside to take the call just as Pam delivered her yogurt and berries.

Hayley stared at Bruce. "Her ring tone is Fleetwood Mac?"

Bruce shrugged. "I guess so."

"Not only Fleetwood Mac. It's 'Gypsy,' your favorite Fleetwood Mac song."

"I know," Bruce said. "I introduced her to Fleetwood Mac. Before me, her musical tastes were atrocious. "We're talking S Club 7 and Hootie and the Blowfish. I educated her on the classic bands of the seventies and eighties."

He noticed Hayley's skeptical look. "Babe, it doesn't mean anything."

She wanted to believe him.

But the dream about them physically pressed together? Her ring tone his all-time favorite song?

Was this just an innocent coincidence?

Was Hayley being utterly ridiculous to even question Tabitha's motives or were these actually subtle signals that Tabitha still had designs on Bruce and was somehow orchestrating a plan to get him back with her sudden interest in Hayley's business?

Either way, Hayley was more than ready for Tabitha Collins to eat that hundred-calorie yogurt and go directly back to Boston.

Chapter 21

Surprised would not be the first word Hayley would use to describe her reaction to being invited to participate in a memorial service at sea for Lonnie Leighton.

Shocked, maybe.

Stunned.

Gobsmacked, even, as the Brits would say.

But here she was, with Bruce at her side, standing on the dock at the Bar Harbor pier waiting to board Lonnie's favorite fishing boat, the *Last Call*, with the two oldest Leighton daughters, Vera and Ruth.

Vera checked her watch. "We should be shoving off soon. I want to get this done before dark."

Hayley looked around.

Other than herself and Bruce, there were no other mourners ready to board the boat.

"Who else is coming?" Hayley casually asked Vera.

"Other than Olive, who is late as usual, just you two. Oh, and Cappy's driving the boat."

Hayley glanced at Cappy, an old geezer of a fisherman, a longtime employee of Lonnie's and a regular barfly at Drinks Like A Fish, at the helm, hand on the tiller, ready to go. Cappy gave her a friendly wave. She noticed he was bleary-eyed and unsteady on his feet, probably the result of an all-night bender which was Cappy's modus operandi. She simply prayed he would be able get them back to shore safely without crashing into a rock or another docked vessel.

Hayley was dumbfounded.

Why were they the only ones who had been invited to this makeshift memorial?

Hayley had actually tried kicking Lonnie out of her restaurant right before she had found him facedown dead in the clam flats.

As if reading her mind, Ruth leaned into her and whispered in her ear, "Daddy didn't have many friends, he spent most of his time with family, but he couldn't stop raving about your cooking during his final days, what a talent you were in the kitchen, so Vera and I thought it would be appropriate that you be here to pay your respects."

"I appreciate that, Ruth, thank you," Hayley said, smiling.

Ruth nodded and then sniffed back her tears. "It's very difficult, knowing he's gone, that we will never see him again."

Vera, impatiently tapping her foot on the wooden dock, checked her watch one more time and then called out, "Okay, Cappy, let's get this show on the road!" She turned to Hayley and Bruce, yelling, "All aboard!"

It seemed ridiculous for Vera to say that considering the only two people waiting to climb aboard the *Last Call* were standing three feet in front of her. But Hayley wisely refrained from making any kind of sarcastic comment, which she was prone to do.

"Vera! We can't go yet. Olive isn't here," Ruth pleaded.

"I'm sorry, Ruth. Olive knew when she needed to be here ready to shove off. I'm tired of waiting around for her all the time!" Vera huffed.

Bruce pointed toward Agamont Park, just above the town pier. "Hold on, there she is!"

Scurrying down the grass toward the pier, they could see Olive frantically waving at them. "Wait! I'm coming!"

Just behind her, Dougie followed close on her heels.

Vera grimaced, eyes narrowing.

Hayley could see Vera's frustration growing as Olive and Dougie got closer, and by the time they were pounding down the dock to board the boat, she was in a state of unbridled rage.

"Stop right there!" Vera bellowed, holding up a hand.

Olive and Dougie came to an abrupt halt.

Vera pointed a finger at Dougie's chest. "He is not getting on this boat."

Olive arched her back defiantly. "He is here with me for moral support."

"He's a Barnes! He hasn't got a moral bone in his body!" Vera spat out.

"Vera, please . . ." Ruth whispered.

Vera spun around and glared at her middle sister. "No, Ruth, this day is about Daddy, and it was no secret he despised the whole Barnes family, especially this little punk who was trying to worm his way into our family for his own financial gain."

"That's not true, Vera, and you know it!" Olive wailed.

"He is *not* welcome here!" Vera snapped.

Hayley and Bruce, who had just walked up the plank and boarded the boat, exchanged glances, both wondering if they should now get off to show solidarity with Dougie, who looked stricken.

"If he can't come, then I'm not coming either!" Olive protested.

Vera shrugged. "Suit yourself." She signaled Cappy, who flipped a switch. The boat engine roared to life.

Hayley stepped forward. "Vera, I'm sure your father—"

But one tempestuous look from Vera shut her up immediately. Hayley knew her place. She was just an invited guest. This was Vera's show.

Dougie gently pushed Olive forward. "Go, I'll be fine."

Olive clutched Dougie's arm. "No, I won't go without you."

"Please, Olive, do this for your dad. I will be waiting right here when you get back," Dougie said.

Hayley marveled at how mature and manly and gallant Dougie was acting. It seemed just like yesterday she was watching him as a toddler squeeze mashed potatoes through his fingers in his high chair when she used to babysit him. He had grown up so much. And she was proud of him.

Olive wavered, still holding on to his arm. "Are you sure?"

Dougie nodded. "It's the right thing to do."

Olive kissed him lightly on the lips, which made Vera snort contemptuously.

"Come on, the sun's going down! We're losing the light!" Vera said, bristling.

Olive finally let go of Dougie and boarded the boat. Ruth, holding the urn with Lonnie's ashes, sat on a wooden bench in the back of the boat. She smiled weakly at Olive, who ignored her. The only people Olive did acknowledge were Hayley and Bruce, offering them a slight nod and a quiet "Hello."

The boat pulled away from the dock and chugged out past Frenchman's Bay to the wide-open ocean.

Olive kept looking back at the dock where Dougie stood at the edge, waving forlornly to her. She blew him kisses until he was a tiny dot and they could no longer spot him. Olive slouched down in a corner of the boat and hugged herself, quietly crying.

The farther they got out to sea, the more the boat rocked as it encountered unexpected choppy waters and a sudden, stiff, cold wind. After twenty minutes, Hayley felt her stomach churning.

Dear God, please don't let me get seasick! Hayley thought to herself. She turned to Bruce. "There wasn't a storm forecast for today, was there?"

"No, I don't think so," Bruce said. "Are you all right? Are you feeling ill?"

"No," Hayley lied.

The last thing she wanted was to be the focus of attention, bent over the side of the boat, vomiting. No. She was not going to let that happen.

But with each wave the boat crested, the more it rocked and the more nauseous she felt. She stumbled over and sat next to Olive, who was turned away from her.

"For what's it worth, Olive, I think you and Dougie make an adorable couple."

Olive slowly turned, a grateful smile on her face. She reached out and squeezed Hayley's hand. "Thank you. You have no idea how much that means to me."

Finally, after what seemed like hours, Cappy turned off the engine and let the boat float quietly in the water. By now the sun had set and it was dusk, a striking orange hue on the horizon before clouds moved in, darkening the sky. Vera snatched the urn from Ruth and stood at the bow of the boat, addressing the mourners.

"I want to thank you all for coming today, it means a lot to the family."

Hayley could see Bruce stifling a laugh.

Outside of the family, it was just him and Hayley.

Unless you counted Captain Cappy, who was only here to drive the boat. He would have much preferred to be sitting at the bar at Drinks Like A Fish already on his fourth shot of whiskey.

"Daddy requested that his ashes be scattered at sea, where, like most Maine fishermen, he was his happiest."

Hayley felt a raindrop on her forehead.

Then another.

And another.

Bruce whispered in her ear. "Yup. We're going to get soaked."

Vera continued talking about Lonnie's hard life, the many challenges he faced as a young man working for a boating company, how he had been fired for no cause and sued, but a biased jury had been swayed by the CEO's blatant lies on the stand. Hayley wondered if that was just Lonnie's side of the story given how ornery and short-tempered he had been his whole life.

A light rain was coming down now.

Hayley expected Vera to speed things up due to the inclement weather, but Vera continued to drone on and on, talking about their dear late mother, the only good thing in her father's life, that is until his three devoted daughters came along. Vera especially took her time describing her own special relationship with her father, how as the oldest, she had the strongest bond with him, implying that as the firstborn, she was somehow the most important, ignoring the peeved expressions of her two younger sisters.

The rain was coming down harder now.

Finally, Ruth decided they needed to move things along. "Vera, perhaps now would be a good time to scatter the ashes."

"Don't rush me, Ruth! I'm not going to give Daddy's life short shrift because of a few raindrops!"

It was pouring down now and Bruce took off his jacket and held it above him, using it as a makeshift umbrella for him and Hayley.

Olive was hugging herself, shivering from the cold, when she finally noticed something and stood up. "Where's Abby?"

No one answered her at first.

Olive stood up. "She should be here. She loved Daddy."

Vera scoffed. "Wake up, Olive. Abby never loved Daddy. She was only after his money."

"Oh, I don't think that's true, Vera," Ruth muttered.

"I was not going to let that opportunistic gold digger spoil this tribute to Daddy. I texted her and warned her to stay away today, to not even think about showing up at the dock."

Olive gasped. "Vera, you didn't . . ."

"Yes, I damn well did!" Vera cried.

There were cracks of thunder.

Cappy jumped, startled, and lowered his black fisherman cap to keep the rain out of his eyes. "Maybe Ruth's right, Vera, we should hurry this along before we have to deal with lightning."

"Cool your jets, Cappy, there won't be any lightning!" Vera shouted over the wind and rain.

On cue, there was a flash of lightning.

Despite Vera's determination to draw out this endless memorial service, everyone else on the boat knew that Mother Nature was going to win, and pretty soon Vera would have no choice but to accept it.

When another bolt of lightning and crack of thunder struck disturbingly close to the tiny boat being batted around in the rough waters, Vera finally relented. She opened the urn and tipped it over the side of the boat, dumping the ashes into the ocean.

"Goodbye, Daddy!" Vera wailed.

And Lonnie Leighton's remains floated away, hopefully to a better place than the one he left.

Chapter 22

About a mile out from shore, the unexpected storm finally began to subside, and the rain was now just a drizzle, as the *Last Call* chugged her way back. Hayley hugged Bruce to keep warm, watching Vera and Ruth chatting quietly and Olive staring at the floor of the boat, keeping to herself. As the lights of the harbor came into view, and there was an end to this journey in sight, Hayley pulled away from Bruce and crossed over to the other side of the boat where Vera and Ruth sat next to each other.

"I just want to say that was a lovely service, despite the bad weather," Hayley said.

Ruth brightened. "Thank you, Hayley. We appreciate you saying that, don't we, Vera?"

Vera continued scowling and grunting.

"I'm sure Lonnie was very proud of all three of you," Hayley continued.

Vera flicked her eyes over to Olive, who was now standing up, craning her neck, looking toward the shore, trying to see if Dougie was still on the dock, waiting for her. Vera angrily mumbled something unintelligible.

Hayley piped in before the sisters had a chance to start arguing again. "I know this is a tough time for all of you, so if there is anything I can do, please be sure to let me know."

"Thank you, Hayley. You're very kind. I just don't know how we're going to go on without him," Ruth lamented. "He was the heart and soul of the family, not to mention the business."

"It's his own damn fault for being dead!" Vera growled. "I begged him to go see a doctor but the stubborn old mule refused, said I was being a worrywart, until it was too late! He'd still be alive if he had bothered to take his health a little more seriously."

"Vera, there is no point in going over this again. What's done is done," Ruth said.

They were closing in on the dock and as far as Olive could see, there was no one standing there, waiting. Dougie had probably gone home when it started to rain. Olive wandered over to them, having heard most of their conversation. "I don't understand, the doctor gave him something like six months and it had only been a month or two."

"Doctors can be wrong, Olive!" Vera snapped.

"But I had just seen him that morning, he was feeling great," Olive pressed. "He had color in his cheeks, he was in a good mood, he didn't even harass me about Dougie, which he usually did like clockwork every day. I just think it's a little weird he died so suddenly."

"Remember our German Shepherd, Major, when he was sick? He had been on his last legs for weeks but on the day he died he had this big burst of energy and then he lay down, went to sleep, and never woke up," Ruth remembered sadly.

"Daddy was not a dog, Ruth!" Olive cried.

"They did an autopsy, Ruth, he died from his illness, so stop trying to make a big deal about this!" Vera warned. "No one wants to hear it."

"Actually . . ." Hayley interjected.

The second the word flew out of her mouth, Hayley regretted it.

All eyes were suddenly focused on her, including Bruce's.

"Actually what, Hayley?" Ruth asked.

"Well, the county coroner, Sabrina Merryweather, she and I are old friends, sort of, she was horrible to me in high school, but that's not the point. She happened to mention to me that your father's autopsy results were inconclusive."

"What does that mean?" Olive gasped, wide-eyed. "Does she think he was murdered?"

"No, of course not, but given all the evidence, there is no way of knowing for certain exactly what happened to your father," Hayley calmly explained, glancing at Bruce who had a look on his face that clearly said, *I can't believe you are getting in the middle of this family drama.*

Vera stood up and glared at Hayley. "And what do *you* think happened, Hayley?"

"Me? I have no idea. I-I probably shouldn't have said anything," Hayley sputtered.

Bruce silently nodded in agreement.

"I mean, you were the one who discovered the body, you and that god-awful Barnes woman," Vera sneered. "Come on, you can tell us, do you suspect foul play?"

"Probably not," Hayley said tentatively, but then relenting, couldn't help but add, "But honestly, I can't be sure, unless I was to unofficially investigate, but that would be a terrible idea. My brother-in-law gets very frustrated with me whenever I do that."

"I think you should investigate," Olive said.

"Me too," Ruth agreed.

They turned to Vera, who knew she was on the spot. Finally, she folded her arms, and said, "If someone did murder our father, then I damn well want to know who done it."

"Will you do it, Hayley? We could pool our resources and pay you some sort of fee if you want," Ruth offered.

"What? No, I could never accept money from you . . ."

Olive lit up, excited. "Then you *will* do it!"

Hayley began frantically waving her hands. "Wait, no, I never said that!"

"Hayley, you just said if there is anything you can do, to just let you know," Vera said. "Well, we're letting you know. There is something you can do. You can look into our father's death, find out what happened, if someone was out to get him."

Hayley could feel Bruce desperately trying to signal her to not get involved. But what could she do? She had already offered. There was no wiggling out of it now.

"I can't make any promises . . ."

Before she could finish, both Ruth and Olive rushed forward to hug her and express their gratitude.

Vera's face darkened. "You can start with the Barnes family. If anyone had a grudge against our father, it was them!"

Hayley exhaled.

This was not how she had expected Lonnie Leighton's memorial service at sea to end.

But like it or not, Hayley Powell was on the case.

Island Food & Spirits
BY
HAYLEY POWELL

I was rushing through the Shop 'n Save last Saturday picking up a few last-minute items I needed for a brunch that I was going to be preparing for Bruce, Randy, Sergio, and myself on Sunday when I hurried around a corner just a little too fast and smacked my grocery cart right into Sally Himes's cart.

I quickly plastered a friendly smile on my face and started to apologize for crashing into her. However, Sally quickly averted her eyes, but not before I spied her rolling them upward with a sigh. Then, she just pushed right past me and disappeared around the corner with her squeaky-wheeled cart with not even a word.

Good lord, I thought to myself. *I make one teeny tiny little mistake almost twenty years ago and that woman still hasn't forgotten or forgiven me for it.*

I am sure a few of you who have lived on the island a long time may remember the incident that I'm talking about. For those of you newer to town, my daughter, Gemma, was about seven years old at the time and she came racing home all excited because there was a new girl in her class from California. California, to Gemma, was like the promised land since one of her all time favorite TV shows on Nickelodeon was produced out in Hollywood, California.

Well, all Gemma could talk about for the next few days was her new friend Kimmy from California. She kept nagging me to let her ask Kimmy over to our house after school for a play-date. She handed me her mom's phone number so I could call and arrange it. I made a mental note to call Kimmy's mother when I got to the office and told Gemma that if it was okay with Kimmy's mom, she could ride the bus home the next day after school with Gemma and we would drive her back to her house around dinner-time.

The following day, I had two very excited little girls jumping off the bus and running into the kitchen for a snack before heading upstairs to Gemma's room to play with Gemma's Barbies.

After a couple of hours, I realized that it was about time that I took Gemma's new friend home before I started dinner.

I was just getting ready to call the girls downstairs when my phone rang.

It was my own bestie Mona calling. I barely had time to pick up when I heard Mona yelling, "Oh my God! Did you hear?"

"Hear what?" I asked.

"It's all over the police scanner! A child has been abducted right here in Bar Harbor! Can you believe it?"

I was stunned. What is going on in this world if there is a kidnapping in our small safe town?

Mona had very few details but the news was spreading through town like wildfire. When I hung up with Mona, I was feeling a little shaken, but I needed to call the girls downstairs so I could take Kimmy home.

My phone rang again.

It was my other bestie Liddy.

"Do you know where Gemma is?" Liddy cried.

"Yes. She's absolutely fine. She's upstairs with a friend, perfectly safe."

I could hear Liddy sighing with relief. "Did you hear about the kidnapping?

"Yes, Mona just called me."

"Oh," Liddy said. I could hear the disappointment in her voice that she had not reached me with the big news first.

Liddy went on to say that she had been in the Shop 'n Save and had heard that some sixth graders had seen a dark van driving by the school. Now police from Ellsworth were setting up a roadblock before the Trenton Bridge to stop and search all the cars leaving the island.

We talked a few more minutes about what a horrible situation this was, and how hopefully with law enforcement all over the county mobilized, this poor child would soon be found.

As I hung up with Liddy, all I could think about was how grateful I was that Gemma and Kimmy were safely playing upstairs. I called the girls to get their coats because it was time to take Kimmy home.

On our way out the door, my phone rang yet again.

This time it was my brother Randy.

"Did you hear?"

"Yes, Randy, I know. It's awful," I said solemnly.

"Well, I heard a rumor that it's more than one kid! People at the bar were saying it might be a weird cult involved that has been hanging around the island for a while now!"

"What? A cult? Seriously?"

That was a tough one to swallow but you just never know!

Randy went on to say he also heard at the bar that the state police had been alerted and they were now combing all of down east Maine for a suspect in a dark van. But there was also another story going around that a woman and a man in a large white car were driving around town looking suspicious, and on top of that, a bag boy at the Shop 'n Save had reported some "sketchy characters" who had been in the store that day purchasing an unusual amount of groceries, perhaps to feed their young kidnap victims! And even more tips were still pouring in on the police hotline!

Randy lowered his voice to a whisper and said, "I wouldn't be surprised if the FBI hadn't already been alerted."

OMG! The FBI! This was definitely serious.

I told Randy I had to go because I needed to get Gemma's friend home but to call me with updates as soon as he heard anything else.

The girls came flying down the stairs, chattering away, as they put on their coats. I got them in the car but I did not want to mention anything to them because I certainly did not want to upset them.

Kimmy told me she lived on Holland Avenue and we headed the short distance to her house. As I turned down the street, I was startled to see that the entire street was lit up like a Christmas tree! There were police cars and emergency vehicles all with their lights flashing and a crowd of people milling around on the sidewalk.

I asked Kimmy which house was hers and she pointed to the one with Police Chief Sergio standing in the middle of the yard next to a woman who was crying and holding onto a man I assumed to be her husband.

Then it hit me.

Like a bolt of lightning.

I suddenly had the worst sinking feeling. I pulled over to the side of the road, stopped the car, turned to Kimmy, and asked, "Kimmy, did you tell your mom you were coming to our house today?"

She shook her head. "No."

Gemma piped in, "You said you were going to call her!"

You can only imagine the scene that unfolded when I walked Kimmy over to her distraught parents holding each other up on their front lawn. Her mom screamed and ran to Kimmy, hugging her while her father looked up to the heavens thanking God for her safe return. Both parents were crying, which, of course, made Kimmy cry. I felt the ears of the whole town listening as I quietly explained "the little mix-up," how I had plum forgot to call to set up the playdate the day before, how it was all my fault, apologizing profusely. I could tell from the nodding of heads from the crowd of on-lookers that they understood mistakes happen and we should all be relieved that Kimmy was now safely home and unharmed.

Unfortunately, Kimmy's parents, Ed and Sally Himes, did not see it that way. They grabbed their daughter and marched inside their house, slammed the door, and never spoke to me again.

Thankfully, I was only the talk of the town for about a week, that is until June Carey drove her car right through the Acadia Restaurant's front window when she saw her husband having lunch with his secretary, and my little mishap was all but forgotten.

Reliving that stressful memory made we want to relax with one of Bruce's favorite cocktails which always does a bang-up job of calming my nerves.

Bruce and I love nothing better on a lazy Sunday morning than to have brunch. Best of all, we start with Bloody Marys, Bruce's favorite brunch cocktail. But every time we made them, Bruce would complain that something was missing. They just weren't beefy enough. That's when I came up with this special recipe, and let me tell you, after one sip, it was now and forever Bruce-approved! So, whenever we brunch, I make sure I serve this delicious concoction that I have lovingly named the Bloody Bruce!

Give it a try and I'm sure you will be adding this to your next brunch menu too!

THE BLOODY BRUCE

INGREDIENTS:
1 ounce vodka
1 ounce tomato juice
1 teaspoon beef bouillon granules (more to taste if
    you like it stronger in flavor)
Dash Worcestershire sauce
2 or 3 dashes of hot sauce
Mix all your ingredients together and pour into an
    ice-filled rocks glass and enjoy!

WOW YOUR GUESTS EASY CLAM CAKES

INGREDIENTS:
2 cans whole baby clams, drained, and save your
    liquid
2 cups flour
2 teaspoons baking soda
1 teaspoon salt
1 teaspoon pepper
2 large eggs, beaten

Mix your clams, flour, baking soda, salt, pepper,
eggs, and 4 tablespoons clam liquid to moisten mixture. Make 12 equal-portioned patties with the mixture.

In a cast iron skillet add enough vegetable oil to
coat the bottom of the pan. On medium-high heat,
fry your patties on each side until golden brown
about 3 to 4 minutes. Remove and move to a paper
towel-lined plate. Serve warm with your favorite tar-
tar sauce, cocktail sauce, or squeezes of lemon.

Chapter 23

The weather improved dramatically the following day with clear, blue skies and the temperature rising to a balmy seventy-five degrees, practically a heat wave by Maine's standards. Mona decided to host a Sunday backyard barbecue, inviting Hayley and Bruce, Randy and Sergio, and Liddy, in addition to her own entire brood, at least those in town. Digger grilled the meats on the barbecue, Dougie kept the cooler filled with icy cold beers and Hayley brought a large bowl of her yummy potato salad to place on the food table along with the huge bags of potato chips, a giant green salad, a pot of baked beans, and a number of other side dishes.

Bruce excitedly bit into a cheeseburger and got ketchup on his cheek, which Hayley dutifully wiped off with a napkin. She noticed he was staring across the yard, distracted, as he took another bite and got more ketchup on his other cheek.

"I am not going to follow you around all afternoon keeping your face clean," Hayley said.

"What's going on with those two?"

Hayley spun around to see what he found so interesting. "Who?"

"Liddy and Dennis Jr. He's been following her around like a puppy dog all afternoon."

"Liddy's helping him find a house."

"Is that all?"

"What else could possibly—" Hayley stopped herself. "Oh, Bruce, come on, he's half her age, less than half her age."

"Stranger things have happened. Especially with this unpredictable bunch."

Liddy and Dennis Jr. were giggling about something, and then she excused herself and scooted over to the cooler to grab a couple bottles of beer for the two of them. Hayley just happened to be standing next to the bottle opener and picked it up and handed it to her. "Looks like you've got a stalker."

Liddy crinkled her face, confused. "What?"

"Dennis Jr. been shadowing you ever since you got here," Bruce said with a grin.

"We're just discussing potential rental properties. He is a client," Liddy said, a bit defensive.

Hayley and Bruce exchanged a quick glance.

"What? Get your minds out of the gutter, will you two? I'm old enough to be his . . ."

"Mother?" Bruce suggested.

"Older sister!" Liddy snapped. "Now excuse me, I need to give him his beer before it gets warm." She stormed off in a huff. Her smile immediately returned when she handed Dennis Jr. the bottle.

Dougie wandered over to the food table, picked up a plate, and started loading up on potato salad and beans.

Hayley gently put a hand on his arm. "I'm sorry you

were barred from the memorial service, Dougie. That wasn't fair to either you or Olive."

Dougie shrugged. "The Leightons are never going to accept me so there's not much I can do about it."

"Now that Lonnie has passed, maybe Olive's sisters will have a change of heart about you and Olive being together."

"Ruth maybe, but not Vera. She hates me more than ever. She's just like her father. Mean and nasty. Trust me, I didn't shed one tear when I heard he kicked the bucket. I just feel bad for Olive, losing her dad like that, but as far as I'm concerned, good riddance."

Hayley took a deep breath. "Dougie, where were you on the day your mother and I found Lonnie's body."

"Why?"

"Just curious."

"You're always curious about something, Aunt Hayley. Do you think I held that old geezer's head down in the mud and suffocated him to death?"

Bruce's eyes widened. "Wow, nobody was thinking that but you sure did paint a pretty clear picture just now."

"I'd be lying if I said I hadn't thought about it when I heard where you found him. I was tired of him trying to keep me and Olive apart. But I never went anywhere near him that day. In fact, I made it my personal mission to stay as far away as I could. I spent the whole day with Olive. We went shopping for fishing supplies at Walmart in Ellsworth. I'm sure the store cameras will pick us up at some point. We were there for almost an hour. Then we went to have lunch at Pat's Pizza. By the time we got back to town, word was already spreading that you had found Lonnie's body. I took Olive straight home in my truck to be with her sisters. I already proved that ring wasn't mine. What more do you want?"

"You're right, Dougie, I'm sorry," Hayley said, grabbing an empty plate and leaving Bruce and Dougie to join Sergio and Randy at the grill where Digger was patting the sweat off his brow with a paper towel while flipping a few burgers and adding some cheddar cheese to a couple of others.

"How do you want your burgers cooked?" Digger asked.

"Medium-well for me," Randy said. "Medium-rare for Sergio."

Digger grabbed some raw patties and slapped them down on the grill. "Hayley?"

"I'll have a hot dog when they're ready."

She was still thinking about that weird dream where she was in a hot dog eating contest with Harry Styles. She looked across the yard to see Dougie now in a deep conversation with his mother.

Uh-oh.

No doubt filling her in on their conversation.

Mona threw her head back and exclaimed, "Oh Lord, she what?" Then she made a beeline straight for Hayley, shouting to Dennis Jr. who was still hovering around Liddy. "Dennis, get over here right now!"

Dennis Jr. scrambled over to his mother, who was now at the barbecue with Digger, Hayley, Bruce, Sergio, and Randy.

Mona put her hands on her hips and said, "Okay, will you two boys kindly tell Miss Marple here where you were on the day we stumbled across Lonnie Leighton's dead body?"

Digger and Dennis Jr. both blinked, confused.

"Go on! Apparently, she's conducting her own personal investigation into the mysterious circumstances surrounding Lonnie Leighton's death even though it's as plain as day that he died from having a terminal illness! But apparently that fact is not good enough for this one!"

"Mona, I was just—"

"Tell her, Digger!"

Digger glanced at his brother then to his mother and back at Hayley. "We, um, we were out hauling traps until about noon, then we washed the boat. After that we stopped at Drinks Like A Fish. Randy was there. He waited on us."

Randy nodded. "That's right. You both came in for a late lunch and were there until around four, *after* the time Hayley and Mona found Lonnie."

"See? So you can stop pointlessly hounding my sons. They all have airtight alibis!" Mona growled. "Which they certainly don't need since at the end of the day, there is no *murder*, despite what you and the Leighton witches might foolishly believe, right Sergio?"

"She's right, Hayley," Sergio said. "The case is closed."

"Okay, I get it. I'm sorry," Hayley whispered.

"Your potato salad had better be mighty tasty, otherwise you might not be invited back the next time I throw an impromptu barbecue! I need another beer! Dougie, bring your thirsty mother a Bud Light!"

Sufficiently shamed, Hayley turned to Digger and offered him an embarrassed smile. "I'm kind of hungry, I'll take a hot dog and a burger. Medium."

Digger nodded and slapped another patty down on the grill.

Chapter 24

After the last table of guests remaining at Hayley's Kitchen had paid their tab and the staff had cleaned up and gone home for the night, Hayley, bone tired, decided to treat herself to the last portion of molten lava cake, tonight's popular dessert special. She carved off half and wrapped up the other to take home to Bruce. She was just raising a generous forkful to her mouth when she received a text.

It was from Randy.

Come to the bar as soon as you can!

Hayley glanced at the time on her phone.

It was almost eleven o'clock.

The last place she wanted to go was Drinks Like A Fish.

She decided to call him to find out what was so urgent.

He picked up on the first ring.

"Are you on your way?"

Hayley stifled a yawn. "No, Randy, I'm exhausted. I've been on my feet for almost eight hours. I just want to go home and crawl into bed. Can't you just tell me what's up over the phone?"

"They're right behind me standing at the bar waiting to order more beers. My back is to them, but I'm afraid they'll hear me if I try to talk over the music."

She could hear Ed Sheeran playing on the jukebox in the background.

"They? Who's they?"

"Please, sis, just come down here," he said cryptically.

"Fine," she sighed, "I'll be there in five minutes."

Randy had a tendency to overdramatize, but she was going to give him the benefit of the doubt because he sounded so serious. She could not imagine who he could be talking about. She scarfed down the molten lava cake in record time and then drove over to Drinks Like A Fish. The second she walked through the door she spotted Digger and Dennis Jr. in the back of the bar, downing mugs of beer and playing darts. Very badly. Their throws were wildly off the mark, nowhere near the bullseye. Both Barnes boys looked completely soused. The bar was otherwise empty except for Captain Cappy, one of Randy's regulars, who Hayley had seen at Lonnie's memorial at sea. He was slouched over at the end of the bar nursing a whiskey, eyes at half-mast. Randy was washing some glasses but stopped when he spotted Hayley and rushed over to her.

"They arrived at six and haven't stopped drinking since," Randy quickly explained, pointing at Mona's sons who were now practically on the floor, laughing at some shared dirty joke.

"So what? You want me to be their designated driver and deliver them home safely?"

Randy shook his head. "No, sis. They have been pretty

lit for hours now from all the beer, and they suddenly got very loose-lipped about exactly what they were doing on the day Lonnie Leighton died."

Randy had been right.

This was important.

"I heard them talking to Cappy," Randy quietly explained. "Cappy was teasing them about playing hooky from work last Thursday. Apparently, Cappy was washing the deck of his boat for hours that day and noticed the Barnes's boat tied to the mooring buoy where it stayed *all* day.

"The boys laughed it off at first, but when they noticed me listening, they got nervous and clammed up real fast. They tried convincing Cappy he was mistaken, that he was confused and his memory just isn't what it used to be, but Cappy was adamant."

"If Cappy's right, then that blows a big hole in their alibi that they were together out on the water hauling traps," Hayley said. She marched over to Cappy, who was staring at the empty bottom of his glass.

"Evening, Cappy."

He squinted at her with watery eyes. "Mona!"

"No, it's Hayley."

"Sorry, honey. Liddy!"

"No, Cappy, it's Hayley. Hayley Powell."

He studied her face a little harder.

"Hayley!"

"That's it! You got it."

"I guess you girls have been friends for so long you're all starting to look like each other."

"Could be, or you have had one too many whiskeys and can't see straight."

"Nah, I like my excuse better."

"Listen, Cappy, are you sure the Barnes's boat never left the harbor last Thursday when you were cleaning the deck of your boat?"

"Yes, those boys are having a little fun messing with me, trying to convince me that I'm some senile old coot, but I know what I saw," Cappy slurred.

"Are you certain it was last Thursday?"

"Oh, yeah, I'll never forget it, because just as I got ready to wash up and come over here for a drink, I heard all these sirens, and by the time I got here to my barstool, it was all over town that Lonnie Leighton had been found dead."

Hayley and Randy stood frozen in place.

Digger and Dennis Jr. were lying.

But why?

Unless they were covering something up for themselves or someone else.

Either way, it did not look good for Mona's two sons.

Chapter 25

When Dennis Barnes Sr. opened the door to his ramshackle two-bedroom apartment located behind a funeral home, his mouth dropped open at the sight of his ex-wife Mona, along with Hayley, standing on his weathered faded welcome mat. He was in boxer shorts with lobsters on them and a ratty stained white tank top because he was not expecting guests. He was scratching his ample belly as he stared dumbstruck at Mona.

"M-Mona, what are you doing here?" Dennis stuttered, giving a quick glance over at Hayley, who offered a quick smile and a wave.

"We're here to see Dennis Jr.," Mona said gruffly.

"Oh, well, he's not here, but please, come in," Dennis said sweetly, yanking the door open wider and gesturing for them to enter.

Mona hesitated, not sure this was a good idea, but ultimately she just sighed and stepped across the threshold into the apartment with Hayley following right behind her.

When Hayley had showed up at Mona's house the fol-

lowing morning to alert her to what Cappy had said about
Digger and Dennis Jr, she fully expected Mona to blow a
gasket and scream at her to get out of her house. But
much to Hayley's astonishment, after calmly explaining
the situation to Mona, how her boys had not told the
truth, Mona had not become instantly defensive. Instead,
she listened quietly, took in the information, then suggested they try to get to the bottom of it by going over to
the apartment Dennis Jr. was currently sharing with his
father.

So here they were.

With Dennis Sr.

Who could not take his eyes off his ex-wife.

The apartment was a pigsty. There was no other way to
describe it. Dirty dishes piled high in the sink. Dust
everywhere. A couch in desperate need of upholstering.
Smudges on the large flat screen TV. Hayley struggled
not to crinkle her nose in disgust.

"Mona, you're looking lovely these days," Dennis said
with a crooked smile revealing a missing tooth.

"I'm wearing the same sweatshirt with the same fishy
smell that I wear six days a week, Dennis. I haven't
changed a bit. But you have. What happened to your
tooth?"

"I walked into a door," he grumbled.

"Drunk from too many beers no doubt," Mona scoffed.

Dennis did not bother to refute her assessment, so that
pretty much confirmed her suspicion.

"Can I get you ladies a drink?" Dennis offered.

"We're not here for a social call, Dennis, we came here
to talk to Dennis Jr. Do you have any idea where we can
find him?"

"No, he left pretty early this morning, I figured he was out on the boat with Digger hauling traps. I hardly ever see him."

"What are you talking about? You're living with the boy!" Mona snapped.

Dennis looked around at the messy apartment. "It's a bit crowded with the two of us staying here. I know he's looking for a place of his own, so he usually just shows up to crash in the guest room late at night, and then he's gone by dawn. I was hoping for a little more father-son bonding time, I love having him around, but it hasn't worked out that way."

"Maybe if you had spent more time with him when he was younger," Mona said but then stopped herself. Now was not the time and place to debate her ex's lackluster parenting skills. "I'm sure Dennis Jr. appreciates you letting him stay here, but he's a grown man now, and he needs his own space."

"No, I get it, especially now that he's seeing someone," Dennis said casually.

Mona snapped to full attention.

"What the hell are you talking about? Dennis Jr. has a girlfriend? How do I not know this? Why wouldn't he tell his own mother he's dating someone?"

Dennis shrugged. "I tried getting him to open up and tell me about her, but he's been real tight-lipped, very shy talking about it, you know what I mean?"

"Why? What's wrong with her?" Mona wailed.

Hayley stepped forward. "Dennis Jr. has always been very secretive about his private life. Maybe he wants to be sure this girl is someone real special before he introduces her to the family."

Dennis pointed a finger at Hayley. "Yeah, that's what I figured. Maybe he just doesn't want to jinx it until he knows for sure that it's serious."

"That's the most idiotic thing I have ever heard! I'm his mother! I need to know what's going on with my children!" Mona roared.

"Technically, Dennis Jr. is not a child anymore, Mona," Hayley offered cautiously.

Mona's nostrils flared but she ignored Hayley's comment, keeping her eyes fixed on Dennis. "So you have no idea where he is right now?"

"Nope, sorry, but now that you're here, why don't you take a seat and stay awhile. I got a Chardonnay in the fridge, I know Hayley likes her wine," Dennis said.

"Take a seat? On *that* couch? I'm not risking planting my butt anywhere in this place and risk carrying home an infestation of bed bugs!" Mona derided.

The insult washed right over Dennis who leered at her. "Mona, you know I would never get rid of that couch. It has sentimental value. Do you know how many times when we first got married that we—"

"Stop right there, Dennis! I will knock another tooth out of your mouth if you dare to finish that sentence."

"Come on, Mona, with all the romance in the air, Dennis Jr. possibly finding true love, maybe it's time we gave it another go," Dennis said with a wink.

Mona looked around the sloppy, filthy apartment, then back at her sloth of an ex-husband who had clearly spiraled since their divorce. "As tempting as your offer sounds, Dennis, I mean clearly I would be treated like a queen if I came back to you, it's gonna be a hard pass."

"Really? We had some good times, Mona. How hard of a pass is it?"

"About as hard as the Rock of Gibraltar! If Dennis Jr. shows up here, tell him to call me! Let's go, Hayley!"

Mona charged out of the apartment.

"Nice seeing you, Dennis!" Hayley said weakly before following Mona out the door.

Dennis called after them. "You know where to find me when you change your mind!"

Chapter 26

When Dennis Jr. showed up at Hayley's restaurant with a delivery of fresh lobsters for her seafood pasta that was on her specials board that evening, he seemed preoccupied. He carried the styrofoam container into the kitchen, slammed it down on the counter, and shoved a paper in front of Hayley to sign confirming her receipt of the order. Hayley had tried to make small talk but Dennis Jr. was not having it.

"See ya," he said with a slight wave.

"Dennis, wait, I was hoping you could stay just for a minute. I just need to ask you about—"

"Sorry, I have an appointment I need to get to, Aunt Hayley, gotta go," Dennis Jr. said, marching out the back door to his truck in the parking lot.

She chased after him, but by the time she caught up to him, he was already behind the wheel of the truck with the engine chugging to life.

"Could we meet up later, maybe for a drink at Drinks Like A Fish, it's kind of important?"

He anxiously checked his watch. "Yeah, maybe, I'll text you."

Before she could get out another word, he was squealing away and she got pelted by some flying bits of gravel. Hayley turned around to go back inside when her phone pinged. She checked the screen.

It was a text from Mona. **Turn around and get in.**

Hayley spun around in time to see Mona pulling up in her white Ford pickup truck.

"Mona, you just missed Dennis Jr., he was here delivering—"

Mona cut her off. "I know, I know, I've been tailing him all day."

Hayley raised an eyebrow. "You *what*?"

"I just gotta find out who this mystery woman is. Come on, get in before we lose him!"

Hayley knew her hostess, Betty, would be arriving momentarily so she would not be abandoning her restaurant, so without pausing to even think about the consequences, she hopped in the passenger's side of the truck and Mona roared off in hot pursuit of Dennis Jr.

"Do you really think this is a good idea, keeping your own son under surveillance?" Hayley asked.

Mona kept her eyes glued on Dennis Jr.'s truck just ahead of them. "Hayley, sometimes desperate situations require desperate measures!"

"How is Dennis Jr.'s dating life a desperate situation?"

"Maybe it's not for him, but it certainly is for me. I don't like my kids hiding things from me. I need to know. Otherwise, I'll drive myself crazy!"

Too late.

Dennis Jr. drove out of town on Eagle Lake Road.

Mona allowed a car to pass her so they were not directly behind Dennis Jr's truck where he could easily spot them through his rearview mirror.

Hayley started to get a sinking feeling.

"Mona . . ."

"Look, if you don't approve of what we're doing, I can pull over right now and leave you on the side of the road and pick you up on my way back!"

"No, I'll ride shotgun, it's just that . . ."

"What, Hayley, what?"

"I think I know where we're going and you're not going to like it," Hayley mumbled.

Mona cranked her head around toward Hayley. "Why? Where do you think we're going?"

Just ahead, Dennis Jr. made a sharp right turning down a side road toward a private property.

Mona's eyes bulged. "Sweet Lord Jesus!"

"I know, I know, I had a bad feeling!"

Dennis Jr. had led them straight to Liddy's house.

Mona slowed her truck down, flipped on the blinker, and turned onto the gravel path that led onto Liddy's property. She stopped far enough from the front of the house so Dennis Jr. didn't notice them as he jumped out of his truck, checked his teeth in his side mirror, his shirt for stains, then ran his fingers through his shaggy hair and shook it out. He then walked like a rooster to Liddy's front door.

"Mona, this could be anything. You know she's trying to find him a rental property. Or maybe she ordered some seafood for a party or something!"

"My boy does not check himself out in a mirror if he's just making a delivery, Hayley!"

He rang the bell.

A few seconds later the door opened and Liddy, with a bright smile, ushered him inside.

"I don't believe it. Liddy is secretly dating my son," Mona gasped, anguished.

"We do not know that for sure. Now, there is nothing we can do at this point, so I think we should turn around and go home, and then you can have a rational discussion with Dennis Jr. later."

"We can do that," Mona said.

A wave of relief washed over Hayley. "Good."

"Or we can confront the little twosome right here and now!" Mona cried, slamming her foot down on the gas pedal, hurtling the truck forward, nearly sideswiping Dennis Jr.'s vehicle that was parked out in front of Liddy's house.

Before Hayley could stop her, Mona clambered out of the truck and was stomping up the steps onto Liddy's front porch. She didn't bother ringing the bell. She just stormed through the front door with Hayley running to catch up to her.

Hayley nearly slammed into her back when Mona suddenly stopped short. She had good reason to be thunderstruck.

There, in the living room, in front of the large picture window that overlooked the wilds of Acadia National Park, Liddy and Dennis Jr. were caught in an embrace. They both had startled expressions on their face, clasping each other's arms as they gaped at Mona who had suddenly burst into the house.

"Mom, what are you doing here?"

"Zip it, Junior! You don't get to speak yet! I want to hear from the cradle robber first!"

Liddy quickly shook out of Dennis Jr.'s grasp. "Mona, this is not what it looks like."

"How many times have people said that when it's *exactly* what it looks like! I guess I shouldn't be surprised! This makes perfect sense given your past history."

"I have no idea what you are talking about!" Liddy scoffed.

Mona laughed derisively. "Oh, please! You've been chasing after younger men your whole life! You nearly married a man half your age. But at least Sonny was on the north side of twenty-five! Dennis Jr's barely old enough to drink!"

Liddy's face darkened. "Mona, how dare you assume such a thing! I am *not* romantically involved with your son, or any of your sons, that I promise you!"

"Then what the hell is going on here?"

Dennis Jr. angrily strode over to his mother. "I can't believe you followed me here."

Mona wagged an admonishing finger in front of his face. "Don't try to change the subject! If you're not in love with Liddy, why can't you just say it?"

"Because I am! I am in love with her!" Dennis Jr. cried.

Mona swayed a bit on her feet, as if she was going to pass out. Hayley took a step forward so she was right behind her to try and catch her if she fell backward.

"I don't believe this . . ." Mona whispered.

Dennis Jr. took a deep breath and continued. "I have had a huge crush on Liddy ever since I was going into my sophomore year in high school and we all went to Sand Beach one summer and she came along with us and wore that sexy orange bikini." He turned to Liddy with adoring puppy dog eyes. "I will never forget that day as long as I live. You looked like a goddess."

Liddy could not help but respond, flattered. "I probably should have worn a more modest one piece that day given that children were present, but I had just finished two months of Jenny Craig and had lost nineteen pounds and I really wanted to show off my new shapely figure. Is there a law against wanting to feel pretty?"

Hayley tried to gently signal Liddy that it might be to her immediate benefit to just stay out of the conversation and let Dennis Jr. do the talking, but as is often the case, she missed the cue.

"Mona, it's hardly my fault if I just happened to get the boy's hormones racing. What do you expect me to do, get thee to a nunnery?"

"All of the girls I've dated since then, they seem so immature and they only talk about superficial things like Kylie Jenner's makeup line or Taylor Swift's latest break up song. It's boring. I've always enjoyed women with a little more life experience, so I went after Liddy." He fixed on his mother's furious gaze, explaining firmly, "And let me be clear. I pursued her. Hard. But she turned me down flat."

The rage slowly began draining from Mona's body.

"I came here again today, just to take one more shot, but she wouldn't budge. She said her friendship with you was too important to her and she would never jeopardize that. She let me down easy though, said I was a great guy and would someday make a girl, or even an older woman, very happy. And then we hugged it out and that's when you came bursting in here like an FBI raid and started yelling like a banshee! That's God's honest truth, Mom, I swear."

Mona nodded, apparently satisfied.

Hayley, however, was not. Still standing close to Mona, she whispered in her ear, "Don't you have something to say to Liddy?"

Mona shook her head. "No, not really."

Hayley pushed her forward. "Oh, I think you do."

Mona sighed. "Okay, fine. I thought you looked pretty good in that orange bikini too, but I didn't say anything because I felt like an elephant in my gray swim skirt."

Hayley shoved her again. "Mona . . ."

"And I'm sorry I assumed the worst, Liddy. That was wrong and I should have known you would never do something like that behind my back."

"Apology accepted," Liddy said. "This is not the first time something like this has happened to me. Lots of young men on the verge of manhood see a smart, sophisticated, gorgeous women and can't help but be drawn to them."

Mona rolled her eyes but kept mum.

Hayley circled around her and walked up to Dennis Jr. "Now that we have cleared that up, I would like you to clear up something else for me."

Dennis Jr. blinked at her, confused.

"Is that why you lied about being on the boat with Digger on the day Lonnie Leighton died? Were you busy chasing Liddy around town?"

"No," Dennis Jr. said nervously. "I hung out at home that day. I was at Dad's playing video games in my room."

"Then why did you tell Sergio that you and Digger were out on the boat when there is an eyewitness who says he noticed your boat was tied to the mooring all day and you and your brother were nowhere to be found? What are you hiding?"

"I'm not hiding anything, Aunt Hayley. Digger was the one who asked if I would just say we were out on the boat."

Mona uttered, flabbergasted. "What? Why?"

Dennis Jr. shrugged. "Beats me. But he's my big brother. I'll say whatever he wants me to say."

Hayley's mind was reeling.

If Digger had gone to the trouble of asking his brother to lie to the police, then there was a good chance whatever he was covering up was big.

Very big.

Maybe even a murder.

Chapter 27

"Mona, promise me you will not confront Digger when he gets home tonight!" Hayley begged as Mona stopped her white pickup truck in front of Hayley's restaurant to drop her off.

Mona's nostrils flared with a deep intake of breath before she let the air out with an exaggerated whoosh. "Why the hell not?"

"Because we don't want to spook him. He might just clam up, and then we'll never know why he lied. He obviously feels the need to hide something, and I just want a little time to figure out what's his big secret."

Mona considered Hayley's plan a few moments, and then slowly nodded in agreement. "You're right. I will keep my mouth shut for now. But if you don't get some answers soon, and I mean real soon, I'm gonna grab him by the scuff of the neck and just shake the truth out of him, is that clear?"

"Crystal," Hayley said, unhooking her seat belt and hopping out of the truck. "Don't worry, Mona, we will get to the bottom of this."

Mona grunted and then sped away.

After a long, busy night at Hayley's Kitchen, Hayley dragged herself home to bed but set her alarm for five thirty, knowing she had to be parked out on the street near Mona's house when Digger left for the morning. Digger had his own place in town but sometimes he stayed overnight at his mother's house in his old room when he would hang out with his brothers in front of the TV and drink too much beer. Mona had texted Hayley late last night that, true to form, Digger was passed out on the couch where he would probably be until morning. She also informed Hayley that Digger had the following day off, so she was banking on the theory that he might use his time off to deal with whatever was secretly going on in his personal life.

Hayley still harbored the fear that Digger might have been the cause of Lonnie Leighton's body ending up face down in the clam flats, but there were still so many unanswered questions, a lack of hard evidence, plus she simply could not fathom the idea that one of Mona's boys was responsible for something so heinous.

Hayley spent most of her morning sitting in her car waiting for Digger to emerge. At seven thirty, Mona's youngest, Jody, skipped out the front door with her Barbie backpack to wait for the school bus. Minutes later, a Volvo packed with teenagers pulled up and Chet rushed out of the house and jumped in as they headed off to the high school. At one point, Hayley spotted Mona peering out the kitchen window, making sure Hayley was outside conducting her surveillance as they had planned. There was still no sign of Digger. Around ten, Dougie ambled out, stifling a yawn and rubbing his eyes as if he had just crawled out of bed. He walked over to his moped that had been parked and locked on the side of the street. He put on a helmet, straddled it, and puttered off down the street, no doubt on his way to a rendezvous with Olive. Finally, around eleven fifteen, Digger sauntered out, bleary-eyed, definitely hungover. He jangled the keys to his Jeep Grand Cherokee. Hayley ducked down in her seat as Digger's eyes seemed to wander over in her direction. She prayed he would not recognize her car and put two and two together.

Fortunately, his mind seemed to be on something else as he got behind the wheel and raced off down the street. Hayley fumbled, trying to start her car, but managed to spin into a U-turn and chase after Digger.

His first stop was at the Shop 'n Save. He found a parking spot near the front entrance and ambled inside, grabbing a shopping cart on his way. About twenty minutes later, he emerged carrying two plastic bags of groceries. But instead of hurling them in the back and taking off, he opened the flatbed and picked up a wicker picnic basket. Then he emptied the bags and began carefully arranging the items in the basket. Cheese, crackers, some artisan bread, a bottle of wine, two wrapped made-to-order sandwiches. A small Bundt cake. A package of plastic forks.

This was looking like some kind of romantic date.

Once he was satisfied with his presentation, he placed the picnic basket in the passenger seat, circled around the back to close up the flatbed, then got into his Jeep and continued on his way. Hayley was in such a rush to keep up with him, she nearly mowed down a bag boy collecting stray carts in the parking lot.

She waved out her open window. "Sorry, Glen!"

And then she slammed her foot on the accelerator after turning onto Cottage Street to catch up to Digger.

When Digger veered onto Eagle Lake Road, Hayley started to sweat. It appeared Digger, like his younger brother Dennis Jr., might be heading to Liddy's house.

Hayley prayed and prayed that Liddy Crawford's abode was not his final destination. She exhaled a huge sigh of relief when he zipped past the road leading down to Liddy's house. He kept going, turning right toward the entrance to Acadia National Park. Hayley allowed a park ranger to pass her and situate herself in between Hayley's vehicle and Digger's Jeep just to keep a safe distance and hopefully not be noticed. But the ranger turned off before reaching the one way road that looped around the park and all its lush greenery and breathtaking ocean views. Hayley hung back as best she could as Digger sped around the wide curves disappearing from view.

Finally, just past the entrance to Sand Beach, Hayley spotted Digger turning into a rest area. She slowed her car down almost to a halt at the side of the road, watching as he got out of his Jeep, grabbed the picnic basket, and then walked across the road and down a dirt path. They were near the scenic Thunderhole, known for its thunderous roar when the strong waves crashed against the rocky cavern below, sometimes sending water forty feet into the air. Hayley knew this was a romantic outdoor spot for young lovers. Digger, like his baby brother Dougie, was seeing someone whom he obviously did not want his mother to know about.

Hayley hustled down the dirt path, sliding behind a tree when she heard voices up ahead. She peered around the large white spruce, rubbernecking to get a better view.

She saw Digger beaming from ear to ear, uncorking a bottle of Pinot Grigio. He was sitting cross-legged on a blanket, the rocky Atlantic coast behind him like he was in a painting. He was with a woman who was wearing a bulky Kelly-green sweater, her back to Hayley. The woman gingerly unloaded the picnic basket, setting the food down in front of them. Digger picked up a plastic wineglass, filled it and handed it to the woman. Then he poured one for himself. The two clinked glasses as Digger made some kind of inaudible toast and they both took a sip. Then Digger took her glass from her and set both of them down on the blanket. He cupped his hand around the back of her neck and drew her closer, passionately kissing her on the lips.

The kiss went on for what felt like an eternity.

Finally, they separated and the woman turned to find a knife to cut the block of Camembert. That's when Hayley got her first glimpse of the woman's face.

She recognized her instantly.

It was Ruth Leighton.

Lonnie's middle daughter.

Island Food & Spirits
BY
HAYLEY POWELL

I was looking through some of my old clam recipes recently when I came across the very first one I ever made. It's absolutely delicious and very simple to make. So simple, in fact, that I almost didn't share it today, but I feel that everyone needs at least one tasty recipe that is a breeze to put together for any type of gathering or occasion.

I also noticed in my notes that I wrote, "Buy clams from Mona," which I can say is something I have been doing for most of my life. Mona has always worked at her family's seafood business ever since she was a little girl. After she finished at a two-year community college with a degree in business administration, her father made her a full-time employee, and now with both her parents retired, she runs the entire business all on her own. She has even built it up over the years, expanding and adding additional seafoods and turning it into one of the most durable and profitable businesses on the whole island to this day!

But I never had any doubt Mona would be a successful businesswoman because even when we were kids, Mona had always had an intense drive to win! I remember back when we were in the eighth grade at Emerson-Conners, our teacher announced that each student in class would be selling Chef Luigi's Make Your Own Pizza kits to raise money for our class trip to Quebec, Canada. Chef Luigi was a national pizza chain, and my brother Randy and I always enjoyed devouring them when our mother didn't feel like cooking, which was more often than not.

Anyway, Liddy, Mona, and I were pretty excited because it was well known that the previous year's eighth grade class had made a killing. Their sale had been a huge hit because most restaurants are closed during the brutal island winters, and so it allowed the locals to stock their freezers with ready to make pizzas.

It was a win-win for everybody!

Just to add an additional incentive, the principal announced at a school assembly that there would be a cash prize of one hundred dollars to the top seller. All three of us, me, Liddy and Mona, squealed with delight. What thirteen-year-old could not use a hundred bucks to buy whatever our hearts desired? We knew exactly what we wanted to do with the money. Liddy and I were fixated on going to the Abercrombie store in Bangor to buy their newest style of jeans with the rips in different places on the legs, which our mothers stubbornly refused to buy for us because they said that it was a waste of money when we already owned old worn out ripped jeans and they had cost five times less than what we would pay at the Abercrombie store. We just rolled our eyes in disgust because our mothers clearly did not understand the first thing about teen fashion. But they did say, however, that if we had our own money we could buy them ourselves. That was all we needed to hear. Mona, on the other hand, loved electronics and games and she had her eye on a new Game Boy, and the only way she was ever going to get one was to buy it herself because her parents believed Game Boys were a huge waste of time and rotted the brain, but they also did agree that, if she used her own money, she could get one.

So when the day came to start selling the pizzas we strategized which neighborhood we would start in and how many houses we could hit before dark and so on. When the bell rang signaling the end of the school day, we were off and running with high hopes and dollar signs in our eyes. We raced from door to door of every house in town with our order sheets clutched in our hands.

Well, one hour later, and after knocking on the doors of at least twenty houses, the three of us stood miserably on the sidewalk, staring down at our nearly empty order sheets, having only sold to one house each. Apparently, what we did not know at the time was that the reason last year's class had been so successful was because it was the first time they had conducted the contest and everyone bought dozens of pizzas to support the kids. Unfortunately, they still had stacks of frozen pizza kits taking up room in their freezers. There just was not as much of a demand this year. Dreams of expensive ripped jeans and brand-new Game Boys began to quickly fade away.

The next day was Saturday and I started out strong selling to three houses in my neighborhood, but by midafternoon, I was getting so tired of people saying no and slamming the door in my face that I finally decided to call it a day.

Liddy called me that night and said she had only sold one pizza and it was to her dad who felt sorry for her. When I called Mona to ask how she did, she mumbled, "Okay." She didn't elaborate much beyond that. I found this highly unusual for Mona, who had always had a mean competitive streak, so I thought since she wasn't bragging about her big sales count, she had probably struck out as well. After a week of pounding the pavement, we had to wait for the orders to come in before finding out who won.

Finally, the big day arrived and all of the eighth graders, along with their parents, gathered in the school gym to pick up their orders and to hear the big announcement of the top seller!

I had never seen a class of kids sit so quietly, waiting with anticipation as Principal Hall thanked all of the parents for their help, how we had raised just enough for our Quebec trip, dragging out the suspense, until finally, he announced that the winner who sold a whopping

seventy-five frozen pizza kits was . . . Mona Butler!

Mona jumped out of the bleachers and raced
down to the gym floor and snatched her crisp
one-hundred-dollar bill right out of Principal
Hall's hand before running back to the bleachers, waving it wildly above her head. Liddy and I
were genuinely happy for her, and I asked her
how she had managed to sell so many kits when
we were having so much trouble. Mona just
gave us a playful wink and then ran off after her
mom to pick up her pizzas for delivery.

Unfortunately for Mona, her victory and
dreams of a new Game Boy were short-lived because as they began dropping off the pizzas to
her customers, all the buyers started asking
where their pound of free clams were, and
that's when Mona realized that maybe she had
not thought her sales plan all the way through.
She had promised a pound of clams to over half
her customers, thinking she could deliver them
at a later time. Much later. Like long after she
had that Game Boy in her pudgy little hands
and had returned from the Quebec trip. Glancing over at her mother's fuming face pretty
much confirmed that she had not thought much
about her plan at all.

When Mona and her mother got back to the
car, her mother held out her hand in front of
Mona. She then sadly reached into her pocket
and handed over her crisp new one-hundred-
dollar bill, which would now be going toward
buying the clams that she had promised her cus-

tomers. And it was still not going to be enough. Clams can be pretty expensive, so Mona was forced to work in the family seafood shop every day after school for a month, until the day we boarded the bus for Canada.

Mona learned a valuable lesson that day, and from that day forward, she never, ever promised anyone something free again unless she knew she could make good on it. I think that lesson helped mold her into the good businesswoman she is today.

On a side note, Mona eventually did buy herself that Game Boy with money that she saved working at the family business and she still has it. Sometimes after a long day at work, she gets it out to play a game of Tetris or two to unwind.

This week I have a yummy cocktail recipe for you that goes great with a big bowl of salty chips and dip.

SALTY DOG COCKTAIL

INGREDIENTS:
1½ ounces vodka
3½ ounces grapefruit juice
Salt for rimming glass

Add your vodka and grapefruit juice to a cocktail shaker and shake to mix.

Pour over ice cubes in a cocktail glass and enjoy.

CLAM DIP

INGREDIENTS:

1½ cups (more if you like a lot of clams) chopped
    cooked clams (a can of minced clams works just
    as well—save some of the juice from the can to
    thin the dip if needed)
1 8-ounce package cream cheese, softened
¼ cup sour cream
2 teaspoons Worcestershire sauce
1 teaspoon minced garlic
1 tablespoon fresh lemon juice

In a stand mixer combine all of your ingredients together until well blended.

Serve with chips, veggies, or crackers and enjoy!

Chapter 28

A tall drinking glass slipped through Mona's fingers
and smashed to bits on the floor, sending small
shards of glass flying as Mona stood frozen next to her
dishwasher that she had been unloading when Hayley
had shown up at her back door to break the news of her
recent discovery.

Mona spoke, her voice crisp. "*Who* did you say Digger
was with?"

"Ruth Leighton."

"Well, it's a small town, Hayley, people are bound to
run into each other." Mona then set about grabbing a
broom and dustpan from the kitchen pantry and sweeping
up the mess she had just made.

Hayley could feel her heartbeat in her throat. This was
the last person she wanted to tell what she had just personally witnessed. "It was definitely not an accidental
meeting, Mona. They were at a romantic spot near
Thunderhole. There was a picnic basket and a bottle of
wine. They were . . . I would say . . . canoodling?"

"*What*?" Mona spat out as if ready to kill the messenger.

"They were kissing, Mona! They were kissing and cuddling and pawing each other all over!"

Mona's nostrils flared. "I don't believe it!"

"Why on earth would I make something like this up? I saw it with my own eyes, I wish I hadn't, but I did!"

Mona took a moment to let the news settle in. Then she slammed the dishwasher door shut, abandoning her plan to put away the freshly cleaned plates and silverware.

"What the hell is going on with my sons? Their hormones are out of control! First Dougie, then Dennis Jr., and now Digger! What's next? Is Chet going to profess his undying love for his math teacher? This is ridiculous!"

"I think you're safe with Chet. He's basically obsessed with Dua Lipa right now."

Mona furrowed her brow. "Is she a local?"

"No, she's a pop star."

"At least Liddy had the good sense to say no to Dennis Jr. But what is it with these Leighton women? Are they some coven of witches casting their spells on my poor, hapless sons? Because the boys seem to be defenseless against their charms. Personally, I don't see it. Whatever their trick is, it must be like some kind of a dog whistle, on a frequency normal people can't hear, just young men in heat who come running!" Mona bounded over to the kitchen table and scooped up her phone. "This is crazy! I'm texting Digger. He needs to come home right now and explain himself."

"Mona, I think we should try to approach this situation calmly and rationally."

"Calmly and rationally are two words that are *not* a part of my vocabulary, Hayley!"

Hayley was certainly not going to argue that point.

Digger must have picked up on the seriousness of his mother's text because not five minutes later he was pulling his truck into the driveway. When he entered the kitchen through the back door, he immediately picked up on the tension.

"What's wrong?" Digger asked tentatively.

"Where have you been all day, Digger?" Mona barked.

"I, um, I went on a run around Aunt Betty's Pond, and then I swung by the pier to gas up the boat."

"Liar!" Mona wailed.

"Digger, I saw you and Ruth Leighton   "

"What do you mean saw us? Way out in the park? What were you doing there? Were you following me?"

"That doesn't matter! What matters is you're sneaking around with a Leighton! At least Dougie was upfront about it!" Mona snapped, pointing an accusing finger at him.

Digger sighed. "Okay, fine. Yes, Mom. It's the truth. I'm seeing Ruth Leighton."

Mona cranked her head toward Hayley. "Tell me, is there a knife sticking out of my chest because I feel like I've just been stabbed through the heart."

"Mona, I think you might be overreacting."

"Hayley's right, Mom. This is exactly why I never said anything. I'm in love with Ruth."

Mona moaned and sank down in a kitchen chair.

Digger bravely soldiered on. "When I saw how you blew a gasket when you found out about Dougie and Olive, there was no way I was going to subject myself to that kind of pain and harassment. Plus, I was worried you might have a stroke. I didn't want to upset you more than you already were."

"So that's why you lied about where you were on the day we found Lonnie Leighton's body in the clam flats?" Hayley pressed. "You were with Ruth?"

"Yes, well no."

"Which is it?" Mona spat out.

"We had been together that morning. Vera took Lonnie to a doctor's appointment and we knew they'd be gone for a while so we took the opportunity to—"

Mona threw her hands up. "All right I don't need to hear all the gory details!"

"I was still there when they got home around noon. I had to crawl out a window so Lonnie wouldn't see me."

"But Cappy said you were gone all day. Where were you that afternoon?" Hayley asked.

Digger's face turned a beet red. "I drove up to Bangor to do a little clothes shopping."

"Shopping for what? I've never known you to go shopping! You own something like two shirts!" Mona exclaimed.

"I wasn't shopping for me. Ruth had seen this negligee in a JCPenney catalogue and I called the store and they had it in stock so I thought I'd drive up there and pick it up for her. I didn't tell you I was going up to the Bangor Mall because I knew you'd give me the third degree and I didn't want to risk slipping up and you finding out about Ruth."

"Okay, Digger, I've heard enough!" Mona groaned. "Is there anything else you're hiding?"

"No, Mom, that's it. That's all she wrote."

Hayley could not help but notice Digger's eyes shooting back and forth between his mother and Hayley like he was watching a tennis match, his body stiff with tension, and she strongly suspected that there was indeed more to this story than he was telling. And she was now fiercely determined to find out exactly what it was that he did not want either of them to know about.

Chapter 29

"Iggy Fennow's been assaulted!" Bruce cried as he bolted from the house just as Hayley pulled her car into the driveway and stepped out.

"What? Where?" Hayley gasped.

"At his office. I just heard about it on the police scanner! I'm heading over there now!"

"Get in, I'll drive you," Hayley insisted, not wanting Bruce to get behind the wheel in his frazzled mental state.

Iggy Fennow was a close friend. He and Bruce had played on the basketball team in high school and remained buddies ever since, occasionally grabbing a beer after work or meeting up for some ice fishing on Eagle Lake during the winter months. It was Bruce's job as the *Island Times* crime reporter to cover an event like this as dispassionately as he could, but journalistic ethics were out the window in this case because of who the victim was.

Bruce nervously tapped his foot on the floorboard as Hayley raced up Ledgelawn Avenue, swinging right onto Mount Desert Street, and then taking a sharp left onto

Main Street where Iggy's offices were located. She nearly plowed into the sign, IGGY FENNOW, ATTORNEY AT LAW, as she pulled into the driveway behind Sergio's police cruiser. Bruce was already flying out the passenger side door before she even had time to put the car into the park position. Then she jumped out and hurried inside the small office where Chief Sergio was already bent over Iggy, inspecting a welt on the side of his face. Sergio stood back up and grimaced at the sight of Hayley and Bruce charging onto his crime scene, but decided to keep silent, knowing Bruce's presence would probably make Iggy more comfortable.

"What the hell happened, Iggy?" Bruce asked.

"That is what I am trying to get to the bottom of myself," Sergio snarled, widening his stance. "But Iggy won't tell me."

"Who called you?" Bruce asked.

"His secretary, Wanda, but she's also not talking," Sergio sighed.

"I told her not to drag the police into this, everything's fine, it was just a small misunderstanding with a client. It's over now."

Wanda sat frozen at her desk just outside the office, nervously wringing her hands. "I'm sorry, Iggy, I just panicked. It was the first thing I thought to do."

Wanda was an elderly woman in her seventies, who should have been enjoying retirement, but her gambling-addict husband died leaving her with a mountain of debt to pay off so she continued working as a secretary, first for Iggy's father, Roy, then Iggy when he took over the law practice. She was a longtime fixture at the Fennow family's firm.

Hayley scanned the office and spotted a stapler lying on the floor. "Did someone throw that stapler at you?"

Iggy's eyes darted to the stapler, then he exchanged a quick glance with Wanda as if to warn her not to say anything.

"I am going to take that as a yes," Sergio said. "Come on, Iggy, fess up. Who was it?"

Iggy shrugged. "I need to respect attorney-client privilege."

"Not when the client hurls a stapler at your face!" Bruce exclaimed.

"I honestly don't think she meant to actually hit him!" Wanda piped in.

Sergio spun around to the shaky secretary. "So it was a woman?"

Iggy's shoulders sank and he rubbed his eyes with his fingers. "Oh, Wanda . . ."

Wanda threw a hand to her mouth and shook her head as if she wanted to kick herself for blabbing too much.

Hayley's eyes wandered to a file on the edge of Iggy's desk. The name Lonnie Leighton was typed on the tab of the brown folder. She then raised her eyes to meet Iggy's. "It was Vera Leighton, wasn't it?"

Iggy bit his lip, determined not to say another word.

But his loyal secretary could not help herself. "My goodness, Hayley, how in the dickens did you know that?"

Iggy dropped his head in frustration.

Hayley tapped the folder. "She was here discussing her father's will, I presume?"

Iggy snatched up the folder and stuffed it in a desk drawer next to him. "I am not at liberty to say."

"Then maybe I will just head over to the Leighton

house and drag Vera down to the station for questioning," Sergio warned.

"Please, Sergio, I'm begging you, do not do that. She just lost her temper, that's all. I'm not hurt so don't expect me to press charges. She is a valued client who just got a little upset when I had to break some bad news."

"A little upset? Have you seen your face?" Bruce cried.

"It's not that bad," Iggy scoffed.

"Listen, if you just explain what happened here, I will back off and forget the whole thing. But you need to tell me."

Wanda pursed her lips. She was not about to make the boss angrier by spilling any more beans.

Iggy touched the side of his face with the big welt and flinched. Despite his protestations, the wound looked very painful. He then nodded, resigned to the fact he had to come clean to the Chief of Police.

"I asked to meet with Vera about an hour ago. As executor of her father's will, I had to inform her that I was in possession of two different wills."

Hayley heard herself blurt out, "Uh-oh."

Sergio shot her an annoyed look before turning back to Iggy. "I assume one of the wills was the cause of her sudden outburst?"

Iggy nodded. "Lonnie signed and filed both of them himself. The first one four years ago and the other one just three weeks before he died. It's the law that I abide by the most recent one filed, and in that one, he left half the business to his girlfriend Abby Weston."

Hayley gasped. "Uh-oh." She raised a hand before Sergio could toss her another admonishing look. "Sorry."

Sergio grimaced. "Well, I can certainly understand why Vera would fly off the knob like that, but—"

"Handle," Bruce interrupted.

Sergio stared at him curiously.

"Fly off the handle."

"Knob, handle, they mean the same thing," Sergio growled.

"Not really," Bruce said, shaking his head.

"You're worse than your wife," Sergio sighed before returning his attention to Iggy and continuing. "But that is no excuse for her to commit an act of violence."

"Those girls have been through the wringer, losing their father, now half the business, I don't want them to endure further stress by you putting Vera behind bars," Iggy pleaded.

"I understand you do not want me to arrest and charge her, but I most certainly am going to give her a stern talking to."

"I'm sure Vera regrets popping off like that," Iggy said. "And given time, I expect her to call me and apologize."

Hayley snickered to herself, highly doubting Vera Leighton would ever say she was sorry to anyone.

"You're a good man," Bruce said, gently patting his buddy on the back. "If it were me, I would have Sergio throw the book at that short-fused harpy."

Hayley watched sympathetically as Iggy winced while touching his face again. She felt bad for him, trying to keep the peace and serve his emotional mess of a client. But she was more worried about Abby Weston and the whole world of hurt that was going to soon come crashing down on her if she tried to claim what now rightfully belonged to her—fifty percent of Leighton Seafood.

Chapter 30

Craving her brother Randy's tasty fried clams from his bar menu at Drinks Like A Fish, Hayley swung in on her way back to the restaurant to treat herself before the long night ahead. When she breezed into the bar, she spotted Randy's manager Michelle chatting up Cappy, who sat scrunched over at the far end of the bar slamming down his usual. Waving at Michelle and about to slide up onto a stool, Hayley stopped suddenly as her eyes flicked to a pair of women sitting at a table near the front window, engrossed in a deep conversation. What startled her was the fact that it was Liddy and Tabitha Collins.

How did they even know each other?

Hayley was just about to turn her back to them and pretend not to see them when Tabitha caught sight of her and broke out into a wide smile, raising her arm. "Hayley, hello!"

Hayley slapped on her best "What an unexpected surprise" face and sauntered over to them. They were each finishing up their own orders of fried clams along with two glasses of white wine.

Liddy's face reddened slightly and she conspicuously cleared her throat before asking in a weak voice, "What are you doing here? Shouldn't you be at your restaurant preparing for the dinner rush?"

"On my way there I had a taste for fried clams. Looks like we're all on the same wavelength."

"Yes, I guess so," Liddy said guiltily.

"I didn't know you two knew each other," Hayley said, eyeing Liddy suspiciously.

"Oh, we just met. I invited Liddy to have a late lunch with me," Tabitha explained in a perpetual cheery voice that now grated on Hayley's nerves. "You never told me you had such fun friends. This one's a hoot!" Tabitha laughed.

A pang of jealousy shot through Hayley. "Oh, Liddy certainly is one of a kind. Well, I don't want to interrupt. I'm going to go sit over at the bar."

"You're not interrupting. We were just about to pay the bill. I have a staff meeting with my Boston crew in ten minutes. I should head back to my rental and get on my computer. It's one of those awful Zoom calls with everybody looking up and down at each other in those small boxes like *The Brady Bunch* credits. It's so annoying." Tabitha popped one more fried clam in her mouth as Liddy shifted uncomfortably in her seat. She then reached for her purse in the empty chair next to her. "Here, Liddy, let me just take care of this."

"Nonsense!" Liddy cried, almost too loudly. "This is my treat!"

"Are you sure?" Tabitha asked, not used to the idea of someone else picking up the check.

"Absolutely!" Liddy declared, snatching the check out

of her hand and slapping her own credit card down on top of it.

"That's very sweet of you, thank you, and will you think about what we discussed?" Tabitha asked.

"Of course. I will call you tomorrow," Liddy answered, nodding, nervously glancing at Hayley.

Hayley's eyes darted back and forth, her heart rate spiking. What were these two cooking up that she was purposefully being kept in the dark about?

"Bye, Liddy! Nice seeing you again, Hayley," Tabitha cooed, dashing out the door to her car.

There was a long silence except for an Elton John and Dua Lipa remix of "Cold Heart" playing on the jukebox.

Finally, Hayley stepped closer to Liddy, who was now avoiding eye contact. "Are you going to just sit there staring at the floor pretending I'm not here or are you going to tell me what's going on?"

Liddy exhaled a heavy sigh. "I swear when she called my office I had no idea who she was. Her name seemed vaguely familiar but I couldn't place it. It was only after we met here at Drinks Like A Fish and she started talking about herself when it dawned on me who she actually was. Mona had told me Bruce's ex was in town and her name was Tabitha and that she was some big cheese at a national seafood company based out of Boston. I barely had time to process it all when you came waltzing in here and saw the two of us together."

"Why did she call you?"

Liddy tensed up, her jaw clenched.

"What? Is she a potential client? Is she interested in buying some property?"

Liddy gave her a curt nod.

"Where?"

"Here. In town."

"She wants to buy a house in Bar Harbor?"

"A really nice one. At least five bedrooms. Preferably with waterfront views. Money does not seem to be much of a concern."

A hot panic seared through Hayley's veins. "Would this be a summer residence?"

Liddy shook her head. "No. Year-round."

"What?" Hayley gasped.

"She told me she is thinking about moving here permanently and work remotely, and only fly back to Boston for in-person meetings when absolutely necessary. But her main desire is to set down some roots in Maine."

"I see," Hayley whispered, her voice scraping the lowest registers, her focus scattered and undefined as her thoughts wandered elsewhere.

"Hayley, sit down," Liddy said sharply.

Hayley ignored her, staring out the window of the bar and watching Tabitha pull away in her fancy Tesla.

Liddy reached out, grabbed Hayley's shirtsleeve and forcibly pulled her down in the chair next to her. "I know what you're worried about and you have no reason to be. This is not part of some master plan of hers to steal Bruce away from you!"

Hayley gave her a deadpan look. "That's not what I was thinking at all, but now that you've said it, it's all I'm going to be able to think about going forward."

"Has she said or done anything that would make you suspect she wants Bruce back?"

"She told us at breakfast the other day she had a dream about her and Bruce together," Hayley said.

"Together as in standing in line to check out at Walmart or something more erotic?"

"I couldn't tell, they were in an elevator holding each other . . ."

Liddy's eyes widened with a sense of dread. "Oh, dear . . ."

"And then The Rock showed up."

"What rock?"

"The movie star The Rock.

"Rock Hudson?"

"No, The Rock. Dwayne Johnson."

"Oh, Hayley, then you have nothing to worry about. If I had a dream about both Dwayne Johnson and Bruce, I would not be paying one iota of attention to Bruce."

"I don't know, I just had this feeling she was sending me some kind of signal."

Liddy squeezed Hayley's hand. "Okay, maybe there is a slight chance she has an ulterior motive for house hunting around here, but Bruce loves you, he's not going to leave you, for anyone, trust me on that."

Hayley hesitated, not as confident. She picked up a stray fried clam off Tabitha's plate and popped it in her mouth. Then she squeezed Liddy's hand back. "You're right. I could be blowing this way out of proportion. Thank you for being such a supportive friend, Liddy."

"Always. That's what I have been put on this earth for. To be the best supportive friend to you that I can be." She paused. "That, and to be the most successful real estate agent in the state of Maine."

Hayley offered her a withering smile. "You want that commission when you find her a place, don't you?"

"Yes!" Liddy cried. "So, so bad. But . . . You come

first, Hayley. If it's going to bother you, I will just refer her to someone else in my office."

Hayley had to chuckle to herself.

Liddy was saying all the right things.

But she desperately wanted the bragging rights of having the super-rich Tabitha Collins as a client.

"You won't be betraying our friendship by working for Tabitha, Liddy, I completely understand this is a big opportunity for you."

"Oh, thank God!" Liddy sighed, hugging Hayley.

As she pulled away and reached for another clam, this time from Liddy's plate, Hayley tried not to think about how deep down, it really did bug her. First her husband. Then her best friend. What else in Hayley's life did Tabitha Collins have her eye on?

Chapter 31

Mona's voice sounded grave on the phone when she called Hayley at the restaurant and asked her to come over to the house just as soon as she could get away. The restaurant was steadily busy but not overbooked and her right hand, hostess Betty, seemed to have everything under control, so Hayley told her staff she was going to just slip out for a bit but be back soon. Stopping by tables to make sure everyone was enjoying their meals on her way out, Hayley then jumped in her car and sped over to Mona's house. When she pulled up, Mona was standing on the porch underneath a light, her grim face illuminated.

Hayley had barely opened the door to get out of her car when she heard Mona moan, "I think Dougie's been lying to us."

"Why?" Hayley asked.

Mona thrust out her fist. "I was doing some laundry and I thought I would wash Dougie's sheets and when I yanked them off the bed *this* clattered to the floor."

Hayley held out her hand and Mona opened her fist,

dropping a gold ring into her palm. She studied it for a moment. "Dougie's class ring. The one he showed to Sergio."

"That's the one all right. I went to put it on top of his dresser when I noticed something odd. Take a closer look."

Hayley raised her hand up to inspect the ring.

"It's definitely from the Class of 2019," she said, noting the inside inscription.

"Look at the size of it."

She turned it over in her hand and it suddenly became so obvious.

Goose bumps spread up both sides of her arms.

The ring was small.

Very small.

A better fit for a delicate-boned feminine finger. Not a tall, strapping, bulky, barrel-chested boy like Dougie, who had a hand the size of a catcher's mitt.

"Where's Dougie now?"

"In the kitchen making a sandwich. He got home right after I called you. I decided to wait until you showed up before I said anything."

"Let's go talk to him," Hayley said solemnly following Mona inside the house and down the hall to the large open kitchen she had just had remodeled. Dougie was sitting at the table chewing a big bite of a giant roast beef sandwich off a plate with some ruffled potato chips on it. He glanced up with sleepy eyes at Hayley and Mona.

"Oh, hey, Aunt Hayley, shouldn't you be at your restaurant?"

"I asked her to come over here when I came across something disturbing in your room."

"What were you doing snooping in my room?"

"I wasn't snooping. I decided to clean your sheets before they got so stiff you can't even fold them. Your room looks like a bomb hit it, by the way. No wonder your sisters called you Pig Pen when you were a kid."

"Mona, let's stay on point," Hayley quietly suggested.

Dougie put his half-eaten sandwich down and leaned back in his chair, arms out. "So, what did you find? I know there're no dirty magazines hidden under the bed because I gave them all to Dad when he moved out. Besides, everything's digital now."

Mona slammed the ring down on the table next to his plate. "Mind explaining this?"

Dougie studied the ring and shrugged. "We've already been over this, Ma. It's my class ring. You were here when I showed it to Chief Sergio."

"Why don't you put it on?" Mona requested, folding her arms.

Dougie stared at his mother, his face suddenly a worrisome shade of red. "What?"

"You heard me. Put the ring on your finger. Let's see how it looks."

He slowly reached for the ring and picked it up before hesitating slightly.

"Forget which one's the ring finger?" Mona snapped.

"No," Dougie grumbled.

He tried slipping on the ring.

It got just past his fingernail before it stopped. Dougie pushed harder and harder, but like Cinderella's stepsisters trying to shove on that tiny glass slipper, or OJ attempting to force the black leather glove over his giant running back hands, the ring just would not budge.

"That ring is obviously way too small to be yours, Dougie," Hayley said. "Who does it really belong to, Olive?"

The blood drained from his face.

"She was in the same year as you, Class of 2019. It looks like it would slide perfectly on her finger, no problem," Hayley said.

"Is it Olive's, Dougie? Spit it out, now!" Mona yelled.

He nodded slightly.

"Sweet Jesus!" Mona cried. "You told Sergio that ring belonged to you! You lied to the police! Dougie, something like that will get you thrown in jail!"

"I had to, he thought I had killed Olive's dad! When I heard they had found that ring in his clam bucket, I knew it wouldn't be long before they came here asking to see mine. But I couldn't find it. I searched everywhere, but it was nowhere to be found. I started to panic! I thought thar if I couldn't produce the ring, it would be enough for Sergio to arrest me. So, Olive came up with the idea of giving me hers to show him, to prove the one Hayley found near Lonnie's body didn't belong to me!"

"Dougie, was that your ring in the bucket?"

"I don't know! Maybe! Maybe not! But I was nowhere near the flats that day! If it's mine, I didn't put it there! I swear! I didn't kill Lonnie! I didn't! You have to believe me!" Dougie screamed, spittle flying out of the sides of his mouth. Then he leapt to his feet, pushing the chair back, and raced out of the kitchen, up the stairs, and into his room, slamming the door shut behind him.

Hayley turned to Mona. "What do you think?"

Her face ashen, her voice tripping over the lump in her throat, Mona managed to choke out, "He's my son. I want to believe him, I really do, but he's changed so much since he started seeing that Olive Leighton, it's almost as if I just don't know him anymore."

Hayley put a comforting arm around her friend's shoulders.

This cover-up did not paint a convincing picture of Dougie's innocence.

It also raised the question, if he lied about the ring, what else could Dougie Barnes be lying about?

Chapter 32

After leaving Mona's house, Hayley immediately called Chief Sergio at the station to update him on the situation. Officer Earl, working the front desk, answered the call.

"Bar Harbor Police Department."

"Hi, Earl, it's Hayley Powell. I need to speak to the Chief."

"He's not here."

"When do you expect him back?"

"I don't. He left for the day."

"Already? Is he okay?"

"He's fine. He just checked out early because of the cocktail party."

"What cocktail party?"

"The one he and his husband are having right now at their house?"

"That's impossible," Hayley declared.

"Why?"

"Because if Randy and Sergio were hosting a cocktail party at their home, I would have been the first person invited!"

There was a long pause on the other end of the phone.

Then Earl managed to squeak out, "I don't know what to tell you, Hayley."

Hayley's head was spinning.

A cocktail party?

She was the Queen of Cocktail Parties.

Everyone always told her she was the life of the party.

How could she ever have been left off the guest list?

Especially her own brother's?

What could she have possibly done to be iced out like this?

Part of her knew she should just call Sergio and leave him a message detailing the new information she had just uncovered. But the nosy part of her personality just could not resist knowing exactly what was going on. She made a sharp U-turn and headed straight for Sergio and Randy's seaside home off the Shore Path with its breathtaking views of the Atlantic.

She considered the possibility that Earl had just gotten his wires crossed. There was really no cocktail party, maybe they were just going to someone else's house for drinks.

Yes, that had to be it.

But as she turned down the side street that led down to Sergio and Randy's sprawling saltbox colonial house, Hayley thrust her chin forward, agape, at the sight of six cars parked in front of the house. She could see people drinking and mingling on the front porch as Randy giddily carried around a plate of appetizers.

She could not believe it.

Earl had been right.

Randy and Sergio were throwing a party.

Without her.

She slammed on the brakes after nearly rear-ending a parked Jeep because she had not been watching where she was going. She leapt out of the car and marched toward the house. As she stomped up the porch steps, she realized she did not know any of the people present. Randy finally spotted her, his blank expression betraying nothing. He walked over to her and held out the plate in his hand. "Stuffed mushroom?"

She shoved the plate away. "No, I don't want a mushroom. Are we fighting and I just don't know about it yet?"

"What? No. Why would you think we were fighting?"

Hayley looked around. "Oh, I don't know, Randy, maybe one clue that comes to mind is the fact you're hosting a party and you didn't invite me?"

"That's not—"

She interrupted him. "I'm hurt. I thought we were close. How many other parties have you thrown that I knew nothing about?"

"This was very last minute. Our friends Ivan and Stephen from Bristol, England, were on a gay cruise and pulled into port this morning. It was a total surprise. They didn't even tell me they were coming. They just walked in the bar before I even opened for the day. They don't have to be back on the boat until ten tonight so I decided to throw a last-minute thing for some of the new friends they've made on board."

Hayley glanced around at the festive crowd.

She finally noticed they were all men.

"Oh, I see," Hayley said. "But they look so fun. You know how much I love parties! You could have invited me."

Randy sighed. "I did."

"When?"

"This afternoon. Right when I decided to throw a party. I left you a voice mail."

"No you didn't."

Hayley checked her phone.

Sure enough, there was a message from Randy at 2:37 p.m. that she had completely missed as she was running around town.

"Oh, look. You did."

Randy gave her a self-satisfied smile.

Embarrassed, Hayley reached out and plucked a stuffed mushroom off the plate. "You know what, on second thought, I would love to try one of these." She then turned to the crowd and announced, "Sorry I'm late, everyone!"

After going around introducing herself to all the guests, Hayley made a beeline for Sergio, bringing him up to speed. He was not initially too keen on discussing a closed case at a cocktail party, but once Hayley told him about Olive giving Dougie her ring in case the cops showed up wanting to see it, he dialed into the conversation pretty quickly.

"He *lied*?"

Hayley nodded solemnly. "They both did."

Sergio stared off into space, a troubled look on his face. "Maybe I got this one wrong. Maybe this was a murder. I mean, why else would Dougie and Olive feel the need to lie? Unless they felt guilty about something and wanted to cover it up."

"What do you think could have happened?"

Sergio shrugged. "I don't know. I mean it's possible Dougie was convinced Lonnie would never allow him to be with Olive and so in order to clear the way for them to be together, Dougie just . . ." He stopped and swallowed, having a hard time believing what he was saying. "Maybe he found Lonnie clamming in the flats, they got into an argument, a scuffle ensued, and Dougie just pushed him down and smothered him in the mud. His ring could have somehow fallen off during the struggle and landed in the clam bucket."

A couple of revelers nearby were eavesdropping, wildly interested in the macabre and ghastly details of their confab.

"I am certainly concerned about why Dougie lied, Sergio, but it's hard for me to picture Dougie Barnes doing something so violent and reprehensible. I've known that boy since he was born and there's not a mean bone in his entire body."

"Then how did his class ring wind up in Lonnie Leighton's clam bucket?"

A thought dawned on Hayley. "Someone could be framing him!"

Randy passed by with shrimp cocktail and Hayley snatched one up and dipped a shrimp in the cocktail sauce in one brisk move before shoving it into her mouth.

"Oh, God, this is good," she moaned as she chewed.

Sergio shook his head. "But why would anyone have to go to the trouble to do that? Sabrina ruled Lonnie's death as inconclusive. I closed the case. There is no murder investigation."

He was right.

A frame-up made no sense.

But Olive had helped Dougie lie to the police and they needed to know why.

It was time to go straight to the source.

Chapter 33

Vera Leighton opened the front door to the family home, a large three-story farmhouse set back in the woods from the Old Crooked Road just outside of town. She was holding a broom and she tried not to look too disturbed by the unexpected presence of Hayley and Bar Harbor's police chief standing on her front porch. Still, Hayley could see Vera's face slowly turning ashen.

"What is it? What's going on? Hayley, did you find out who killed Daddy?"

"No, Vera, I'm sorry, not yet. We're here to see Olive, if she's here."

"Yes, she's here. Why? What's this all about?"

Sergio was losing patience. "I would just like to talk to her."

Vera looked as if she wanted to argue some more, but the stern, all-business expression on Sergio's face discouraged her from the effort. She cranked her head around and called back into the house. "Olive, there are some people here to see you!" She then swung back around and said with a sniffle, "We're just here cleaning out a few of Daddy's things to donate to Goodwill. I think that's what he would have wanted."

Hayley nodded sympathetically but knew Lonnie Leighton had never donated anything to charity in his long, miserable, miserly life.

"Come in," Vera said, motioning them to enter. Olive tentatively trundled down the stairs carrying a cardboard box of her father's clothes. She stopped halfway at the sight of Sergio in his police uniform, her bottom lip trembling slightly.

"Hello, Olive," Hayley said warmly, trying to calm her down. "Thank you for seeing us. This will only take a minute."

Ruth came in from the kitchen, wiping her hands on a dish towel, a look of concern on her face. "What's happening? Is this about Daddy?"

"They need to talk to Olive," Vera said warily.

Olive had been living at home with her father since graduating high school, which had made it even more of a challenge to keep her forbidden relationship with Dougie a secret. Ruth had a place in town and Vera bunked in the small studio apartment they had renovated above the garage adjacent to the main house. But when Lonnie became ill, Ruth and Vera moved back into the family home to help look after him, according to local gossips.

Usually this would be the point where they would be offered something to drink, maybe a cup of coffee, but the Leighton sisters were not in the mood to play hostess. They were determined to get straight to the point.

"Okay, she's here. Fire away," Vera said impatiently.

"It's about your class ring," Sergio said flatly.

Olive noticeably flinched.

"What about it?" Vera snapped.

Ruth put a hand on her older sister's arm. "Vera, please, let Olive answer his questions."

"Do you have it? Is it here?" Sergio said, folding his arms.

Olive shook her head tentatively.

Sergio leaned his body slightly forward. "Would you mind telling me where it is?"

Tears welled up in Olive's eyes.

She pursed her lips.

"Well, where is it, Olive? Tell him!" Vera snapped.

The tears were now streaming down her face and her whole body was shaking.

Ruth rushed to her younger sister and enveloped her in a hug. "It's okay, Olive, it's best if you just tell him the truth."

"I can't!" Olive wailed.

Sergio exhaled a sigh. "Did you give it to Dougie?"

Olive buried her face in her sister Ruth's shoulder.

Vera's eyes widened. "*Did* you?"

"Yes!" Olive cried, clutching Ruth.

Sergio turned to Vera. "We found a Mount Desert Island High School ring in your father's clam bucket. When we went to ask Dougie about it, he produced a ring to prove it wasn't his," he calmly explained. "Except it turns out, the ring he showed us was too small for Dougie's finger, but I presume it's a perfect fit for Olive."

Ruth gently took Olive by the shoulders and held her at arm's length. "Honey, why would you do that?"

"Because I was scared! Dougie overheard his mother talking about the class ring they had found at the scene and when he went to find his in his room, it was gone. He searched and searched but had no luck. We started to panic, we knew it would look bad if he couldn't find it, so I gave him mine in case the police came looking for it."

"Well, I guess that's it then," Vera said, her eyes dancing, overjoyed. "We know the killer. It's Dougie Barnes. Don't you think it's high time you arrested that murderous cretin, Chief?"

Sergio raised a hand. "Hold your cows, Vera."

"What do you think this is, the Yellowstone Ranch? We don't have cows here!" Vera snapped.

"Hold your ponies, then!" Sergio sighed.

"Horses. It's hold your horses," Hayley interjected.

Vera turned to Hayley. "Is he for real?"

Hayley held up a hand. "He means let's just all take a beat."

"It wasn't Dougie!" Olive wailed. "We were together that whole day! He couldn't have done it!"

Vera rolled her eyes contemptuously. "Olive, please, don't you think it's time you stopped covering up for that sorry excuse for a man. He *killed* our father for heaven's sake. If you don't stop lying, the chief could arrest you as an accessory. Isn't that right, Chief?"

Olive gasped. "Accessory? What is that?"

"Helping someone who has committed a crime, lying for them, assisting in the cover-up, all of which you are one hundred percent guilty of, I'm afraid to say, Olive," Vera barked.

Olive was sobbing now, her hands planted firmly over her face.

Ruth just gave Vera a withering look.

"Now let's not get ahead of ourselves," Sergio said. "I'm not here to arrest anyone. We're just trying to get to the facts."

Vera's eyes blazed. "The fact is, Olive is a traitor to this family for dating a Barnes boy in the first place!"

Hayley scoffed.

What a rich irony.

Vera accusing Olive of being a traitor.

Blissfully unaware that her mousy, inconspicuous sister Ruth was also romantically entangled with another Barnes boy.

If she only knew.

"Am I the only one confused as to why you are still here talking to us when you should be out there trying to track down Dougie Barnes?" Vera shouted.

"We need more evidence than a class ring in your father's clam bucket," Sergio sighed, tired and annoyed at having to deal with the exhausting Vera. "And if Olive is telling us the truth, then we need to find out who else your father saw that day."

"We know he had a doctor's appointment in the morning," Hayley offered.

"Yes, I drove him there myself," Vera said.

"And after that?" Sergio asked.

Vera shrugged. "I went to make some deliveries and Ruth went to her knitting circle at Rosana Moretti's house, isn't that right, Ruth?"

"Um, yes, that's right," Ruth mumbled.

"So, Lonnie stayed here at home until he went clamming sometime in the afternoon?" Hayley asked.

"Yes," Vera said emphatically.

"No," Ruth whispered.

Sergio raised an eyebrow. "No?"

"No," Ruth said louder. Something in her memory bank seemed to stir. "No, he didn't. I completely forgot. When he got home from the doctor's, before I left, I re-

member Daddy saying he had to go in town to see someone."

"Do you remember who?" Sergio pressed.

Ruth nodded. "Yes, because I found it so odd. He was
going to meet with Dennis Barnes of all people."

Hayley's heart nearly stopped. "Dennis Jr.?"

Ruth shook her head. "No, senior."

Mona's ex-husband.

Island Food & Spirits
BY
HAYLEY POWELL

Have you ever noticed that the older you get, the busier you seem to be?

I know, right? Me too.

I always thought that after my two kids left the roost things would slow down considerably, but no, instead my schedule has been more packed than ever, especially writing this column for the *Island Times* and running an open-year-round restaurant.

Two things that I love doing, by the way.

After one particularly exhausting week, however, I came home and collapsed on the living room couch. About ten minutes later, Bruce followed suit, dragging himself through the front door and dropping into his Barcalounger across from me. We looked at each other and marveled at how we had not seen each other or spent even a couple of hours together in the last month or so and it was only the end of May. The busy summer season in Bar Harbor was not even in full swing yet!

So, I decided that my husband and I desperately needed one whole day together, just the two of us, no groups of friends, no interruptions, no phones, nothing! Except the two of us enjoying some long-needed, uninterrupted quality time as a couple.

Bruce was totally onboard with this plan, and so we checked our schedules and planned to take the upcoming Monday off to be together and reconnect.

Bruce suggested we drag his old canoe and paddle out from behind the garage where it had been stored since the day he moved in with me after we got married a few years ago. Bruce loaded the canoe, the long paddle, and some lifejackets into the flatbed of his truck while I prepared a lovely old-fashioned picnic lunch in the kitchen. Then we set out to Long Pond for a day of canoeing, swimming, and a romantic picnic, both of us excited for a blissful day of peace, quiet, and togetherness.

Just what the doctor ordered.

In hindsight, we should have gotten a second opinion.

After arriving at Long Pond, we were delighted to see there was only one other car besides ours in the parking area and not a soul in sight. Within just a few weeks, the kayak rental place that was across the street would have cars lined up and down the side of the road.

We unloaded the canoe and got it in the water where we then added our cooler filled with our lunch and drinks. Once we climbed in and got ourselves situated, Bruce slowly paddled us out on the quiet, serene lake, barely making a ripple in the water as we glided along.

I couldn't stop marveling at what a beautiful day it was and how nice it was to have this picturesque setting to ourselves. An hour passed as we floated across the lake and the only people we saw were a couple of kayakers who waved at us from a distance as they sailed past us. We were so caught up in our pristine surroundings, before we even knew it, we had paddled roughly three miles, almost to the very end of the four-mile pond.

Bruce thought we should stop at this point for our picnic lunch, and more importantly, our bottle of wine, before heading back. My stomach was already grumbling, so needless to say, I did not argue. We spotted a small opening that had a few large flat rocks that would give us some footing to go a short distance into the woods. We pulled up and Bruce hopped out, and when his feet were firmly planted on the rock and I was sure he would not fall into the water, I handed him the cooler, which he set down beside him so he could hold out his hand to give me an assist out of the canoe.

Once on shore, I looped the rope that was tied to the canoe around a tree branch, and we carefully picked our way through the trees and brush in search of the perfect lunch spot.

It must have been our lucky day because we had not gone more than fifty feet or so from shore before the woods opened up to a small clearing with tall, magnificent trees surrounding a small patch with the sun shining brightly down upon it. It was incredibly romantic!

We eagerly spread out our blanket on the ground and unpacked the food and opened the bottle of wine, and yes, of course, I did not forget to bring two plastic wineglasses. Lunch was a loaf of French bread, cheeses, meats, my favorite clam dip that I had made the night before with our leftover steamed clams, and a chilled bottle of Pinot Grigio. In other words, heaven!

We realized that this was the most relaxed the two of us had been in months as we laughed, talked, cuddled, but mostly ate and drank! In fact, our bellies were so full of food and wine we both lay back on the blanket and promptly fell asleep.

I was not sure how long I had been asleep when all of a sudden I felt water dripping on my face, which woke me up with a start! *Oh no,* I thought to myself, *It's starting to rain!*

I looked up at the sky to see dark, ominous clouds rolling in that had not been there earlier. The thunderclap that followed finally woke Bruce up. There is a saying in Maine, "If you don't like the weather, wait a minute!"

Well, this storm looked as if it was going to hang around a lot longer than a minute. It was here to stay awhile.

Bruce glanced at his watch and gasped. "We've been napping for over two hours!"

We hurriedly gathered our belongings, stuffed the leftovers in the cooler, folded up the blanket, and raced through the thick underbrush

back to the canoe. As we reached the edge of
the water, Bruce suddenly stopped short, causing me to run right into the back of him.

Even with the winds whipping around us, I
heard him shout, "Oh no!" I honestly did not
want to know, but I peeked around him anyway
to see what the problem was.

Our canoe was gone.

I knew what had to be coming next.

He slowly turned around and looked at me.

Before he could say a word, I cried, "Yes,
Bruce, I remember tying up the canoe!"

But in my head, I was starting to panic because I knew I had just looped it around a tree
branch in a hurry because my mind was on that
clam dip I had such a craving for! However,
there was no way I was going to admit that in
this moment.

Just then, I swore I heard someone call my
name.

"Hayley!"

But the wind was blowing harder and the
rain was coming down now in buckets making
us both miserable so I chalked it up to wishful
thinking.

Bruce suddenly brightened. "I gave you my
phone to carry. Give it to me and I'll call for
help."

I just stared at him, not daring to tell him
that I had put it in the glove compartment of
his truck so no one could bother us on our romantic getaway. Of course, he had been mar-

ried to me long enough to guess my expression and figure it out for himself. He just rolled his eyes, annoyed, which only made me mad.

That's when the fireworks started.

Not real Fourth of July fireworks, but the kind of fireworks that explode when a couple starts fighting. We yelled and screamed and blamed each other to the point where we were arguing about things totally unrelated to our predicament! How he never remembers to put the toilet seat down and how it ticks him off when I use his razor to shave my legs!

Fed up, Bruce finally hollered, "I wish we had never come out on this godforsaken lake together!"

Well, then I just burst into tears, startling Bruce.

He felt so bad for making me cry he immediately said he was sorry, and that he loved me so much, and we would find a way out of this even if we had to spend the night and go trekking through the woods in the morning after it stopped raining and it was light out in search of a road.

This only reminded me how dire our situation was and it just made me cry harder. Poor Bruce, not knowing what to do, just took me in his arms and kissed me, trying to console me.

All of a sudden, we heard a loud booming voice through a loudspeaker shouting, "Are you two serious? The whole town is looking for you, and here you are canoodling on rocks in the middle of a rainstorm!"

We both jumped back and looked out at the water where Mona was standing at the bow of the police rescue boat with a megaphone in one hand and her other hand on her hip while Police Chief Sergio guided the boat toward us.

Luckily, our canoe had been spotted drifting by a pair of kayakers and then when they got back and saw our truck was the only vehicle parked on the side of the road, they put two-and-two together and called the Bar Harbor police station to report it.

Sergio immediately alerted emergency personnel and fired up the police boat. Mona had heard the report on her scanner and jumped in her truck and raced to the entrance to Long Pond to join in the search. I may have casually mentioned to Mona earlier about our planned romantic excursion so she instantly knew who had gone missing.

What we were not prepared for was how many boats and searchers were at the scene when we got back.

Bruce just had this hangdog expression on his face, mumbling, "I will never, ever live this down at work."

"You should just be happy to be alive!" I reminded him.

"Right now, I wish I wasn't."

I laughed, knowing full well he was right. He was never going to live this down.

On a side note, I made a ton of my clam dip, homemade crackers, and platters of ham sandwiches and delivered them to all of the emergency personnel involved in appreciation for everything they do each and every day.

Especially that day when they saved us both before we got pneumonia.

I also came up with a cocktail for Bruce, who still is taking a lot of guff at work since our rescue was front page news in the *Island Times*! I decided to mix two of his favorite drinks together to hopefully get him in a better mood.

Margarita Beer for Two

INGREDIENTS:
4 ounces tequila
2 ounces Cointreau
2 ounces fresh lime juice
8 ounces Corona beer
Ice
Kosher salt for rim (optional)

Divide your tequila, Cointreau, and lime between two ice filled glasses and give them both a good stir. Divide the beer between both glasses and enjoy your refreshing Margarita Beer.

CLAMS CASINO DIP

INGREDIENTS:
¾ cup crushed Ritz cracker crumbs
⅓ cup grated parmesan cheese
12 ounces canned chopped clams drained and
　　rinsed (By all means use cooked chopped clams
　　if you have them.)
8-ounce bottle clam juice
5 slices cooked and crumbled bacon
2 tablespoons lemon juice
1 teaspoon garlic powder
½ teaspoon black pepper
2 teaspoons sriracha or your favorite hot sauce.
6 ounces shredded mozzarella cheese divided

Preheat your oven to 375 degrees.

In a bowl, mix your cracker crumbs and parmesan
cheese. Set aside.

In a mixing bowl, add your clams, clam juice, bacon,
lemon juice, garlic powder, pepper, hot sauce and 3
ounces of mozzarella cheese.

Spread your clam mixture evenly into a 9-inch deep-
dish pie pan.

Sprinkle crushed crackers over the top of the mixture and then sprinkle the mozzarella cheese over
the top of the cracker crumbs.

Bake in the oven for 15 to 20 minutes until crackers are golden and dip is hot and bubbly.

Serve with chips, veggies, or crackers of your choice and enjoy!

Chapter 34

Sergio turned in to the Big Apple convenience store and gas station and pulled up to a pump in his police cruiser with Hayley buckled into the passenger seat.

"You need to gas up?" Hayley asked.

"Yes," Sergio said, climbing out and stretching. "I also heard Dennis Barnes has been working part time a few weekday afternoons here to make a little extra cash."

"Really? I had no idea!" Hayley exclaimed, eagerly hopping out.

Sergio slid his credit card into the slot, selected the premium unleaded button, and then shoved the nozzle into the tank. When the numbers started running up on the screen, Sergio sauntered into the store, Hayley close on his heels.

The bell rang as Sergio pushed open the door and Hayley could see Dennis crane his neck around to get a peek at his new customers.

"Afternoon, Chief," Dennis mumbled before eyeing Hayley suspiciously. He did not like the fact that Hayley was tagging along with the Chief of Police. That was never a good sign. Although there was no judgement on Hayley's face as far as she could tell, Dennis's whole body stiffened and his voice had a defensive tone as he spoke.

"I know what you're thinking, Hayley," Dennis spat out.

"You do?" Hayley asked, genuinely surprised.

"Yeah. What's Dennis doing working at the Big Apple? Well, I'll tell you . . ."

"You really don't have to, Dennis. What you do is your own business, I honestly don't—"

He did not let her finish her thought. "It's all because of Mona. She and that fancy-pants lawyer of hers played hardball during our divorce negotiations, like twenty-six years of marriage meant nothing, bubkes, even after fathering nine children . . ."

Was it really nine?

Hayley swore it was only eight.

Who was she forgetting?

It was impossible to keep track of Mona's brood anyway.

Dennis was now riled up as he continued. "Staying faithfully by her side since high school . . ."

His voice trailed off during that last thought.

Faithful was one thing Dennis Barnes was not.

Mona had put up with his laziness and general malaise for years, but when she caught him cheating on her a few Christmases back, that had been the last straw.

"Mostly!" Dennis quickly added. "I'm not perfect, I know that, but I didn't deserve to get royally screwed in the settlement. I can barely pay my bills. And now that my son's moving out and won't be splitting the rent with me, I got no choice but to make extra cash where I can!"

"I know Mona pays you a generous monthly alimony, Dennis, so maybe this is more about your addiction to playing the slots in Bangor which might better explain your depleted bank account."

"I thought you said this was none of your business."

"You opened the door, Dennis."

He decided he was done talking to Hayley and quickly flicked his eyes back to Sergio. "Coffee, Chief? Just made a fresh pot. Donuts are a bit stale, but still tasty. Had one just a few minutes ago."

"No, thanks, Dennis. I didn't come in here to buy anything. I'm here to ask you a few questions."

Dennis nervously shifted his weight to his left foot and planted the palms of his hands down on the counter. "Oh? About what?"

"Lonnie Leighton."

Dennis's eyes darted back and forth now between the chief and Hayley.

"What about him?" Dennis asked, shifting his weight back to his right foot and agitatedly scratching his face as if he were about to break out into a case of shingles.

"It's come to my attention that you two got together on the day he died," Sergio said.

"Uh-huh, Uh-huh, that's right. I remember that."

Hayley's steely eyes focused on Dennis like a laser, which just made him more anxious. "You two weren't exactly drinking buddies. Mind explaining why you met up?"

"Sure, Hayley, sure. I was worried about my boy. Dougie. That poor kid. He was so head over heels for that Olive girl and it was killing him that the stubborn old coot wasn't having it. So I decided to try and help Dougie out, you know, go talk to Lonnie, try to get him to see that

Dougie was a good kid and would make one hell of a son-in-law!"

"Oh, please!" Hayley scoffed.

Dennis narrowed his eyes, seething. "You got something to say, Hayley?"

"Yes, Dennis, I don't believe that pile of crap you're shoveling for one second!"

Dennis stood upright, offended. "And why not?"

"Because it's a selfless magnanimous gesture."

"So?"

"And you are utterly incapable of doing anything magnanimous, Dennis! Come on, what's the real reason?"

"I just told you!" Dennis whined.

"Dennis, lying to an officer of the law could get you into a whole world of trouble," Sergio reminded him.

"I'm not lying to you, Chief."

Sergio gave him a stern, penetrating, threatening glare that made Dennis's whole body shiver like he was suddenly struck by a debilitating bout of malaria.

"I was talking to her!" Dennis squeaked, pointing at Hayley, who could not help but smirk. She knew they had him right where they wanted him. "Technically I was not addressing you, so you can't say I was lying to the police."

"So you admit you just lied to Hayley?" Sergio asked, his fingers touching his baton attached to his belt just for show.

Dennis was melting behind the counter now.

He was too stupid to try and outwit them any longer. His poor brain just didn't have the bandwidth. "Okay, I didn't go talk to Lonnie because of Dougie. I went to see if he might consider hiring me on at his company!"

Hayley gasped, appalled. "You wanted to stick it to Mona by going to work for the enemy!"

"No! I owe on some gambling debts! I went to Mona first to see if she might increase my alimony, but she just laughed in my face. I was pretty desperate so I suggested she hire me part-time so I could make a little extra to pay down what I owe. Well, she said no! She didn't want to have to see my face, even for just a few hours a week."

"So you went to Lonnie," Sergio said.

"Yeah, maybe a small part of me wanted to get even with Mona, but the cold hard fact was I needed to make money and fast. There are a couple of three-hundred-pound bruisers up in Brewer who have been calling me and threatening to break my legs if I don't start making a few payments."

"Was Lonnie open to taking you on?" Hayley asked.

Dennis shook his head, shoulders slumped, down-hearted. "Are you kidding me? He wanted nothing to do with me. Called me a no-good loser. Ordered me to leave his shop or he was gonna call the cops and have me arrested for trespassing. He was wicked mean, a nasty old bastard! He made me so mad!"

Hayley and Sergio exchanged brief glances.

Sergio took a step forward. "Mad enough to kill him?"

Dennis suddenly stood upright. "No! I swear, Chief, when I left Lonnie, he was still alive!"

In Hayley's opinion, she somewhat agreed with Lonnie's assessment. Dennis was in many ways a loser. Lazy, selfish, self-destructive. She had always marveled at Mona's patience for staying with him all those years, especially since patience was not something in Mona's wheelhouse. But something about those marriage vows had stuck with Mona and she rode it out for as long as she possibly could, until the relationship was no longer tenable, when it was irrevocably broken. But for all of Dennis's faults, he had never raised a hand to her, never demonstrated anything close to suggesting he was a violent man.

And now, watching him cower behind the counter at the Big Apple, a shell of a man, just trying to stay afloat and not drown in drink, debt, and disappointment, Hayley found it difficult to believe that he actually had it in him to kill anybody. Other than himself if he didn't clean up his act.

Chapter 35

A disembodied voice crackled through the police cruiser, "Chief, we have a ten-thirty-one at sixty-two Ledgelawn Avenue."

Sergio scooped up his wireless mic. "Ten-four. On my way."

Hayley, who owned her own police scanner and kept it on top of the fridge even before she married crime reporter Bruce, swiveled her head around.

"Crime in progress?"

Sergio cranked the wheel, spinning the car around in a sharp U-turn, and speeding back down Mount Desert Street toward Ledgelawn Avenue.

Hayley sat up in her seat, alert, ready for whatever they might be heading straight into.

Within two minutes, Sergio was slamming on the brakes, the cruiser screeching to a stop, the blue light on top of the hood flashing.

"Wait here," he said, jumping out and cautiously making his way across the cement walkway toward the house.

The front door was wide open but no one was there waiting for the police to arrive.

Hayley suddenly realized who lived in this house, and hurried out of the cruiser.

She whispered urgently to Sergio, who was now at the front door. "Sergio, this is Abby Weston's house!"

Lonnie Leighton's girlfriend and apparently the heir to half his small fortune.

Sergio stopped, slowly turned around and put a finger to his lips, but nodded in acknowledgement before poking his head through the doorway. "This is the police!"

Hayley could make out a muffled voice coming from inside the house. Sergio seemed to relax a little and disappeared down the hallway. Hayley glanced around to see a few neighbors staring out their windows at the police cruiser. A woman walking her poodle across the street was distracted watching the scene while her little dog lifted his leg up next to a bush.

Sergio suddenly reappeared at the doorway, waving at Hayley. "It's all clear. You can come in."

Hayley trotted after Sergio, who led her inside and down the hall to the kitchen where they found Abby Weston with a mop, sopping up spilled milk from her floor and squeezing it into a yellow bucket. Heads of lettuce, flattened tomatoes, a couple of onions, some cereal and a few canned goods littered the floor along with a crushed milk carton and a brown paper bag with the bottom ripped open.

It was a mess.

"Abby, what happened?" Hayley gasped.

Abby, almost nonchalantly, replied, "I arrived home from the Shop 'n Save to find an intruder in my house. I just walked into the kitchen carrying my bag of groceries and there he was just standing there by the refrigerator. I screamed at the top of my lungs and dropped the bag. I must have spooked him because then he just tore right on out of here, ran past me, and back out the front door."

"Did he steal anything?" Sergio asked.

"I really don't know. I didn't have time to take inventory. It all happened so fast."

"And then you called the police?" Hayley asked, bending down to pick up a few of the squashed tomatoes.

"No, that was my neighbor next door Gladys Kravitz."

Sergio reached for his notepad and pen in his pocket. "Kravitz. How do you spell that?"

"No, Sergio," Hayley said with a chuckle. "I'm assuming that's not her real name."

Sergio cocked an eyebrow. "Why not?"

"Because Gladys Kravitz is a character from that old TV show *Bewitched*," Hayley explained.

"Be-what?"

"She was a neighbor who was always sticking her nose into everybody's business on the street, especially—"

"I'm sorry, we did not get that show in Brazil!"

Hayley turned to Abby for help.

"Hillary Higgins," Abby muttered.

"Is that another character in the show?" Sergio sighed.

"No, that's my neighbor next door. She was the one who called the police when she heard me scream."

Sergio scribbled the name on his pad, annoyed.

Abby stopped wiping the floor and leaned the mop up against the kitchen counter. "Is this going to take long? I have a meeting with my lawyer in twenty minutes."

"I just want to get as much information as possible so we can catch this guy," Sergio said.

Abby, with a stiff upper lip, replied, "I probably forgot to lock the door when I left. I'm sure it was just some stupid kid looking for cash to buy weed. Nothing appears to have been taken, no harm done, why don't we forget the whole thing?"

Sergio and Hayley exchanged curious looks.

"Abby, someone broke into your home, that's very serious," Hayley said somberly.

"I know, but I'm fine," Abby sighed and then looked down at the crushed milk carton on the floor. "What is it they say, why cry over spilled milk? I wasn't even going to call you, but then that meddlesome busybody Hillary had to get involved."

"I just have a few more questions. It won't take long, I promise," Sergio said.

Abby sighed, checking her wall clock.

"You say you might have left your front door unlocked?"

Abby nodded. "Yes, I forget sometimes. It's usually very safe around here."

"Not today," Hayley noted.

"So the intruder was standing by the refrigerator when you walked into the kitchen and first saw him?"

Abby thought about it for a moment. "Yes, that's right."

"What did he look like? Can you describe him?"

"He was wearing one of those, what do you call them, hoodies? Hoodies, yes. I didn't get a good look at him."

"But he was facing you?" Sergio asked.

Abby hesitated. Then she nodded slightly. "I guess so. Like I said, it all happened so fast."

"Even with the hood up, you probably were able to at

least get a glimpse of his face before he took off running," Sergio said, a slight suspicion now in his voice.

"No, I didn't because I wasn't wearing my glasses at the time," Abby explained. "I can't read anything without my glasses. Look, Chief, I really need to go—"

"So you wear reading glasses?" Hayley asked.

"Yes, Hayley, I do, otherwise everything is blurry."

"But if they're reading glasses, that means you're farsighted, not nearsighted, so if you walked into the kitchen from over here and the suspect was way over by the refrigerator, you should have been able to make him out quite clearly."

"Well, I didn't! What is going on here, am I on trial now? I didn't see anything! Maybe his back was to me when I walked in, I don't remember! I told you, I screamed and she just ran out before I could—"

"*She*? It was a woman?" Sergio asked.

"No, I didn't mean that. It was a man."

Sergio grimaced. "Then why did you just say—?"

"I don't know!" Abby wailed. "I need to go. I trust you can let yourselves out."

Abby Weston rushed out of the kitchen and out the front door.

Sergio turned to Hayley. "What was all that about?"

"I get the feeling she might know the person who broke into her house but she doesn't want to tell us," Hayley said.

They walked out of the house where Hillary Higgins, in her late sixties, wearing a baby-blue housecoat and carrying a sack of empty returnables, hovered on the lawn next door, a cigarette dangling from her cracked lips. "Did you get a description of the guy?"

Sergio shook his head. "Not a good one, but you said *guy*, can you confirm it was a man, at least?"

Hillary took a puff of her cigarette and blew smoke in Sergio's direction, causing him to cough a little. "Nope. He was wearing a gray hooded sweatshirt and jeans and was running down toward Glenmary Road by the time I spotted him. His back was to me the whole time."

"Okay, call me at the station if you remember anything else," Sergio said.

"Can you believe she didn't even want to call the cops? She didn't want to get you involved. Isn't that the craziest thing? We don't know how dangerous this person could be! My house could be next! There was no way I was going to let it go!" Hillary cried.

"Thank you, Mrs. Kravitz," Sergio said.

"Kravitz? Who the hell is Kravitz? My name is Higgins!"

"Sorry, my mistake," Sergio mumbled, making a mad dash for his police cruiser.

Hayley had to stifle a laugh.

But Hillary Higgins was right.

Any clear-eyed victim of a home break-in would instantly call the police, not stall and make up excuses.

Which meant, in her mind, that Abby Weston was definitely hiding something.

Chapter 36

"This just might be the best pasta dish I have ever tasted!" Bruce gushed as Hayley bristled sitting next to him at the dining room table at Tabitha Collins's very expensive, high-end rental house.

Tabitha giggled as she took a long sip of her Chardonnay. "Oh, Bruce, stop!"

Hayley glared at Bruce. "Yes, Bruce. Stop."

There was a brief silence except for the sound of Bruce's fork scraping the china plate as he twirled it, wrapping more linguine around it, and eagerly shoveled it into his mouth, chewing loudly. He swallowed and turned to Tabitha. "What is this called again?"

"Linguine Pasta Alle Vongole," Tabitha replied, beaming.

"Basically, Linguine with Clams. It's on the menu at my restaurant. You've ordered it dozens of times. It's a very simple recipe," Hayley said, fuming.

Bruce suddenly realized he was in hot water with his wife. "Yours is great too, babe . . ." He stopped himself.

Hayley leaned forward. "*But*?"

"No buts. It's just . . . this has a real kick to it."

Tabitha shot Hayley a triumphant smile. "That's because I'm very generous with the garlic and pepperoncini. My mother was Sicilian and she loved anything spicy. Plus, I make my own pasta, but I can't take credit for the clams. I got those from your friend Mona, who has the freshest seafood in town."

"Don't tell that to Vera Leighton," Bruce cracked.

Eager to change the subject, Hayley glanced around their posh surroundings. "This is a lovely house, Tabitha. How did you find it?"

"Can you believe Airbnb? Who would have thought?" Tabitha said, slapping her hand down on the table. "I got lucky it was available this month." Her eyes drifted to Bruce's empty plate. "Another helping, Bruce?"

Bruce wavered, not sure if saying yes would be some kind of betrayal, but he just could not resist. "Yes, please."

Tabitha stood up, grabbed his plate, gave him a wink, and bounced off toward the kitchen.

Was that a wink or did she just have something caught in her eye?

No, Hayley was fairly certain it was a deliberate wink. She tried not to scowl but wasn't sure if she was entirely successful. When she turned to her husband, he fumbled for his wine, not wanting to make eye contact.

Hayley knew this was all her fault.

After Sergio had dropped her off at her house, she had found Bruce pacing in the kitchen, not sure what to do. Tabitha had called and invited the two of them to dinner and he was not sure how to respond. He had told Tabitha he needed to talk to his wife, stressing the word *wife*. For Hayley's part, she had already alerted her staff she was

taking the night off from the restaurant because she
wanted to cook Bruce dinner. But she had spent the whole
day running around playing detective and had not given a
single thought about what to make. She had not even
gone grocery shopping and her cupboards were essentially bare. Bruce's inclination was to pass on the offer,
but Hayley insisted he call back and accept. Not because
all she had to serve Bruce was a box of Hamburger
Helper, but because she was determined to find out for
herself what Tabitha's true intentions were when it came
to her husband.

They had barely sat down at the gorgeous New
England farm table in walnut when the full-court press
flirting began. Tabitha casually touching Bruce's hand
with her own, cracking a few private jokes that Hayley
would never be able to understand, keeping his wine
glass full hoping he might get tipsy and return her long-
ing gaze. It was becoming quite clear that Hayley's initial
misgivings were spot-on. Tabitha Collins wanted to steal
Bruce away from her.

The one silver lining had been Bruce's resistance to
her charms. After all, he had suspected what might be
coming and wanted to just stay home and avoid any potential land mines. But no, Hayley had been adamant.
And so he had remained rigid, sitting there quietly, carefully choosing his words whenever he was forced to
speak. That is, until he had taken his first bite of Tabitha's
Linguine Pasta Alle Vongole. That's when everything
went off the rails. And it was clear from the pained expression on his face that he wished he was anywhere else
but here.

By the time dessert rolled around, a delicious tiramisu
which Tabitha quickly pointed out was another recipe

given to her by her Sicilian mother and not store-bought, Bruce was ready to finally end this torture. He began to rub his temples with his fingers. Tabitha shot out a hand, touching his shoulder before Hayley even had the chance. "Are you all right, Bruce?"

He nodded. "Just a headache. It kills me to have to end this wonderful evening early but I think I need to go home."

Tabitha blinked, crestfallen.

Hayley thought she might cry she was so relieved.

"Really? I have some Tylenol in the medicine cabinet. Are you sure you don't want to stay for coffee? This place comes with a very nice espresso machine."

Of course it does.

Bruce knew better than to drag this out. "I'm sorry, but we really should go." He turned to Hayley. "Sorry, babe."

"I was having such a nice time. I hate to cut this lovely evening short, but if you're not feeling well . . ." Hayley paused, then followed up with a fake sigh. "What a shame. I was having such a nice time."

Bruce stood up fast, practically bolting for the door, before realizing he was supposed to be under the weather, so he readjusted, slowing his gait. "Thank you for dinner, Tabitha. Sorry to leave so abruptly."

"Of course, I understand. Call me tomorrow and let me know if you're feeling better."

He ignored that last request.

Hayley did too.

She gave Tabitha a stiff hug. "You must share that tiramisu recipe with me."

Tabitha mimed zipping her lips shut. "Family secret."

"Oh, well, I tried."

Hayley actually didn't care. She was just being polite.

Unlike the spectacular Linguini Pasta Alle Vongole dish, in her opinion, Tabitha's tiramisu was a bit dry, not nearly as moist and tasty as her own, which she found immensely satisfying.

Tabitha had to chase down Bruce to get a hug good night, which he gamely obliged with, if ever so briefly. Then he was racing for the car.

"This was fun," Hayley said. "We should do it again before you go back to Boston."

Hayley could have kicked herself.

Why did she have to say that?

It just opened the door for Tabitha to have another chance to hook her claws into Hayley's husband.

Tabitha gave her a tantalizing smile. "Who knows? We may have a lot more opportunities in the future to get together."

Hayley knew she was teasing her permanent move to Bar Harbor, but she refused to take the bait.

"Good night!" Hayley chirped, jumping in the car with Bruce. As they pulled away, she could see through the side mirror Tabitha standing in the doorframe, watching them go, her smile slowly fading, as if she was disappointed about how her well-planned evening had played out.

Hayley and Bruce rode in silence for a few minutes before Hayley shifted in her seat to look directly at Bruce. His hands gripped the steering wheel so tight she could see the whites of his knuckles. "Tell me honestly, do you enjoy the attention from her?"

He glanced in her direction, a look of dread on his face. "Seriously? You want to do this now? I wasn't lying back there, Hayley. I really do have a headache."

"Fine," Hayley pouted. "We don't have to get into it."

More silence.

Finally, Bruce flicked his eyes back to her. "You were the one who made us have dinner with her tonight. I was happy just staying home."

She could not argue with that.

"It's just so obvious she wants you back. I guess it's making me feel a little insecure so what I'm looking for is a little reassurance."

More silence.

Hayley sat up in her seat.

Where was the reassurance she had been expecting?

Why wasn't he telling her she had nothing to worry about like he had before?

Bruce pulled into their driveway, braked to a stop, and shifted the car into the park position. He unbuckled his seat belt and turned to his wife. "I am not going to lie to you. Yes, Hayley. Yes, I do enjoy it."

Hayley's stomach knotted. "Okay."

"I have my writing career. You have your restaurant. We're both super busy and don't have a lot of time to spend together as much as I'd like to. But that's life. That's most marriages. But I will admit, when you run off investigating crimes for kicks, and you're not there for that precious rare time when we're both not working, then yeah, sometimes I feel neglected."

This was a wallop Hayley had not expected.

And it rendered her speechless.

Bruce reached out and took her hand. "I'm not saying I can't deal with it, or even that it's a big problem, but sometimes a guy needs a little validation, something to make him feel like he's still got it."

Hayley finally found her voice. "And Tabitha gives you that validation?"

"Maybe a little. But it's all very innocent."

"Is it?"

Bruce sighed. "It's all very innocent because I don't love Tabitha." He leaned in and kissed her softly on the lips. "I love you."

Hayley knew he was not just trying to make her feel better.

He meant what he said.

But she was still going to worry.

That was just her nature.

She suddenly noticed Bruce waiting for her to respond, a tentative look on his face.

She squeezed his hand. "I love you too."

They kissed again.

Her heart fluttered.

"By the way, you do, Bruce."

"I do what?"

"You still got it."

Bruce smiled and started getting out of the car but Hayley grabbed his arm. "Wait, Bruce. I have to know one thing. Does her spaghetti with clams really taste better than mine?"

Bruce paused, thought about it, and then said with a playful wink, "I plead the Fifth."

"Wrong answer!" Hayley cried.

Chapter 37

When Hayley's eyes fluttered open after a fitful night's sleep, she rolled over to discover Bruce was already out of bed and gone to the *Island Times* office. He had probably slipped out extra early this morning to avoid any further discussion about their evening with Tabitha Collins. Frankly, Hayley could not blame him. She stretched her arms and contemplated lounging in bed for at least another hour, but of course that's when her phone started vibrating on the nightstand next to her alerting her that she had a new text. She closed her eyes, deciding to read it later, but then a few seconds later, the phone vibrated again. Then again. And again. Her curiosity finally got the best of her. She sat up and reached for the phone. The texts were from Mona.

Code Red! Code Red!

Where are you?

Why aren't you answering my texts? We have an emergency!

Instead of typing a reply, Hayley just called Mona, who picked up on the first ring.

"Where the hell are you? I've been texting you all morning!"

"Mona, you texted me three minutes ago. I got back to you right away! What's wrong?"

"It's Dougie!"

"Oh no! What's happened now? Is he okay?"

"I wouldn't know! He's missing!"

"What do you mean missing?"

"Missing! Gone! Vanished! I don't know how many ways to say it, Hayley! He's usually up at five every morning, but today he didn't come down for coffee so I thought I'd let him sleep in, but now it's seven o'clock, he should have already hauled his butt out of bed and gotten his day started so I went upstairs and banged on his door. He didn't answer so I went in his room and he wasn't there. His bed hadn't even been slept in!"

"Maybe he stayed over at Digger's last night."

"No, he was here last night. We played a game of Scrabble. I saw him go upstairs to bed. I just called over at Digger's place and he said he hadn't seen Dougie since yesterday afternoon. He must have snuck out in the middle of the night."

"Mona, there really is no cause for alarm," Hayley assured her. "He probably just—"

Mona interrupted her. "I checked his closet. His suitcase is gone."

Okay, so there was now cause for alarm.

"I'll be right over."

Hayley ended the call and then shot out of bed, grabbing her clothes off the floor where she had shed them last night and hastily got dressed. She downed a quick cup of coffee for a caffeine kick and dashed out the door to her car, driving straight over to Mona's house.

When she burst through the front door, she found Mona pacing back and forth in her living room, a stricken look on her face.

"Eight kids, Hayley, I've raised eight kids, and this is the first time one of them has run away!" Mona wailed.

"Dougie's twenty-one. Technically he's too old to run away," Hayley said quietly. "And you raised nine kids."

"Oh, right, you'd think I'd remember how many times that good-for-nothing Dennis knocked me up!"

"Any ideas where he might have gone?"

"I'm sure wherever he is, he's with Olive Leighton!"

Hayley nodded, plucking her phone from her pocket. She had Ruth Leighton in her list of contacts and put a call into her. She thought she would get her voice mail but after a few rings, Ruth answered. "Hello?"

"Hi, Ruth, it's Hayley Powell. I hope I didn't wake you."

"Good morning, Hayley, no I've been up for hours. I'm just on my out. I'm going over to my—"

She suddenly stopped herself.

Like she did not want Hayley to know where she was heading, which only piqued Hayley's curiosity.

Ruth quickly changed the subject. "It doesn't matter. How can I help you?"

There was no time to press Ruth on what she was up to so Hayley just plowed ahead.

"Ruth, is Olive there with you?"

"No, I believe she's still upstairs in her room sleeping."

"Could you do me a favor and check for me, please?"

"Why? What's wrong?"

"I'm at Mona's house and Dougie's not here and she's

a little bit concerned about where he might be, so I thought Olive might have some idea."

"Hold on," Ruth said, suddenly concerned.

Hayley heard pounding as Ruth hurried up the stairs, then some knocking on a door and Ruth calling, "Olive? Olive?" Then the sound of a door opening and a surprised yelp. "She's not here. That's so strange. I didn't hear her leaving this morning."

"Did she pack a bag? Are any of her clothes missing?"

More footsteps and a door creaking open.

There was a long pause before Ruth spoke again. "Yes, she bought a new dress at Talbots last week. That's not here. A couple pairs of shoes are gone." More shuffling sounds. "I'm looking inside her jewelry box. Also, her favorite earrings and a necklace are missing. Why would she go somewhere without telling us? She knows how I worry."

"Ruth, I will call you back just as soon as I know anything," Hayley said.

"Please do, thank you, Hayley."

Hayley ended the call and then began scrolling down her contacts list before tapping a number and pressing the phone to her ear.

"Who are you calling now?"

"Ed Seavey."

"Why would Ed Seavey know where they are?" Mona cried.

"Because your truck is still parked outside and so is Dougie's moped. If he left town, he'd need a ride and Ed operates the only taxi service in town."

Mona nodded vigorously. "Smart thinking. It's not like we have Uber or Lyft way up here in the sticks."

"Ed's Taxi," a man answered before hacking a few times with a disconcerting smoker's cough.

"Ed, it's Hayley Powell."

"Hey there, Hayley, having car trouble this morning? Need a ride somewhere? I'm afraid you're going to have to wait. I did an early morning airport run to Bangor and I'm still a half hour from the Trenton Bridge," Ed said, violently trying to clear his throat before taking an audible puff on the cigarette he was no doubt sucking on.

"Airport? Ed, were your passengers Dougie Barnes and Olive Leighton?"

"Why, yes! How on God's green earth did you know that?"

"Just a wild guess. Did they happen to mention where they were flying to?"

"Not at first. They were real secretive. They just sat in the backseat holding hands and smiling like two Cheshire cats. But by the time we hit Ellsworth, I made a comment about them looking like a pair of lovebirds sneaking off to get married."

"And?"

"Olive started giggling so I knew I had guessed right although neither would confirm it. Then Dougie got a text on his phone that their flight out of Bangor to Boston had been delayed and I heard him say to Olive that he was worried they might miss their connection to Vegas."

"*Vegas*?" Hayley gasped.

Mona's eyes popped open. "Vegas? They're going to Las Vegas?"

"Thanks, Ed," Hayley said, lowering her phone and raising a hand to try and keep Mona calm, a decidedly impossible task at this point.

"People only go to Vegas for two reasons, Hayley," Mona yelled. "Either to gamble away their hard-earned money or to get married! And the only compulsive gambler in the family is Dougie's good-for-nothing father!"

"Maybe they got tickets to one of the Cirque du Soleil shows," Hayley offered weakly.

Mona glared at her. "Dougie hates the circus! Especially those high-falutin' French ones! So he must be getting married!"

After all the heartache and conflict they had endured from their families for just wanting to be together, it made perfect sense that Dougie and Olive would just skip town and elope.

Why didn't any of them see that coming?

Chapter 38

"**M**ona, watch out!" Hayley screamed, thrusting her hands out to grab the dashboard of Mona's truck before impact. Mona cranked the wheel, but not fast enough, and her Ford pickup truck shot up over the sidewalk curb and smashed into a mailbox, uprooting it and sending it sailing into the air only to come crashing down on the top of Mona's hood. Hayley and Mona sat in silence for a moment, both catching their breath.

Finally, Mona turned to Hayley. "You okay?"

Hayley nodded, still in a bit of a daze.

"Good," Mona snorted, pushing open the driver's side door. "I'm going to go find out just what the hell is going on here!"

"Mona, wait!"

But it was too late.

She was already out of the truck and pounding across the lawn toward her son Digger's house.

With the hope that Dougie might have shared his plans to elope with his older brother Digger, who he idolized, Hayley had suggested they drive over to Digger's place and talk to him. Perhaps Dougie had shared key details, like what hotel they would be staying at, or the wedding chapel they were going to get married in. Mona thought that was a pretty good idea so the two of them hopped in Mona's truck and hightailed it over to Digger's.

It was still a few minutes before eight o'clock in the morning, but Mona knew Digger was not out early lobstering today, so there was a good chance he would be home. And he was.

When they rounded the corner onto Digger's street, they spotted him standing outside his house in his underwear and a ratty old tank top.

And he was not alone.

Hiding behind him was Ruth Leighton in a revealing silk negligee, ducking down, her head below his shoulders as Digger tried calmly talking to a wild-eyed, enraged Vera Leighton. At least she was fully dressed in a plaid shirt and jeans and clutching a brown paper bag. She appeared to be yelling at the top of her lungs, waking up the whole neighborhood.

It was suddenly obvious to Hayley who Ruth was off to meet when she had called her earlier that morning.

Obviously the shock of seeing both Leighton women on her son's front lawn, one of them in a sexy nightie, caused Mona to lose control of her vehicle and crash into the mailbox.

Hayley contemplated just staying in the truck and letting Mona handle this, but her curiosity got the best of her and she scrambled out of the passenger's side, chasing after Mona.

His mother annihilating his mailbox and nearly flattening a black cat darting across the street, had certainly gotten Digger's attention. He stared at her dumbstruck as

Mona flew across the lawn, adrenaline giving her an assist.

Vera, still in the middle of a major meltdown, was focused on her sister Ruth, who was trying to will herself to be invisible behind Digger. "You pig! You cheater! You liar!"

Digger barked at Mona, "Mom, go home! You're the last person I need here right now!"

"I most certainly will not, Digger, not until you tell me what the hell is going on here!" Mona wailed.

Vera whipped her head around to Mona. "You want to know what's going on? I'll tell you what's going on! Your two-timing spawn of Satan just got caught red-handed sneaking around with my own backstabbing sister!"

Mona and Hayley stood frozen on the lawn.

This was a lot to take in.

First, Hayley silently prayed Mona had not picked up on the fact that in Vera's version of events, Mona was cast in the role of Satan.

Luckily that sticky point seemed to sail right over Mona's head.

Second, if Digger was cheating on someone with Ruth.

Clearly the aggrieved party was Vera.

That little tidbit unfortunately did not escape Mona's attention.

"Wait, hold on now just a minute," Mona cried, turning to Digger. "Is she saying . . . ?"

"Yes, Mom," Digger solemnly explained. "I was seeing Vera, but now I'm seeing Ruth."

"And nobody bothered to tell *me*!" Vera roared, eyes blazing.

"Maybe I should go inside and let you all work this out," Ruth muttered, modestly folding her arms and backing away toward the front door.

"You stay put, Ruth!" Vera snapped. "That's so like you, always trying to avoid conflict! Well, this is your mess too, and you need to deal with it right now!"

"Digger, are you kidding me? Not one, but *two* Leightons?" Mona howled, clutching her chest as if he had just driven a stake through the middle of it.

Digger nodded. "Yes. Vera and I were dating on the down-low for a few months . . ."

"*Ten* months! That's not a few! Ten!" Vera hollered.

"Okay, ten," Digger conceded. "But then I ran into Ruth and we got to talking and there was this spark nei-ther of us could ignore, so we got together a few times, and then a few more, and pretty soon I couldn't deny the fact that I love her, I honestly love her!"

"Enough! This isn't some sappy Olivia Newton-John song, Digger! Why the hell didn't you just tell Vera?" Mona sighed.

Digger sized up Vera. "To avoid a scene just like this one."

Vera sniffed and looked away, refusing to show how hurt she was, but Hayley could tell she was fighting back tears.

"I kept meaning to have a talk with Vera and let her down easy, officially end things, but I was scared. I'm sorry, Mom, but I just didn't have the guts to do it. Everyone in town knows how crazy she can get."

Hayley found herself nodding in agreement.

Vera Leighton's volatile nature was now legendary.

Mona laser-focused on Ruth, whose whole body trem-bled. "And what about you? Why didn't you break the news to her? She's your own sister!"

"I didn't dare! She was already incredibly upset over Olive and Dougie! Can you imagine how she would react if I told her I was dating a Barnes boy too?" Ruth cried. "But little did I know, she started the whole trend and was sneaking around with Digger months before Olive and Dougie got romantically involved with each other!"

Vera raised the brown paper bag she was holding. "I'd noticed Digger was being distant lately, but I didn't know why, so I thought I'd stop by the Morning Glory bakery for some freshly baked muffins and come by here to maybe rekindle things, never expecting Ruth to answer the door looking like Elizabeth Taylor from *Butterfield 8*!"

Mona turned to Hayley. "What's *Butterfly 8*?"

"I will explain later," Hayley said softly.

Ruth took a tentative step toward her sister. "Vera, I am so sorry. We meant to tell you, we really did, we were just waiting for the right moment—"

"Save your breath!" Vera barked, spinning around, her back to everyone in order to hide the tears now streaming down her cheeks before fleeing to her car and speeding away.

"Mom, what brings you here so early in the morning anyway?" Digger asked.

"We think Dougie and Olive have eloped to Las Vegas!"

Ruth gasped.

"Did he say anything to you?"

Digger shook his head. "No. Not a word."

Mona threw her hands in the air. "What did I feed those boys as kids that would make them all turn out to be such Don Juans? They certainly didn't get it from their father!"

Chapter 39

When Helen Woodworth led Hayley into the den of her small cozy house on Snow Street, six ladies sitting around clicking away with their knitting needles in unison raised their eyes in surprise. The last person any of them had ever expected to show up at their weekly knitting circle was Hayley Powell. It was pretty much the same reaction she had received when she crashed Sabrina Merryweather's book club. One knitting circle attendee, Doris Crimmons, actually dropped her needles in shock and had to casually bend over to pick them up off the Persian rug.

"Ladies, look who decided to join us today," Helen cooed. "We happened to run into each other at the post office this morning, and Hayley just mentioned she had recently taken up knitting and was working on a knit bowtie dog collar for her cute shih tzu Leroy, so I insisted she come and try out our little knitting circle."

The ladies all smiled and nodded, welcoming Hayley to the group, except one. Abby Weston, Lonnie Leighton's girlfriend, who sat in a wooden rocking chair near the closed-up fireplace. She rocked back and forth, suspiciously eyeing Hayley, not buying the whole random run in at the post office excuse. She knew exactly why Hayley was here, even if all the other gullible ladies were fooled.

And Abby was absolutely right.

When Hayley had learned Abby belonged to Helen's knitting circle, she had hunted down Helen like an expensive Arabian horse that had somehow broken free from the barn. She put the word out to family and friends, and within minutes Randy was texting her with his own sighting of Helen heading into the post office to mail a package. Bar Harbor was such a small town it only took Hayley five minutes to get there, just in time to nearly collide with Helen on the steps outside as Helen was coming out the door on her way to take care of her next errand. Hayley had rummaged for her half-finished knit bowtie from her bag to get Helen's opinion, feigning frustration that she needed to make more time to finish it, and of course, also planting the seed that a weekly knitting circle might just be the solution. She had secured an invite to Helen's circle in less than two minutes.

"I'm hopeless with a pair of knitting needles so any advice you can give me would be greatly appreciated," Hayley said, showing everyone her knitted doggie bowtie.

There were lots of ooohs and aaaahs and words of encouragement from the group. Hayley declined to mention that this half-finished bowtie project had actually been started by Liddy, whose therapist suggested she take up a hobby to calm her nerves, which she did, deciding to knit something for Hayley's dog. It lasted a day and a half before she abandoned the whole project out of boredom, but had given it to Hayley anyway to prove she had at least made the effort. She thought Hayley might want to finish it herself one day.

Hayley could tell from Abby's face that she wasn't buying any of this. She just lowered her eyes and returned to knitting her red ski cap.

"Hayley, why don't you take a seat and get to work, and if you have any questions, any one of us would be happy to help you," Helen said.

"Where should I sit?" Hayley asked, glancing around and zeroing in on the empty rocker next to Abby.

"Anywhere you like," Helen said before shoving a plate of sweets in her face. "Sugar cookie?"

"Thank you," Hayley said, plucking one from the plate and shoveling it into her mouth.

After making a big show of deciding whether to sit in the middle of the couch between Betty Dyer and Esther Willey, both of whom were patting the empty cushion next to them, eager to tutor Hayley in the fine art of knitting, or the empty rocker next to Abby, Hayley swallowed her cookie and nonchalantly wandered over to the rocker, catching Abby scowling out of the corner of her eye.

Hayley plopped down in the chair and pulled out her knitting needles and tried to figure out just how to get started, sighing loudly. "It's been a while since I did this."

Abby ignored her.

Betty Dyer, who was practically bursting out of her gray cardigan that she probably knitted herself, desperate to be Hayley's mentor, called from across the room, "Hold the knitting needle with the cast-on stitches in your left hand, wrap yarn in around the needle, slide the right needle with yarn on it, and slip the old stitch off the left needle. It sounds complicated but it's not. You'll get the hang of it. If you want to come sit next to me, I can show you."

Hayley fumbled but pretended she was making progress. "No, I think I got it. Thank you, Betty."

As the other ladies gossiped about the latest happenings in town and Helen served coffee spiked with brandy, there was an icy silence from Abby, who kept her eyes trained on her half-finished ski cap. Hayley finally turned to Abby, but before she could speak, Abby whispered under her breath, "I know exactly why you are here, Hayley."

"I was just going to ask if you could hand me another sugar cookie," Hayley said, batting her eyes innocently.

Abby noticed the plate of cookies Helen had set down on the side table next to her, scooped it up, and shoved it front of Hayley, who smiled and took one, saying sweetly, "Thank you, Abby."

"You're not here to knit. I should out you to the rest of the circle about why you're *really* here," Abby muttered.

"Fine, you got me. I was hoping you might talk to me, but if Leroy gets an adorable bowtie out of it, even better."

Abby stole a quick glance at the bowtie in Hayley's lap. "That is going to be adorable. I can picture him wearing it."

Finally, a little ice was breaking.

"Abby, I am not here to make you uncomfortable, I just want to know what's going on, why you lied to Sergio."

Abby nervously moved her needles at lightning speed, reaching down into her tote bag for more red yarn. "I have no idea what you're talking about. I would never—"

Hayley leaned closer and whispered, "It wasn't some random stranger who broke into your house, was it? It was Vera."

"How did you know that?" Abby cried as Esther Willey's ears perked up, curious to know why they were whispering and being so secretive.

"Educated guess," Hayley murmured. "Was it about Lonnie's second will?"

Abby nodded, then glanced around the room to make sure no one was eavesdropping. Luckily Betty Dyer had just engaged Esther Willey in a discussion about rising gas prices. Then Abby turned to Hayley. "She showed up at my house, trying to threaten and intimidate me. I swear, Hayley, I knew nothing about that second will. Lonnie never shared his intentions with me. I just loved the man. I didn't care one whit about his darn business, pardon my French."

"But Vera was so fearful you might now try to force your way into the family business, she wanted to scare you away."

"She was already waiting inside my house when I got home from the store. She must have known Lonnie had a key. I was so startled to see her standing there in the kitchen I dropped my bag of groceries. Vera was prepared to write a big fat check in exchange for me signing away any rights to Leighton Seafoods. Part of me was prepared to do it right then and there, but then cooler heads prevailed, and I told her I should consult with a lawyer first before I signed anything. Well, you can imagine that didn't sit very well with Vera. She started yelling and screaming and at one point she physically shoved me. I screamed and that seemed to scare her and she ran out of the house. That's when my neighbor spotted her tearing down the street and called 911."

"Why didn't you just tell Sergio the truth?"

"Because I did not want to make things any worse by being the one responsible for Vera getting arrested. Now that Lonnie's gone, I just want to forget the whole thing, wash my hands of Vera Leighton, and the whole Leighton family, and their business."

"Why do you think Vera was so threatened by you being a part of the seafood company?"

"She has never liked me. She was always convinced I was just trying to get my hooks into her father for his money, which could not be further from the truth. Despite his many faults, I truly did love the man." Abby paused, a forlorn look on her face, before casually adding, "And then there was the sale. That was a whole other rift."

Hayley sat up in her rocker. "Sale? What sale?"

"Lonnie told me about it. Vera came to him one day wanting to sell the business to a national food chain for oodles of money. They would be set for life, but Lonnie was on the fence about it. He had built that business up from scratch and wasn't sure he wanted to just give it all up. I advised him to follow his heart. It was his company and his decision. After mulling it over for weeks, he told Vera no, he didn't want to sell."

"Oh, boy . . . Vera must have erupted like Mount Vesuvius," Hayley remarked.

Abby nodded. "It wasn't pretty, I can tell you that. Then we found out Vera had already been in talks to sell long before she had even mentioned it to her father. Can you believe that?"

Hayley suddenly felt a sense of dread in her gut.

"Who was the buyer?"

"Some bigwig out of Boston. A woman. Tabitha some-body."

"Tabitha Collins?"

"Yes, that's it. How did you know?"

Hayley, flabbergasted, accidentally stabbed her hand with a knitting needle, drawing blood.

Island Food & Spirits
BY
HAYLEY POWELL

My BFFs Liddy and Mona joined me for one
of our twice-weekly deck chats one evening recently. Liddy provided a nice bottle of wine for
a batch of my lemon wine spritzers and Mona
brought some cooked clams for my clam casserole, a recipe I had been making ever since I
tasted it years ago at one of my favorite local
seafood restaurants.While enjoying our spritzers
and clam casserole, we were, as usual, reminisc-
ing about the past.

Mona started chuckling.

Liddy asked, "What's so funny?"

Mona turned to me, still laughing, and asked
me if I remembered the night that Danny (my
first husband and the father of my children)
proposed to me.

I nearly choked on my wine spritzer. How
could I ever forget that night? It was one for the
history books.

It was an ordinary Friday night. Danny and I
would save money from our paychecks so that
once every two weeks we could actually go out
to a restaurant and have a nice dinner. It sure
beat the usual Friday night menu of frozen

Tony's pizzas we could pick up at the Shop 'n Save that were always on sale—two for five dollars!

Unbeknownst to me, Danny had been planning to ask me to marry him and had been saving extra hard to buy a small diamond ring. He had also chosen my favorite seafood restaurant down on the waterfront that sat out on a pier with lovely views of Frenchman's Bay and outer Porcupine Islands.

And Danny had come up with the perfect idea of how he wanted to propose to me!

Fortunately, I am an unapologetic creature of habit so he knew that I would, like always, order the garlic and wine clams appetizer as I had just about every time we dined at this lovely establishment. Since I love talking about food, I even told him two days before that I was going to order the clams appetizer because it was so delicious and it was all I could think about!

Danny went to the restaurant earlier that day and asked the chef if he would be willing to slip the ring in one of the clam shells so that when I opened the clam, I would find the ring instead, and that would be Danny's cue to get down on one knee and ask me to be his wedded wife.

Luckily the chef was a big fan of young love and readily agreed, but not before he asked how he would know it was Danny's order when it came into the kitchen. Danny told him that he would order for himself the mozzarella sticks with a request to hold the marinara sauce.

No one ever holds the marinara sauce so that way the chef definitely would know it was him.

Fast forward a few hours later. Danny and I were being escorted by the sweet-natured hostess to a romantic corner table near the large bay windows. I was so excited to be eating at my favorite seafood place that at first I didn't notice how nervous Danny was acting, tapping his fingers on the table, barely looking at his menu, his eyes darting back and forth between me and the kitchen. I was too busy perusing the menu, casually mentioning that perhaps tonight I might try a different appetizer instead of my usual steamed garlic-and-wine clams.

As I said this, I glanced up from my menu and saw a panic-stricken Danny suddenly stuttering, "B-B-But you always order the clams!" I shrugged and replied, "Yes, well, maybe it's time to try something different. I shouldn't always be such a creature of habit."

"But you *love* the clams! Why wouldn't you order the clams? You should get the clams! Please, order the clams!"

Poor Danny looked so devastated, I just laughed and leaned over to pat his hand that was now nervously playing with his fork. I told him, "Of course I'm ordering the clams. I just don't like being so predictable all the time."

There was such a look of relief on his face as he muttered, "I happen to like predictable."

The waitress came to take our order, and of course, I ordered the steamed clams appetizer with the seafood casserole and another wine spritzer. Danny followed by ordering the mozzarella sticks with no marinara sauce, which I found odd, and the Seafood Alfredo.

I sat there chatting and sipping my drink and gushing about the gorgeous view, but Danny just sat across from me in stony silence, looking as nervous as a long-tailed cat in a roomful of rocking chairs. He didn't even pretend to be paying attention to my scintillating conversation. At least in my mind it was scintillating.

Finally, I asked him if there was something wrong, and he mumbled something about just being very hungry and how that was something I should understand since I am not the most patient or pleasant person to be around when my stomach was grumbling. I was about to argue, but then realized he had a very good point.

Just then, I spotted our waitress emerge from the kitchen with our appetizers. I told Danny to hold on, help was on the way. The waitress was coming with her tray. But instead of stopping at our table, she made a beeline right past us and served the appetizers to the couple sitting at the next table.

I looked at Danny, who now looked positively sick, and said, "Sorry, hun, I guess that couple ordered the same appetizers as us."

Danny was staring at their plates, looking like a deer caught in headlights, and whispered in a hoarse voice, "Yeah, what are the odds?"

At that moment, the chef came hurrying out of the kitchen and was racing toward us with a plate of steamers in his hand, but before he had a chance to reach us, the girl at the next table let out a shriek and was holding up a ring in her hand. She jumped out of her seat, bouncing up and down, screaming, "Yes! Yes! I will marry you!"

The whole restaurant broke out into enthusiastic applause. Everyone except her date, who was sitting across the table from her looking dumbstruck with his mouth hanging open and shaking his head slowly back and forth, not sure what to say. Danny just leaned back in his chair, a shocked and miserable expression on his face.

I leaned toward Danny and whispered, "That poor guy sure doesn't look very happy for someone who just proposed!" Danny threw down his napkin, and frustrated, sighed, "That *your* ring!" It didn't quite register yet. The chef carrying the plate of steamed clams came to a screeching halt between our tables and was frantically pivoting back and forth between Danny and the other man.

It took a few beats for Danny's words to finally sink in, but then, after assessing the situation with two different plates of clams, they finally did, and like the girl at the next table, I jumped out of my chair with a shriek and started yelling, "Yes! Yes! I will marry you!"

Well, the whole restaurant once again broke into thunderous applause as Danny and I just grinned at each other and clasped hands.

It took a few more moments for the poor girl next to us to finally realize that her boyfriend had not said a word up to this point. She tentatively glanced over at Danny and me, then at the chef holding another plate of clams, and you could finally see it registering on her face what had just happened.

She spun around to her red-faced boyfriend and screamed, "Five years! I have given you five years! Enough is enough, you coward!" Then she held the ring out to me and sniffed, "I believe this belongs to you!" I took the ring and thanked her, feeling happy, but also feeling sorry for her at the same time as she turned her back on her boyfriend and marched out of the dining room, leaving him alone at the table.

Danny then took the ring from me, got down on one knee, and formally asked me to marry him. I said yes. Again. There was more applause. We even asked the jilted boyfriend at the next table to join us so he would not have to eat alone. Which surprisingly, he did.

You all know how our story ended. Maybe not happily ever after, but I did get two great kids out of it, and as frustrating as that man can be, Danny and I are still friends to this day. On a side note, the couple at the next table reconciled, got hitched, and are still happily married with four kids.

So enjoy this week's recipes since they are a salute to my past and my present.

LEMON WHITE WINE SPRITZER

INGREDIENTS:
Pinot Grigio or your favorite bottle of white wine
   chilled
Club soda
1 lemon sliced

Fill your glass with 6 ounces of the chilled wine, 2 ounces of club soda and 1 lemon slice.

This refreshing cocktail is the perfect accompaniment with the casserole below.

When I am asked to bring a casserole to a potluck, you can never go wrong with my easy Clam Seafood casserole. The best part is, there is practically no measuring, you can use leftover seafood, and with Ritz crackers and butter in it, there is no way you can go wrong. The clams can be substituted with lobster, shrimp, or even fish, or if you are feeling especially decadent, use a mixture of the seafood listed.

This has been a favorite of my friends and family for years. So, give it a try and I guarantee your own friends and family will thank you for it.

HAYLEY'S CLAM CASSEROLE

INGREDIENTS:
1 sleeve Ritz crackers, crushed
8 ounces minced cooked clams (canned is fine too)
4 tablespoons butter melted
½ teaspoon pepper
Lemon to taste

Preheat your oven to 350 degrees.

In a bowl, mix your crushed crackers, clams, melted butter, and salt and pepper and put in buttered casserole dish and squeeze some lemon over the top.

Bake for 25 minutes, remove, serve, and enjoy!

Chapter 40

Hayley leaned back against the headrest in the passenger seat of Abby Weston's silver Buick Enclave, taking deep breaths and with her eyes closed.

"Hold on, Hayley, we're almost there!" Abby cried, panic rising in her voice.

"I'm fine, Abby, really, there's no need to go to the hospital," Hayley sighed.

"Nonsense! You shouldn't take any chances! You need to see a doctor! Don't you remember what happened to Karen Linscott when she went skiing at Sugarloaf last winter? She fell on the bunny slope and hit her head, said she was fine, went to have a hot apple cider at the lodge, and two hours later she was dead from an epidural hematoma!"

When Hayley had stabbed her hand and drew blood with the knitting needle, there was really no cause for immediate concern. She had punctured the skin, but it did not look too serious. However, Helen Woodworth, perhaps fearing a lawsuit, leapt to her feet and tried to drag

Hayley to the bathroom where she could run water over the wound with soap and water to avoid infection. She ordered Esther Willey to go to the pantry in the kitchen and get the emergency first aid kit that was stocked with some bandages and petroleum jelly. Helen had been so alarmed by Hayley's knitting related injury, and possibly fearful Hayley might spill some blood on her solid snow-white area shag rug, she pulled Hayley toward her a bit too aggressively, causing Hayley to trip over the leg of the coffee table and fall face forward in a ridiculous pratfall, banging her head on the floor, her bloodied hand smearing the hardwood. The one thought in Hayley's head at the moment was, *"At least I didn't get any blood on the rug."*

It was complete pandemonium after that as all the ladies in the knitting circle jumped to their feet and rushed over to help Hayley, who insisted she was fine. She did, however, admit to feeling a bit woozy once they all helped her back up to her feet.

Abby had seen enough.

She announced she was taking Hayley to the hospital immediately despite her protests.

And now they were speeding into the Bar Harbor Hospital parking lot, screeching to a halt at the emergency entrance. Abby fumbled out of the car and scurried around to assist Hayley, who was already out of the passenger side, still asserting to Abby that she was not about to die from a brain injury.

Hayley's general practitioner, Dr. Cormack, happened to be on duty when they arrived, and so after a neurological exam to test Hayley's thinking, motor function, sensory function, coordination, eye movement, and reflexes, she was whisked off for a CT scan and then returned to the exam room to await the results. Abby stayed in the emergency waiting arca texting the ladies of the knitting circle with constant updates.

As Hayley shifted uncomfortably on top of the exam room table, crinkling the white paper underneath her, her mind kept going back to what had caused her such a shock.

Tabitha Collins.

It seemed a rather glaring coincidence that she was trying to buy Leighton Seafood, and right after Lonnie declared that he did not want to sell, the old geezer wound up dead in the clam flats.

The door to the exam room swung open and Dr. Cormack entered with his intrepid, loyal nurse Tilly right on his heels as usual.

"You're very lucky, Hayley, the CT scan came back negative. No sign of internal bleeding. They're not always one hundred percent accurate detecting a traumatic brain injury, but coupled with your neurological test results, I'm fairly confident you're going to be just fine."

"Thank you, Doctor," Hayley said. "That's quite a relief."

Dr. Cormack sat down in a metal chair next to the exam table and gingerly took Hayley's hand. "Now, let's redo that bandage, shall we? Helen Woodworth may knit nice sweaters, but she's a lousy medic." He unwrapped the hastily applied bandages and examined the wound on Hayley's hand. It had stopped bleeding but still looked like a nasty cut. "So how did this happen?"

"I'm almost too embarrassed to say. I had a mishap with one of Helen's killer knitting needles. I'm a beginner, it was my first day, but in my defense, I heard some surprising news that caused me to jab myself."

Dr. Cormack cocked an eyebrow, curious. "Oh?"

Hayley knew this was her one chance to steer the conversation into fertile territory where she might learn something useful. "Abby Weston, you know Abby, she was dating poor Lonnie Leighton before he sadly passed . . ."

"Of course I know Abby," Dr. Cormack said, dabbing an antibiotic ointment on Hayley's hand before wrapping it up in fresh bandages the correct way.

"Well, she told me that a woman I know was trying to buy Leighton Seafood and Lonnie didn't want to sell."

Dr. Cormack finished wrapping the bandage around Hayley's hand and stood up from his chair. "And you found that surprising, why?"

"Well, poor Lonnie was dying. I don't see why he would be so against selling the business if he wasn't going to be around much—"

"Oh, he wasn't dying!" Tilly said in a chipper voice.

Hayley sat upright on the exam table. "What?"

Appalled, Dr. Cormack shot Nurse Tilly an admonishing look. "Nurse Tilly, it is strictly against hospital policy to discuss a patient's medical records."

Nurse Tilly blanched. "I am so sorry, Doctor, I just assumed now that he was no longer with us—"

"Any patient! Alive or dead!"

"Yes, Doctor," Nurse Tilly muttered, her face flushed with embarrassment.

"I have another patient waiting. Get some rest, Hayley. If you experience any persistent headaches, I want you to come back here, okay?"

"Promise," Hayley said, feeling bad for Tilly.

Dr. Cormack gave his nurse one more blisteringly stern look before walking out of the exam room.

"Oh, me and my big mouth!" Tilly wailed. "Why do I always put my foot in it?"

"It's not your fault, Tilly. He just seems to always be in a foul mood. He should really work on his bedside manner."

"But he's right. I told you before. I should never discuss a patient's medical history with anyone. He could write me up for such a huge blunder or even terminate me! When am I ever going to learn?"

"Don't beat yourself up, Tilly. You weren't gossiping. You just absent-mindedly corrected me when I thought Lonnie was suffering from a terminal illness. Anyone could have slipped up and made that simple mistake. But now that the cat is out of the bag . . ."

"Please don't pressure me with any more questions, Hayley, I don't want to get fired, nursing is everything to me!"

"I would *never*, Tilly! You don't have to tell me anything that would compromise you ethically."

"Okay, good."

"You can just nod."

"I beg your pardon?"

"Nod if I'm in the ballpark. When I saw you out with Donnie at Drinks Like A Fish, you were under the impression that Lonnie's condition was terminal . . ."

Tilly frowned. "Gosh, you're right! I spilled the beans then too! That's twice now!"

"So, when Lonnie came in for this last appointment, something must have changed. He found out he was in remission from whatever was wrong with him? He was suddenly getting better?"

Tilly just stood frozen in place, her head still, not sure what to do. Then, she nodded ever so slightly.

"So he knew he wasn't going to die!"

Another barely perceptible nod.

But enough to confirm Hayley's suspicions.

Lonnie Leighton was going to live.

And that did not sit well with somebody.

So perhaps he needed to be helped along.

Chapter 41

Armed with this new information, Hayley raced over to the law office of Iggy Fennow, the Leighton family lawyer. His secretary Wanda's face dropped at the sight of Hayley bursting through the door.

"Wanda, I know he's a very busy man, but—"

"Yes, Hayley, he is and I am afraid Mr. Fennow has no time to see you today!" Wanda sniffed, the first line of defense between herself and the boss to whom she was resoundingly loyal.

"But this will only take a second—"

Wanda stood up from her desk and Hayley thought for a minute she might throw herself in front of the door to Iggy's office, but her feet remained planted behind her desk as she wagged an admonishing finger at Hayley. "Please don't make me call your brother-in-law and have him come over here to physically escort you off the premises. Now, I understand whatever it is you need to discuss with Mr. Fennow must be important, but he has a packed schedule today and you're just going to have to make an appointment." She sat back down and clicked a few keys on her desktop computer. "Now, let me see, he does have an opening a week from Friday at four." She looked up at Hayley, smiling sweetly. "Does that work for you?"

Hayley grimaced, already plotting how she was going to have to leave the front office, sneak around back, and tap on Iggy's window to get his attention.

But fortunately, that was not going to be necessary because the door to Iggy's office opened and he stood there with a half-eaten pastrami sandwich in his hand, some mayo on the side of his mouth, and a napkin stuffed down his shirt collar. Despite his secretary's claim, Iggy did not look all that busy. With a heavy sigh, he said to his secretary, "It's okay, Wanda, let her in."

He had obviously been eavesdropping on their entire exchange from behind his door.

"Thank you, Iggy, thank you," Hayley said, zipping past a snarling Wanda and into Iggy's office.

"Can I get you anything, Mr. Fennow?" Wanda cooed, trying to worm her way into the office out of her own curiosity as to what all this hoopla was about.

"No, I'm good, thank you, Wanda," he said, shutting the door in her face and turning around to face Hayley, who hovered near his large desk. "Now, Hayley, what's this all about?"

Hayley took a deep breath. "Did you know Lonnie Leighton was *not* dying?"

"Of course. He called me with the good news the minute he got the test results back."

"And Vera knew as well that Lonnie's condition was not terminal?"

"She most certainly did know. She's his daughter. And the number two in charge at the family business. All his daughters knew. They could not have been happier or more relieved."

"I'm not so sure about that. Have you heard of a woman by the name of Tabitha Collins?"

Iggy rolled the name over in his mind. "It sounds vaguely familiar. Didn't Bruce date a woman named Tabitha? It was a long time ago."

"Yes, that's the one. More recently she's been here in Bar Harbor meeting with Vera about buying the family business."

Iggy's eyes widened in surprise. "I was not aware of that."

"In Lonnie's will, did he say who would take control of the company in the event—?"

Iggy held up a hand. "Stop right there, Hayley! As executor of Lonnie's will, I cannot discuss the contents of that will with anyone who is not a beneficiary. I could be disbarred."

Hayley nodded, frustrated. "I understand." She paused, her mind racing, then continued. "Okay, can you at least confirm something that's *not* in the will?"

"What are you talking about?"

"You're legally prohibited from discussing what's *in* the will, but is there a law about discussing what's *not*?"

Iggy looked at her warily. "Somehow, I think I am going to regret playing this little game, but I will play along as a favor to Bruce. No, Hayley, there is no law stopping me from telling you what's *not* in Lonnie's will."

"Super! So tell me, did Lonnie put anything in his will requesting to be cremated after his death?"

"No, I don't think so. I can check again, but off the top of my head, there was no specification about what to do with the body."

"Then why was he cremated?"

"That decision was ultimately left to the family."

"Who in the family?"

"Well, I can't be sure. Ruth was the one who told me they had decided to cremate him, but I assume all three daughters had a say. Although I was surprised they went that route."

Hayley perked up. "Why is that?"

"I always just assumed Lonnie would want to be laid to rest in the cemetery plot he had reserved next to his late wife."

Hayley gasped. "Vera . . ."

"What about her?"

"I bet she strong-armed Ruth and Olive to cremate their father."

"Why?"

"To erase any evidence of foul play!"

Iggy's face went pale. "Hayley, what are you saying?"

"Vera murdered her own father so she could sell the family business for a huge sum to Tabitha Collins!"

She was out the door like a shot leaving behind a thunderstruck Iggy.

Chapter 42

Hayley swung her car to the left off the south side of Route 233 and down to the boat launch on the north end of Eagle Lake in Acadia National Park. She spotted Digger's truck pulled over to the side of the parking area. After leaving Iggy Fennow's office, she had immediately called Mona to ask where she might find Digger. Mona had told her it was Digger's day off, and Hayley knew exactly where to find him if he wasn't sneaking around with Ruth Leighton. For his entire adult life, any day Digger didn't have to work, rain or shine, hail or snow, he would go fishing for brook trout out on Eagle Lake, either in a canoe or during the winter through a big hole in the ice. Every year Digger was first in line at the Town Hall to renew his fishing license. "Fishing is my therapy," he once told Hayley. "The only place in the world where I can clear my head of all the troubles in the world."

Hayley knew it would be dark soon and Digger would be returning so she stood at the edge of the lake, watching and waiting, constantly checking the time on her phone. Finally, after about twenty minutes, she spotted a red Old

Town Saranac 146 canoe gliding toward her, rippling through the otherwise still water, Digger using his dual-wood Beavertail paddle Mona had bought for him last Christmas from L.L. Bean.

As he got closer and made out the figure standing at the water's edge to be Hayley, she could not tell if he was happy to see her or dreaded her presence. When he hopped out of his canoe with his waders on and dragged it out of the water and onto solid ground, Hayley knew it was the latter.

"Fish ain't biting much today, Aunt Hayley. I only caught one threespine stickleback and one rainbow smelt I threw back." He then proceeded to unload his rod and fishing equipment from the canoe.

"You know Bruce is the fisherman in the family, I just fry 'em up in a pan. I'm here because I need to talk to you."

"Yeah, I figured as much. I don't mean no disrespect, Aunt Hayley, you know how I feel about you, but frankly I'm not in a talking mood. I've got everybody piling on me right now. I got two gals fighting over me and destroying what's left of their family, not to mention Mom, who's madder than a three-legged dog trying to bury a turd on an icy pond."

Digger got his talent for painting such vivid mental pictures from his mother.

"I understand what you're going through, Digger, and I don't mean to add to your troubles. I just want to ask you one question."

Digger sighed, resigned to the fact that Hayley was not going anywhere until she got the answer she came for. "All right, shoot."

"When you were with Vera, was there any time she might have had the opportunity to get her hands on Dougie's class ring?"

"No, not that I recall," Digger said, shaking his head.

"Are you sure?"

"Yes, it's not like Mom ever invited her over for tea. I mean when would she . . . ?" his voice trailed off.

"What, Digger, what is it?"

His face suddenly went pale.

"When was she at the house?"

"When the Leightons found out Dougie and Olive were in love, Vera told me she feared Olive had run away and was hiding in Dougie's room. At the time, I thought that was crazy because why would Olive hide right under my mother's nose?"

"You're right. Nothing gets by Mona Barnes. She would've smoked her out in no time at all."

"But Vera just wouldn't stop going on about it, so to put her mind at ease, I drove her over there when I knew nobody was home so she could see for herself. We were only there a few minutes, in Dougie's room, and there was no sign of Olive hiding there obviously. I could tell Vera wasn't satisfied so I offered to go down and check the basement, which was Dad's man cave when he and Mom were still together, now we just store our hunting and fishing gear down there."

"So you left her by herself in Dougie's room?"

"Yeah, but not long at all. Just for a minute or two."

"Long enough for her to pocket something of Dougie's that she could use later to frame him. Something small enough to slip into her pocket. Like a class ring."

"Why didn't I think about that the moment you found

that ring in Lonnie's clam bucket? Of course, Vera could have swiped it to pin the blame on poor Dougie. It's all my fault! I'm such a friggin' idiot!"

"No, Digger. There was no reason for you to be suspicious, especially after Sabrina Merryweather's results were inconclusive. There was no murder investigation. But that ring was Vera's insurance policy just in case the police were out looking for a killer."

"Which means . . ." Digger said in a raspy, hoarse voice, his face stricken. "Vera killed her own father."

"It's starting to look that way," Hayley said solemnly. "But I'm not sure just the class ring is going to do the trick. Vera can simply deny taking it. We're going to need more proof."

Digger thought hard, the shock slowly fading into grim determination. "How about a confession? Will that do the trick?"

"Of course. But how—?"

"She's been calling and texting me almost every hour since she found out Ruth and I are an item. She's desperate to see me. I'm sure she wants to persuade me to dump Ruth and come back to her. What if I arrange a meeting and record the conversation on my phone, try and get her to slip up and admit to what she's done?"

Hayley hugged him. "Your mother would be so proud of you!"

"Let's hope so," Digger said doubtfully.

After letting him go, Hayley noticed her clothes smelled fishy, but there was no time to worry about that now. They were on the verge of catching a cold-blooded killer.

Chapter 43

Hayley huddled behind Balance Rock, a large boulder left unsettled by a past ice age, just off the shore path with a direct view of the exact spot where she and Mona had discovered Lonnie Leighton's body. Digger waited nearby for Vera, who had agreed to come meet him. With her phone clamped to her ear, Hayley called the police station to alert Sergio of their plan so he could provide backup if needed.

"Good afternoon, Bar Harbor Police Department. Sergeant Earl speaking."

Earl had just been promoted from officer to sergeant, but it still stuck in his craw that his best buddy Donnie, who had come up in the ranks with him, was already a lieutenant. It might have had something to do with his habit of reading comic books when he was supposed to be manning the front desk and his overall laziness and general lack of ambition. But that was just Hayley's unbiased opinion.

"Hi, Earl, it's Hayley Powell. I need to speak with Sergio, it's very important."

"I'm sorry, Hayley, he's not here right now. Is there something I can help you with?"

Fat chance.

The last thing she needed was Earl showing up at the scene and screwing up her whole plan. Although Sergio was perhaps the best police chief the town of Bar Harbor had ever seen, some of his underlings, Earl included, more closely resembled *Paul Blart: Mall Cop*.

"No, thank you, Earl. Just have the chief call me back as soon as he can!"

Hayley ended the call and stuffed her phone in the back pocket of her jeans. She peeked around the large rock to see Vera approaching, dressed to the nines in a dusty-pink, notched-neck, pleated blouse and black slacks, as if ready for a romantic evening, except for the thigh-high waders to protect her from the mud as she trudged through the clam flats. She had obviously made an effort for her meeting with Digger. Even her hair was combed back and parted to the side instead of just hanging over her face, which was a first.

Hayley strained to hear their conversation, grateful it was low tide so she did not have to contend with the thunderous crashing waves rolling in.

"You look nice," Digger noted as she stopped a few feet away from him.

She brushed some lint off her black slacks. "Thank you. I was so happy when you texted me. I knew in my heart you would finally see the light, how much better I am for you than boring old Ruth." She glanced around, her eyes falling on the exact location where her father's body had been found. "But why did you want to meet me out here?"

He ignored the question. "You're right, Vera. You're so much more exciting and dynamic than Ruth. I kind of always knew I'd eventually come crawling back to you."

Vera's whole face lit up. She was so delighted to hear him say those words she didn't seem to notice how they got stuck in his throat before he managed to finally spit them out.

Digger reached out and took her hand. She looked as if she expected him to get down on his knee and propose right there in the clam flats, but he did not and Hayley could detect the slight disappointment on Vera's face.

"How did Ruth take the news?" Vera asked, although there was no trace of genuine concern in her voice.

"I haven't told her yet. But I will, I promise."

"I will do it, if you want," Vera eagerly offered. "No sense putting it off. She's gonna have to find out and deal with it sometime."

"I'm not worried about Ruth. She's strong. She'll get over it eventually," Digger said. "I just want to make sure you and I are starting off on the right foot."

Vera crinkled her nose. "What do you mean?"

"I know you're not a big fan of my mother, but the one thing she taught me was, in any relationship, the key ingredient is trust. We gotta have trust and be honest with one another."

"I wholeheartedly agree, Digger. I trust you completely. Do you trust me?"

Digger hesitated.

Vera gasped and ripped her hand out of Digger's. "You don't trust me?"

Hayley noticed the phone in Digger's other hand that he held casually by his side, presumably recording their conversation as he attempted to secure a confession.

"I do trust you, but I have to ask you, point blank, and I need you to tell me the truth, did you swipe my little brother Dougie's class ring from his bedroom when you were over at the house?"

"N-No!" Vera sputtered, before repeating even less convincingly, "No . . ."

Digger stared hard at Vera, who quickly averted her eyes and self-consciously crossed her arms, avoiding eye contact. "I mean . . . Why is that so important to know now?"

"Because I don't want any secrets between us. Secrets tend to fester and they always find a way to destroy relationships."

"Is that another pearl of wisdom from your dear mother Mona?" Vera scoffed.

"Yes. I don't want to end up divorced like my parents. I want us to last. I need to know everything if I'm going to one day be your husband."

Vera gasped. "*Husband*?"

Digger nodded with a shy smile.

He was playing his part to perfection.

But Vera was still vacillating, not sure how much she should tell him and risk losing him.

Digger could sense her wavering too.

"Nothing you say could ever make me love you any less, Vera," Digger said softly.

He was not lying. He could not love Vera any less at this point. But there was another moment of hesitation so Digger decided to try a different tack.

"There was no love lost between me and your father, you must know that. Frankly, I'm glad the old geezer's gone. I saw what he put Olive and Dougie through. He was never going to accept us either. He would have made our lives miserable. But now we don't have to worry about that anymore."

Vera studied Digger's face. She finally seemed to buy his sincerity, which was a true testament to Digger's innate acting abilities. He should have joined the drama department in high school rather than fracturing a knee and an ankle playing football and gaining fifty pounds recovering at home in front of the TV.

"Yes, Digger, I took the ring."

"How did it end up in your dad's clam bucket?"

"Because I put it there."

"Why?"

"As an insurance policy. In case the police decided to investigate his death," Vera said coldly. "With that ring as a clue, they'd be completely focused on Dougie as the number-one suspect. I'm sorry, I know he's your brother."

Digger took a step back. This was what he had come for, but hearing Vera admit it out loud was still a bit of a shock.

"But why would you have to do that unless—?"

"Yes, we did it."

Hayley gasped and threw a hand over her mouth.

Digger cocked his head to the side. "*We*? Who's we?"

"Me and Ruth."

Digger's jaw dropped. "R-Ruth was in on it?"

"Of course. I couldn't have done it without her."

Hayley could see a wave of emotions washing over Digger's face. He was utterly bereft. The last thing he had ever expected to hear was that the woman he actually was in love with was also a murderer. He opened his mouth but could not speak. Vera did not seem to note the horror on his face.

"I had a hell of a time persuading her to help me. You know what a squeamish, faint-of-heart wimp Ruth is, but I finally got her to go along."

Hayley could not believe it.

Two sisters plotting a murder.

It was like something out of *Arsenic and Old Lace*.

"Daddy treated Ruth something awful, almost as bad as he treated me. Olive was always the apple of his eye, who could do no wrong, which is why he was so livid when he found out Little Miss Perfect was sneaking around behind his back with a Barnes boy! That was a big reason why I kept mum about you and me and what we had going on. I have worked too hard building up this business over the years to get written out of the will at the last minute if he was to find out about us. Now I know Ruth was probably thinking the same thing."

Suddenly a loud voice cut through the air like the crack of a ricocheting bullet. "Hayley!"

Hayley suddenly froze, pressing herself against the rock formation, closing her eyes, wishing herself invisible.

"Hayley, what in sweet Jesus are doing hiding behind Balance Rock?"

She was intimately familiar with that voice.

It could only be one person.

Mona Barnes.

Hayley slowly turned around to see Mona tromping through the flats toward her in a heavy flannel shirt, muddied jeans, a Red Sox cap and her waders, lugging her clam rake and a plastic bucket. Since Lonnie was dead and could no longer give her any grief about clamming in this spot, Mona had apparently decided that today was as good as any to take advantage.

The jig was up.

Vera knew Hayley had to be in the vicinity.

And so left with little choice, Hayley stepped out from behind her hiding place, now in full view of Digger and Vera.

Vera's eyes shot daggers at Hayley as the realization slowly sunk in that she was being set up.

Chapter 44

Mona dropped her rake and bucket and charged past Hayley and toward Digger and Vera, who both stood frozen in the mud. Vera's eyes darted back and forth nervously, not sure what her options were at this moment. She was suddenly surrounded and outnumbered.

"Would somebody mind telling me what the hell is going on here?" Mona bellowed.

"It's kind of complicated, Ma," Digger muttered.

"No, it's not!" a voice cried, causing everyone to spin around to see who else had just joined the group.

It was Ruth, her hand holding a gun, drooping slightly.

"Ruth!" Digger called out as if no one else had recognized her.

Ruth was shaking, tears streaming down her cheeks. With the back of her free hand she wiped her nose, still clutching the gun in the other but now pointing it toward the ground. Everyone kept their eyes glued on the gun.

Digger took a tentative step forward. "Ruth, baby, what are you doing with a gun?"

Remembering she was holding a weapon, Ruth suddenly jerked her arm upward, pointing it at Digger and Vera. "I had a sneaking suspicion after you acted so mysterious when I called you earlier, and you said you couldn't talk because you had something important to do, but wouldn't tell me what it was, that Vera was somehow involved, and so I followed you here!"

"Ruth, you gotta believe me, it's not what it looks like!" Digger said evenly, his eye still trained on the gun.

"I don't believe anything you say anymore! I should've known it wouldn't work out between us. Vera always gets what she wants! Always! I was such a fool thinking you were going to end things with her to be with me! How could I be so *stupid*?"

"Ruth, what the hell are you doing with that pistol?" Vera shouted.

Ruth's eyes narrowed, she casually pointed it in her sister's direction, causing Vera's whole body to stiffen. "I got it from Daddy's gun cabinet. He kept it loaded in case anyone tried breaking into the house."

"So what's your plan, you're going to shoot all of us?" Vera sneered.

Ruth's bottom lip quivered. "I don't have a plan, I'm just so confused, I honestly thought I had finally met the man I was going to marry, and then you had to take that away from me, you're always taking things from me, Vera, even Daddy . . ."

"You can't pin that solely on me, Ruth! You *helped*!"

"You *made* me!" Ruth wailed.

"It's not like I held a gun to your head. You're the one with the gun, Ruth!"

Hayley could see Mona inching her way toward Ruth with the intention of attempting to wrestle the gun out of her hand. Ruth sensed the motion behind her and spun around, aiming the gun at Mona, who quickly backed off.

"Come on, Ruth, you hate guns, you don't have it in your soul to shoot anybody, why don't you just give it to me?" Vera said gently, holding her hand out.

"No, Ruth, whatever you do, don't give Vera that gun!" Hayley cried.

Unlike Ruth, Hayley suspected Vera would have no compunction about using it.

Ignoring Hayley, Vera stretched her arm out even farther, closer to Ruth's trembling hand holding the gun. Just as Vera's fingers were about to touch it, Ruth jerked it away.

There was quiet except for a few seagulls nearby and Ruth's uncontrollable sobs.

Finally, Hayley cut the silence, folding her arms and eyeing Vera and Ruth accusingly. "Poor Lonnie. Betrayed by his own *daughters*."

Ruth sniffed, then looked up at the sky to heaven. "I'm sorry, I'm so sorry, Daddy, I never should've listened to Vera's rantings and ravings."

"Maybe he might hear you if you look *down*," Mona whispered under her breath before Hayley shot her an admonishing look.

"No wonder Olive was Lonnie's favorite. That's why her relationship with Dougie threatened him so much. He didn't want to lose her. She was the only one he really trusted. And he was right. Look what happened to him," Hayley said quietly.

"You have no idea what you're talking about!" Vera snapped.

"Okay, let me give it a shot then," Hayley said, pointing a finger at Vera. "You were in the middle of selling Leighton Seafoods to Tabitha Collins. You thought your father was going to die soon and you wanted to cash out because you knew you and your sisters would be left with the family business anyway. But then there was an unexpected glitch. Lonnie's illness went into remission. He was going to be around a lot longer than you expected, which put a huge crimp in your plans to sell."

Hayley studied Vera's face.

Although Vera fought hard to keep a poker face, Hayley could detect a whiff of fear.

"So you crushed up a bunch of sleeping pills and added them to Lonnie's whiskey. Who wouldn't believe an accidental overdose? You both knew Lonnie took them by the fistfuls day and night. But my guess is it didn't work. It wasn't a lethal dose. It just made him groggy. Am I warm, Vera?"

Vera stoically stood her ground, lips pursed.

Ruth's shoulders sank. "Yes, then Vera put him to bed and tried suffocating him with a pillow!"

"Shut up, Ruth!" Vera roared.

But Ruth was done listening to her sister. She continued, her voice cracking. "But he fought back. So she made me go get a washcloth. I didn't know what she was going to do with it but she grabbed it from me and stuffed it in his mouth and held his nose!"

Everyone stood around, aghast.

Whatever they had imagined had happened to Lonnie Leighton, this was far worse.

Ruth simpered and cried, a hand over her face while the other gripped the gun by her side.

"Fearing what the police might find if they combed the

house, you forced Ruth to help you move the body," Hayley said solemnly.

"I didn't force Ruth to do anything! She knew what would be coming to her if Daddy was out of the picture! She's not as innocent as she's pretending to be!" Vera shouted scornfully.

"So, you drove the body out here, Lonnie's favorite clamming spot, and left him face down in the mud to suggest he had suffocated. Isn't that right?"

Vera glared at Hayley, refusing to admit anything.

"My God, Vera," Digger muttered. "How could I not see how cold-blooded—"

"It wasn't some master plan! It just happened!" Vera cried defensively.

"That's not true," Hayley said. "It was completely premeditated."

"You can't prove that!" Vera howled.

"Of course we can. Digger recorded you admitting to stealing Dougie's class ring from his room. You had to have done that before killing Lonnie in order to plant it in his clam bucket in case the police needed a suspect. That means you were considering killing him before he even found out he was in remission. You were impatient and wanted to speed things up!"

"Oh, Vera, what have we done?" Ruth cried.

"Don't listen to them, Ruth! We put him out of his misery!" Vera shrieked.

"Except he wasn't in any misery," Hayley reminded her. "He had a healthy relationship with Abby, he was recovering from his illness, he probably had years left on his life, which you cruelly took away from him, you and Ruth."

Ruth sunk to her knees in the mud, bawling.

Hayley almost felt sorry for her, but the reality was Ruth was still a willing accomplice.

Digger just stared at both women, wide-eyed, in a total state of shock, most likely now questioning his taste in women.

Hayley turned to Vera. "I just have one question."

Vera glanced at Hayley derisively. "What?"

"Why on earth did you ask me to investigate if you were guilty of the crime all along?"

Vera threw her head back and laughed disdainfully. "Honestly? To throw everybody off the scent. I thought you were too dumb to actually figure it all out." She contemptuously gestured toward her sister on her knees in the mud. "Ruth disagreed. She warned me about your impressive track record. I guess I should've listened."

Ruth stuck a foot out in front of her and used it to haul herself up, her long skirt covered in mud. "I regret everything, my role in all that's happened, but most of all, I regret listening to my older sister!" Ruth sniveled. "Someone call the police. I want to confess. And please, Digger, take this."

Ruth went to hand him the gun, but in a flash, Vera flew forward, knocking Digger to the side, snatching the gun out of Ruth's wobbly grip.

They all slowly raised their hands in the air as Vera swung the weapon around, crazed and determined to get control of the situation.

"What are you going to do, Vera? Shoot us all?" Mona sighed.

She thrust the gun in Mona's direction. "Don't test me, Mona! I'll tie up any loose end I have to!" She swung the weapon back toward Ruth. "Even my own loose-lipped sister!"

Digger suddenly stepped in front of Ruth, using his body as a protective shield.

Out of the corner of her eye, Hayley saw Mona tense up with fear in her eyes that one of Mama Bear's cubs might get shot.

"You're going to have to go through me first, Vera," Digger said bravely, although Hayley knew on the inside he was probably scared out of his mind.

Vera hesitated, then waved the gun around. "Get out of the way, Digger!"

It was so obvious.

Despite everything, Vera still had feelings for Digger.

And she just could not pull the trigger.

Seizing upon the moment of distraction, Hayley delivered a roundhouse kick, her shoe slamming into Vera's hand holding the gun. Vera cried out in pain, splaying her fingers, and sending the pistol flying into the mud. Hayley lunged for it.

Vera, now unarmed, had no other choice but to turn around and make a run for it. Mona wasted no time chasing after her. Hayley, Digger, and a sniffling Ruth watched in awe as Mona darted through the heavy mud at lightning speed, catching up to Vera, and grabbing at the back of Vera's blouse, slowing her down enough for Mona to tackle her like a Patriots defensive lineman and take her down. Kicking and screaming like a wildcat, Mona managed to climb on top of Vera, straddling her to keep her immobile on the ground.

"See, Vera? I am, and always will be, a faster runner than you! I would've proved it at that high school track meet if you hadn't tripped me up on purpose!" Mona shouted, victorious.

Hayley could feel her phone buzzing.

She scooped it out of her back pocket.

It was Sergio finally returning her call.

"Hey," Hayley said.

"So what's the big emergency?"

"You're a little late, Chief," Hayley said. "But come join the party. I have a lot to catch you up on."

Chapter 45

There was much to celebrate at Mona's backyard barbecue a few weeks later. First and foremost, was her son Dougie's engagement to Olive Leighton. Although the young couple in love did fly to Las Vegas to elope, they chickened out at the last minute in front of the Elvis impersonator ready to marry them. In his heart, Dougie knew he just could not disrespect his mother, and if he was going to get hitched, he wanted her to be there. So, after taking in a show and splurging on a steak dinner, Dougie and Olive got back on a plane and flew home. Although Mona tried her best to maintain her typically tough exterior, Hayley was there to witness the moment when Dougie told her why they decided to wait, and there was no denying Mona's emotions were getting the best of her. Her eyes were quite noticeably moist with tears, although she would vociferously deny it.

The second reason they were celebrating was the impending merger of Mona's business with Leighton Seafoods. With Vera and Ruth now in jail awaiting trial for Lonnie's murder, Olive was left to run the business. Her first decision was making Abby Weston a silent partner since she had inherited a healthy chunk of Lonnie's estate including part ownership of the company. But neither Olive nor Abby were all that eager to take over, and so after discussing her options with her fiancé, Dougie, Olive decided to combine forces, merging the Barneses' business with the Leightons' business and forming a new company, Bar Harbor Seafoods, making it one big, local, family-run business once Dougie and Olive made it official.

Mona, who had been looking forward to stepping back and allowing her sons autonomy running the company, welcomed the merger with open arms almost as much as she did her soon-to-be daughter-in-law.

Dennis Jr. worked the grill, flipping the burgers, while Digger served the drinks on this bright sunny Sunday afternoon. Hayley had brought her famous potato salad and Bruce brought a six pack of beer which he promptly unloaded into the cooler after keeping one for himself. After the tension of the last few weeks following Lonnie's death, it was a real treat to just kick back with a low key barbecue, catching up with friends.

It was a perfect day.

Mona stuffed a handful of potato chips into her mouth and took a swig of her Bud Light. "So, Olive, I'm dying of curiosity, how did that bigwig from Boston take the news that you weren't going to sell?"

Tabitha Collins.

Hayley smiled tightly.

She had almost forgotten all about her.

Almost.

Olive shrugged. "Okay, I guess. She said she understood but I could tell she was disappointed."

Liddy, who was also there, sighed, resigned. "I guess

that was the reason she decided not to buy a place here. One minute I'm showing her million-dollar properties in Seal Cove and the next, she's hightailing it back to Boston."

"Good riddance!" Mona snorted.

Hayley noticed Bruce had a knowing smile. "What?"

"Nothing," Bruce said, taking a swallow of his beer.

"I know that look. Tell me," Hayley pressed.

Bruce knew he was never going to get any peace until he came clean. "That may not have been the *only* reason she left town."

Hayley cocked an eyebrow. "Oh?"

"Right after Olive informed her she wasn't going to sell, Tabitha showed up at the *Island Times* office to see me."

Hayley's heart skipped a beat.

"She wanted to know where she stood with me, if there was any chance I might feel the same way about her as she felt about me after all these years . . ."

Everyone stopped eating and drinking, on edge to hear what Bruce would say next.

"So I told her in no uncertain terms that I am, and always will be, hopelessly in love with my wife."

He then kissed Hayley on the lips.

And that's when the perfect day got just a little more perfect.

Island Food & Spirits
BY
HAYLEY POWELL

In light of the recent untimely death of Lonnie Leighton and the awful revelation that his two eldest daughters were involved, our town of Bar Harbor had been turned upside down with gossip. It was all anybody could talk about at the supermarket, the post office, on practically every street corner. But once a month passed by, in true island fashion, things returned to normal as people moved about in their day-to-day business. And I, for one, have been so busy, I have hardly had a moment to myself.

Between the busy restaurant and writing my column, it's been a hectic time, so the other night after checking in with my ace hostess Betty and seeing that she had everything under control, I decided this would be a good night for me to sneak out early. With Bruce being away on business, I could have a date night with myself, binging reruns of my favorite TV show *NCIS* starring Mark Harmon without having to listen to Bruce making snide comments about my obsession with that man every time he came on the screen. As if I would ever have the opportunity to meet the man, but one can always hope.

I also decided to go in the restaurant kitchen before I left to grab a to-go container of Kelton's Clams and Sausage Spaghetti, which was our special of the evening. I already had a pitcher of Mai Tais in my fridge at home so, all in all, this was going to be a wonderfully decadent night. I left the restaurant with my supper and headed home to an excited Leroy, who was thrilled to see me home early for once.

I poured myself a yummy cocktail, warmed up my spaghetti, set everything on my TV tray, and turned on one of Mark's earliest episodes, one where he hadn't gone completely gray yet, although I defy anyone who would argue he is not sexy at any age.

I was so involved with my dinner and the show's plot, I did not notice Leroy looking up toward the stairs right away. But then, moments later, he was gritting his teeth and growling softly, and pacing back and forth. After he failed to come when I called him, I paused my show to listen and hear what was upsetting him so much.

At first there was just silence, but then, I heard what I thought sounded like shuffling and scratching sounds from upstairs. I hopped up from the couch and walked over to the foot of the stairs to listen some more.

Sure enough, I could hear constant scratching and thumping around. I walked slowly up the stairs being careful not to hit the creaky step as I went up.

When I reached the top, I stopped, not hearing anything for a moment. Then suddenly there was more rustling and lots of pitter-patters of little feet above me. That's when I knew it was squirrels! They had been getting into the attic every now and again. Bruce had promised to find out where they were getting in from and block it, but obviously forgotten to do it. The few times we heard them, Bruce would open the attic window and they would eventually leave through there. But he wasn't here now, so it was going to be up to me! This was not exactly how I had planned to spend my evening, shooing squirrels out of the attic. They may look cute but they can be vicious, and I was not looking forward to facing off with an angry trapped squirrel. But if I did nothing, they might tear everything up we had stored there, making homes in the boxes.

I pulled on the rope that lowered the attic stairs from the ceiling and took a deep breath before heading up.

My plan was to scoot over to the window across the room as quick as I could, open it halfway, then dash back down the attic steps and close them up because I did not need any squirrels bunking with me in my bedroom.

I was silently cursing Bruce in my head for not finding the entrance point that they were using to get in and I was also cursing myself for forgetting to turn on the light at the bottom of the stairs. But luckily it was a clear night out so I could see the window. I hurried over to it, listening for noises as I went. I reached the window and gave it a push but it would not budge. I tried again, but just then, something ran right across my feet. I was so startled, I jumped, and stumbled for the stairs, forgetting all about the window. I was halfway across the room when I spotted the biggest squirrel I had ever seen running straight at me!

Without thinking, I turned and ran toward the back corner of the attic with no plan in mind. I just wanted to get away from that monstrous thing.

I glanced over my shoulder and did not see him. Maybe he and his other squirrel friends got scared by my presence and escaped back out from where they came.

That's when I saw him.

A big, tall man hovering in the shadows, not more than three feet away from me. I screamed bloody murder and started to run away from him but tripped over a stack of boxes and went crashing to the floor. The next thing I knew, the big man jumped on top of me from behind. Now I was screaming and thrashing around trying to fight him off of me.

I could hear Leroy barking like crazy at the bottom of the steps as I was kept screaming and fighting for my life and trying to crawl toward the stairs, but the weight of the man was holding me down!

Just then I heard people calling my name.

It was my brother Randy and his husband Sergio.

I had forgotten they were stopping by to drop off a card table they had borrowed for a party. Crying with relief, I yelled for help and heard footsteps pounding up my stairs, then they raced up the attic steps and mercifully yanked the intruder off my back, holding him, as I quickly scrambled to my feet, utterly breathless.

I whipped around to face my attacker, secure in the knowledge that Sergio and Randy had him under control. Randy and Sergio were trying hard not to laugh at this point. Then they just lost it, howling uncontrollably. They were holding a large black diving wet suit, the exact one that Bruce wore when he went scuba diving which he had not done in years. Apparently, he had hung it up in the attic, which I mistook for an intruder. How it fell on top of me I will never know. On the floor was a scuba tank that must have fallen on top of me too along with the diving suit, which would explain why it was so heavy and felt like the weight of a man.

After Sergio finally managed to pry the window open, we all went back downstairs to a very relieved Leroy, who was jumping all over us and wagging his tail and barking happily. We went into the kitchen and enjoyed slices of cheesecake, which the boys had brought as a thankyou for me lending them one of my card tables.

Definitely a night to remember. In fact, Randy relived the hysterical story of finding me wrestling with that wet suit three times as we ate our dessert, not to mention texting it to all his friends.

At least a good time was had by all.

Mai Tai Cocktail

Ingredients:
2 ounces pineapple juice
1½ ounces white rum
1 ounce orange curaçao
1 ounce dark rum
Pineapple and cherries for garnish (optional)

Fill a glass with ice and then mix all your ingredients
in a shaker glass and pour over ice. For a festive
look, add a garnish with a slice of pineapple and a
couple of cherries.

CLAMS AND SAUSAGE SPAGHETTI SPECIAL

INGREDIENTS:
2 pounds little neck clams, steamed and removed
   from shells
½ onion finely diced
1 clove garlic, minced
2 hot Italian sausages, skin removed
2 tablespoons olive oil
½ cup white wine
8 ounces spaghetti noodles
1 cup pasta water (as needed)

Boil your spaghetti noodles in a pot of salted boiling
water.

In a large skillet warm your olive oil on medium heat.
Add your onions and cook until just beginning to
soften. Add your garlic, stir, and cook for one minute.

Add your two sausages and break up in chunks as
they cook, breaking them up more as you go along.

Once the sausages are browned, add your wine and
deglaze the pan, stirring up all those bits at the bottom of the pan, which will add flavor.

Add your cooked clams and stir in to warm.

Add your drained pasta to the sauce and mix all together (adding a little of the reserved pasta water if
it seems too dry).

Serve in bowls with some crusty bread and enjoy!

Private Investigator Poppy Harmon can see through the charms of Southern California's trickiest criminals. But when she and the Desert Flowers Detective Agency go up against a dashing dating show murderer, they may have finally met their match!

While sidekick Matt Flowers shoots a film abroad, Poppy dusts off her own acting chops to break up a Gen Z crime ring targeting seniors in Palm Springs. Tanya Cook and her gal pals have been swindling susceptible residents for all they're worth—until the gang meets Poppy undercover. Yet, with the case cracked, the desert heat is on full blast as new terrors take the lead . . .

Poppy's already sweating over a menacing mystery stalker when a shocking death proves she's in serious danger. As suspicions fall once again on Tanya, finding answers may mean pulling off the most challenging performance of her career . . .

Now, with Poppy's unknown stalker rumored to be posing as one of several bachelors on a glitzy reality series, a disguised Poppy must reveal his true identity on set before he realizes hers. Does Poppy have what it takes to catch the coldblooded killer in time for the season finale . . . or should she start planning for her funeral?

Please turn the page for an exciting sneak peek of Lee Hollis's newest Poppy Harmon mystery POPPY HARMON AND THE BACKSTABBING BACHELOR, now on sale wherever print and e-books are sold!

Chapter 1

Poppy Harmon was having a devil of a time operating her electric wheelchair. When she pushed the joystick forward, the wheels seemed to veer right, not straight ahead, and she banged into a wall in the hallway after maneuvering out of the bedroom, trying to steer herself toward the living room.

Poppy sighed.

She was never going to get the hang of this.

She tried cranking the knob to the left, but only managed to drive the wheelchair away from one wall and crash it into the opposite one. The noise alerted someone in the kitchen, and within seconds a young woman in her twenties with long, straight black hair, emerald green eyes, and a bright smile that mostly disguised a somewhat hardened face suddenly appeared in front of her.

"Oh, you're up. How was your nap?"

"Fine," Poppy spit out, frowning, continuing to push the knob forward but getting nowhere. "I hate this new wheelchair. My old one was a lot easier to operate."

"Here, allow me," the young woman said, slipping behind Poppy and manually pushing the wheelchair by the handles out to the living room and parking it in front of the large flat-screen TV hanging on the wall. "I have some tomato soup heating up on the stove for your lunch. Would you like Ritz crackers or saltines to go with it? I have both."

"Saltines, please," Poppy answered gruffly.

"Coming right up," the woman said before snatching up the remote and turning on the TV. "Now you just relax and watch your British Bake Off show, and lunch will be ready in just a few minutes."

She bounded back to the kitchen.

Once she was gone, Poppy adjusted the itchy, stringy gray wig she was wearing, straightened her burgundy housecoat, and checked out her face in a wall mirror across from her. The retired Tony Award–winning Broadway makeup artist the Desert Flowers Detective Agency had hired to transform Poppy into a ninety-two-year-old woman had done an incredibly convincing job using liquid latex, eyeliner, and face paint. Poppy looked at least thirty years older than her actual age.

And more importantly, Tanya Cook, the self-described "professional home care nurse" who'd answered her ad to help out with shopping, errands, meals, and to administer medications, was totally buying the disguise.

Poppy heard a thump.

It had come from down the hall, the small guest bedroom that she had set up as her office.

Poppy tried to pick up the remote off the coffee table to lower the television volume but couldn't quite reach it. She stretched her fingers as far as they would go, but the remote was still about an inch away from her grasp.

Frustrated, Poppy swiveled her head around to make sure Tanya had not wandered back into the living room, and then, with lightning speed, she jumped out of the wheelchair, grabbed the remote, and quickly sat back down. She muted the TV and waited.

Sure enough, she heard another thump.

Poppy pulled back on the joystick, the wheelchair rolled in reverse, and then she buzzed back down the hall. The door to the guest room was closed. She leaned forward, turned the handle, and pushed the door open, surprised to find two more young women, both around Tanya's age, and just as pretty. One was blond and the other auburn haired. The blonde was seated at a desk meticulously going through drawers while the other one held a half-filled plastic garbage bag that she appeared to be stuffing with valuables.

"Who are you? What are you doing here?" Poppy cried.

The two girls froze in place, not quite sure what to do.

Tanya appeared in a flash. She stepped in front of Poppy's wheelchair and knelt down so they were at eye level, a reassuring smile on her face. "There's no cause for concern. These are my friends, Bella and Kylie. I invited them over to help tidy up the house. Don't you want your lovely home to be nice and clean for when your grandkids come to visit?"

"I suppose so," Poppy said. "How much is this going to cost me? I used to do my own housework. . . ."

"Oh no, Edna, this is included in the service. You don't have to pay anything extra. I am just here to make things easier for you."

Poppy nodded. She had momentarily forgotten her

cover name was Edna Greenblatt, so she was grateful that Tanya had just reminded her. She smiled warmly at the two nervous-looking women in the office. "Thank you, girls. I may have some gingersnap cookies in the kitchen. Would you like one?"

They exchanged quick glances, and then the one with the garbage bag, Bella, shook her head and muttered, "No, we're fine."

Tanya firmly gripped the handles of the wheelchair and rolled Poppy out of the room and back down the hall. "Come on, Edna, time to eat your soup."

"I spotted some dust bunnies underneath the desk. Do you think they can sweep those up, too?" Poppy asked.

"Of course, the whole house will be spotless when they're done, I promise," Tanya said, parking Poppy back in front of the TV in the living room. "Now stay put while I finish preparing your lunch tray."

Poppy detected a slight annoyance in Tanya's tone. She was obviously getting tired of being nice to this high-maintenance old crow.

Because the fact of the matter was Tanya was no professional home care nurse. Tanya Cook and her two cohorts, Bella and Kylie, were professional criminals, allegedly running a massive financial fraud and theft scheme by infiltrating the homes of susceptible senior citizens and gaining access to their bank passwords, cash, checks, credit cards, valuables, and personal documents. Basically bleeding their victims dry right in their own homes! Tanya would scout out a vulnerable target, someone in need of in-home care; apply for the job with forged credentials; then show up at the door with a friendly smile and a promise to take good care of them. She would play nursemaid for about a week, gaining the trust of her charge before bringing in her two accomplices to rob the unsuspecting senior blind, even insidiously redirecting social security direct deposits to a dummy bank account.

Their last mark, however, a feisty widow by the name of Cecile LaCrosse, an eighty-nine-year-old battle-ax who unfortunately fell victim to the scam, was not about to let them get away with it. And so she brought in Poppy and her crew at the Desert Flowers Detective Agency to set up a sting and bring this evil coven of Gen Z witches down.

Poppy, along with her two partners, Iris Becker and Violet Hogan, took a very personal interest in this particular case because they felt a strong kinship with the victims. Although still in their sixties, they knew it was only a matter of time before they themselves might be confused, defenseless elderly victims preyed upon by opportunistic, heartless swindlers.

And so Poppy had insisted that she pose as an elderly widow, drawing on her years of acting experience from when she was a starlet in the 1980s, in order to bust up this enterprising, depraved crime ring.

And so far she had played it to perfection.

Tanya was confident enough after only three days of playing nursemaid to bring in her two sidekicks to finish the job by pillaging poor Edna Greenblatt's home until she was left with nothing but her electric wheelchair, which had a mind of its own.

Tanya appeared with a wooden tray and set it down in front of Poppy. "I garnished the soup with a few garlic croutons. My own grandmother used to love the extra kick."

"It looks lovely," Poppy said, picking up the spoon with a shaky hand and scooping some up, making sure to dribble a little on her housecoat just to be convincing.

"Can I get you anything else?" Tanya asked.

"Oh, no, dear, you've done quite enough," Poppy said with a thin, knowing smile.

And she meant it.

Tanya and her friends had certainly done enough.

And they were about to discover just how "done" they actually were.

Chapter 2

Violet's loud, piercing, high-pitched voice of concern blasted through Poppy's ear. "Poppy, Poppy, what's happening in there? Are you okay?"

Poppy dropped her spoon on the tray and raised her hand to adjust the small earbud resting in the crevice of her right ear, and urgently whispered into the tiny microphone that had been pinned on the inside of her housecoat, "Violet, turn down the volume on your mic, you're going to burst my eardrum!"

"Oh, sorry," Violet said, lowering her voice. "Iris, how do you adjust the volume on this thing?"

"Here, let me do it," Iris snapped.

There was a pause.

"Hello? Hello? Is this better?" Violet bellowed, even more deafening than before.

Poppy sighed. "No, she just made you even louder."

"Hold on," Violet said.

Poppy could hear her two friends and partners bickering in the background away from the microphone that they were using to communicate with Poppy.

"Is that better?" Violet asked, almost whispering.

"Yes, much," Poppy said.

"Who are you talking to?"

The stern voice came from directly behind her. Poppy used her joystick to turn her electric wheelchair around.

Tanya stood staring at her, a plate of gingersnap cookies in her hand.

"What?" Poppy asked innocently.

"I heard you whispering to somebody," Tanya said suspiciously, eyes darting around to see if anyone else was in the room before returning her mistrustful gaze back to her charge. "Who was it?"

Her tone was unsettlingly sinister.

"Abe," Poppy said softly.

"Who's Abe?"

"My late husband. He comes to talk to me every now and then," Poppy said with a sad, drawn face. "I miss him so much. He would have loved this tomato soup." Poppy picked up her spoon to take another sip, making sure to get a garlic crouton. As she slurped and crunched, Tanya seemed to size her up, ultimately opting to believe her story, then held out the plate of gingersnaps toward her.

"Cookie?"

Poppy slowly reached out with her trembling hand and took a cookie, then shoved it into her mouth and talked with her mouth full. "Yummy."

"I'm going to see if Bella and Kylie would like one," Tanya said, turning around to head down the hall, but stopping at the window. "Have you noticed that van parked across the street?"

"What van?" Poppy asked innocently.

"Desert Florists," Tanya said, staring out the window.

Poppy swallowed hard.

The van had been rented by the Desert Flowers Detective Agency. They had slapped a fake florist shop decal on the side so as not to arouse suspicion. Inside were Violet and Iris, keeping a careful watch over the house. However, they had underestimated how smart and observant Tanya Cook could be.

"If they're just here to deliver flowers to a house in the neighborhood, it's taking them a really long time," Tanya said warily, checking her wristwatch. "It's been there since I arrived this morning."

"Oh, that van is parked there all the time," Poppy quickly explained. "It belongs to one of the neighbors. That's his business. He's always leaving it there and getting a ticket because he forgets to move it on street-cleaning day."

Tanya peered at the van a few more seconds before deciding to buy Poppy's on-the-spot made-up explanation. She then continued on down the hall with her tray of cookies.

"Is everyone in place?" Poppy whispered.

There was silence.

"Violet?" Poppy asked.

Still nothing.

She had lost communication.

Either her earpiece battery had suddenly died, or there was a problem with the transmitter in the van.

"Violet?"

"I'm here, Poppy, I accidentally hit the mute button! Sorry! Yes, we're ready, it's go time!"

"I knew I should have been in charge of the communication equipment!" Iris snorted.

Poppy braced herself just as Tanya returned from the guest bedroom/office with her empty plate. Something outside caught her eye and she raced back to the front window in time to see a uniformed police officer ducking down and circling around the house. Tanya gasped, her mouth dropping open in surprise. She quickly found her voice and started yelling, "Cops!"

Bella and Kylie came crashing out of the guest room, Kylie holding a stuffed garbage bag in her arms.

"Are you serious?" Bella asked nervously.

"Yes!" Tanya cried. "I just saw one sneaking around the side of the house! Run!"

Bella sprinted toward the kitchen, Kylie following close behind but weighed down with the bag. She finally let go of it and it dropped to the floor with a thud as she raced to catch up with Bella.

Poppy heard a man yell, "Police! Put your hands up!"

Tanya's eyes popped open in surprise and she made a mad dash for the front door. Poppy, anticipating the move, jammed the joystick of her wheelchair all the way forward, full speed, and whizzed over in front of the door, blocking her escape.

"What are you doing? Out of my way, old woman!" Tanya screeched, furious, struggling to get around her.

Poppy sprang up to her feet and forcefully pushed Tanya back.

The miraculous sudden strength and agility of the ninety-two-year-old stymied Tanya briefly, but she was still not to be deterred. She charged forward, trying to physically shove Poppy out of the way. Poppy held her ground, knowing she was no match for the young, physically fit woman, but determined to keep her from getting away. Poppy and Tanya grappled, Tanya trying to scratch Poppy's face with her nails in the hope she might release her grip, but as Tanya withdrew her nails, she was stunned to find latex hanging off them, not blood.

"What the—?"

Two uniformed cops suddenly bolted into the living room from the back door off the kitchen, their guns drawn.

"It's over, Tanya!" one of the cops yelled.

She shuddered at the mention of her name because she knew at this moment this had all been a sting.

A con job. A trap.

And she had willfully, stupidly, walked right into it.

Tanya slowly raised her hands in the air while glaring defiantly at Poppy, who busily wiped the old-age makeup off her face with the napkin from her lunch tray.

One of the cops, a boyish, inexperienced one, struggled to unhook a pair of handcuffs from his belt loop. Finally, he glanced apprehensively over at his more seasoned partner. "Sarge?"

The older cop sighed, and assisted him in releasing the handcuffs from the officer's belt so he could snap them on Tanya's wrists.

Once her face was free of powder and latex and added wrinkles, Poppy removed her gray wig.

Tanya gaped at her, undoubtedly kicking herself for so easily buying into her now obvious disguise.

The older cop studied Poppy, then stepped forward with a big smile. "Hey, I know you . . ."

The younger cop snapped to attention and stared at Poppy, still clueless. "You do?"

"*Jack Colt, PI*!" Sarge crowed, slapping his forehead. "You're Daphne, Jack's secretary!"

The younger cop still appeared totally confused. "Who?"

"The TV show, it was on in the nineteen eighties!" Sarge exclaimed.

"I wasn't born until nineteen ninety-seven," the younger cop said.

Both Poppy and Sarge chose to ignore him.

Sarge was almost giddy. "Detective Jordan said he had recruited an actress to help with this operation. I just never imagined it would be *you*! This is so cool!"

Of course, Poppy knew that it was she who had contacted Detective Jordan, bringing him into the case, not the other way around, but why clarify such things and potentially bruise Jordan's fragile ego?

"I am a private investigator these days," Poppy felt the need to explain.

"Wait, a *real* one? Are you joking?" Sarge asked, still beaming from ear to ear.

Poppy nodded shyly.

Sarge fumbled for his phone. "Hey, do you mind if I get a selfie with you? My poker buddies are never going to believe this!"

Poppy did not feel this moment was appropriate for that kind of thing, but she also did not want to disappoint a fan.

Sarge basically bodychecked a handcuffed Tanya out of the way to get to Poppy.

"Maybe I should read this woman her rights first, Sarge," the younger cop quietly suggested.

"That can wait, kid, hold on a sec," Sarge barked before holding his phone up and beaming while snapping a photo. He checked it and frowned. "It's a little blurry. Do you mind if I take another one?"

"No, not at all," Poppy said, keeping one eye on Tanya, who glowered at her menacingly.

Sarge tried again, this time satisfied. "Thank you, Daphne, you made my day!"

"Of course," Poppy said, grabbing the handles of the wheelchair and pushing it out of the way so the officers could escort Tanya Cook outside to their waiting squad car.

The young officer gripped Tanya by the arm to lead her out, but she refused to budge, her eyes angrily fixed on Poppy. "So you're telling me the cops recruited some washed-up, old has-been Hollywood *star* to take us down?"

Sarge nodded. "Yeah, and unfortunately for you, it worked like a charm, didn't it?"

Tanya sneered and looked dismissively at Poppy. "Why bother with the old lady makeup? You're already old enough to be my grandmother."

Poppy bristled on the inside, but was not about to show any emotion on the surface to give this she-devil the satisfaction. Instead, she calmly replied, "Yes, Tanya, you may have many more years ahead of you in life than I do, but a lot of them will no doubt be spent behind bars . . . so there's that."

Poppy opened the front door, allowing the two officers to leave with Tanya, who looked as if she wanted to smack Poppy right across the face but couldn't because her hands were handcuffed behind her back, so instead, she just raised her head high contemptuously and began to softly whistle the children's nursery rhyme "Twinkle, Twinkle, Little Star."

Poppy scoffed at Tanya's labored attempts to ridicule her Hollywood past. But given what was about to come, that unfortunately would turn out to be a very grave and dangerous mistake.

Index of Recipes

Visit our website at
KensingtonBooks.com
to sign up for our newsletters, read
more from your favorite authors, see
books by series, view reading group
guides, and more!